Father's Notebook

Kader Abdolah (a pen name created in memoriam to friends who died under the persecution of the current Iranian regime) was born in Iran in 1954. While a student of physics in Tehran, he joined a secret leftist party that fought against the dictatorship of the shah and the subsequent dictatorship of the ayatollahs. Abdolah wrote for an illegal journal and clandestinely published two books in Iran. In 1988, at the invitation of the United Nations, he arrived in the Netherlands as a political refugee. He now writes in Dutch and is the author of novels, short stories and works of non-fiction.

Susan Massotty is a translator of Dutch into English. She has translated works by Kader Abdolah and Margriet de Moor, as well as Anne Frank's *The Diary of a Young Girl*. She won the Vondel Prize for *My Father's Notebook*.

Translated works by Kader Abdolah

Fiction
The House of the Mosque
The King

Non-fiction
The Messenger: A Tale Retold

My Father's Notebook

KADER ABDOLAH

CANONGATE

This Canons edition published in Great Britain in 2021
by Canongate Books

First published in Great Britain in 2006 by
Canongate Books Ltd, 14 High Street,
Edinburgh EH1 1TE

Published in association with HarperCollins US

Originally published in Dutch
as *Spijkerschrift* by Uitgverij De Geus bv,
Postbus 1878, 4801 BW Breda, Nederland

canongate.co.uk

1

This translation has been published with the support of the
Foundation for the Production and Translation of Dutch Literature.

Rutger Kopland, 'Suppose', translated by James Brockway, in *A World Beyond Myself*.
London: Enitharmon Press, 1991. Originally published as 'Stel', *Dit Uitzicht*.
Amsterdam: G. A. Van Oorschot, 1982.

Excerpt from *Max Havelaar*, by Multatuli, reprinted with permission.
Translated by Roy Edwards and edited by E. M. Beekman.
Copyright © 1967 by Roy Edwards and published by the University of
Massachusetts Press, 1982.

British Library Cataloguing-in-Publication Data
A catalogue record for this book is available on request from the British Library.

ISBN 978 1 78689 898 2

Designed by Linda C. Dingler

Typeset by Palimpsest Book Production Ltd, Falkirk, Stirlingshire

Printed and bound in Great Britain by Clays Ltd, Elcograf S.p.A.

Contents

BOOK I

The Cave

And so it went until the men of Kahaf finally sought refuge in the cave. "Grant us Thy mercy," they said.

In that cave We covered their ears and their eyes for years.

And when the sun came up, the men saw it rise to the right of the cave. And when the sun went down, the men saw it set to the left, while they were in the space in between.

They thought they were awake, but they were asleep.

And We turned them to the right and to the left.

Some said, "There were three of them, and a fourth watched over them."

Others, hazarding a guess, said, "There were five of them, and a sixth watched over them."

And there were those who said, "There were seven of them." No one knew.

We woke them, so that they might question one another.

One of them spoke: "We have been here for a day or part of a day." Another said: "Allah alone knows how long we have been here. It would be best to send one of us to the city with this silver coin. We must be careful. If they find out who we are, they will stone us."

Jemiliga then left the cave with the silver coin in the palm of his hand.

When he reached the city, he saw that everything had changed and that he did not understand the language.

They had slept in the cave for three hundred years and did not even know it. And some say there were nine more.

This was God's word, God's story. And "The Cave" was one of the stories in the Holy Book in Aga Akbar's house.

We have started with His word before trying to decipher Aga Akbar's secret notebook.

There are two of us, Ishmael and I. I'm the omniscient narrator. Ishmael is the son of Aga Akbar, who was a deaf-mute.

Even though I'm omniscient, I can't read Aga Akbar's notes, so I'm going to tell the story up to Ishmael's birth, then leave the rest to him. But I'll come back again at the end, because Ishmael can't decipher the last part of his father's notebook.

The Cave

From Amsterdam it takes a good five hours to fly to Tehran. Then you have to travel another four and a half hours by train to see the magical mountains of the city of Senejan loom up, like an age-old secret, before your eyes.

Senejan itself is not beautiful and has no history to speak of.

In the autumn an icy wind whips through the streets, and the snowy mountaintops form a never-changing backdrop.

Senejan has no special foods or products. And since the Shirpala River has dried up, the children play in the riverbed to their hearts' content. The mothers keep a watchful eye on them throughout the day to make sure no strangers lure them into the hollows.

The city's only poet of significance—long since dead—once wrote a poem about Senejan. It's about the wind that carries the sand in from the desert and deposits it on the inhabitants' heads:

Oh wind, oh wind, alas there's sand in my eyes,
Oh my heart, oh my heart, half-filled with sand.
Alas, there's a tiny grain of sand on her lip.
Sand in my eyes, and oh God, her rosy lips.

The rest of the poem goes on in much the same vein.

Whenever a poetry reading was held in one of the buildings in the old bazaar, it was bound to be attended by old men rhyming about the mountains. Their favourite topic was an ancient cuneiform relief that dated back to the time of the Sassanids.

An Anthony Quinn movie about Muhammad was once shown in Senejan. It was quite an event. Thousands of country bumpkins who didn't know what a movie theatre was rode their mules through the mountains to stare in wonder at *Muhammad, Messenger of God.*

Hundreds of mules were tethered in the marketplace. The authorities were beside themselves. For three months the doors of the movie theatre were open night and day, while the mules ate hay from the municipal troughs.

Although Senejan didn't figure prominently in the nation's history, the surrounding villages did. They brought forth men who made history. One of these was a great poet, Qa'em Maqam Farahani, whose poetry everyone knows by heart:

Khoda-ya, rast guyand fetna az to-ast
wali az tars na-tavanam chegidan
lab-o dandan-e torkan-e Khata-ra
beh een khubi na bayad afaridan.

Though I would never dare to say it aloud, God,
The truth is that You are a mischief-maker,
Or You would not have made the lips and teeth
Of the Khata women as beautiful as they are.

The girls born in these villages make the most beautiful Persian carpets. Magic carpets you can fly on. Really fly on. This is where the famous magic carpets come from.

Aga Akbar was not born in Senejan, but in one of these villages. In Jirya. A village covered with almond blossoms in the spring and with almonds in the fall.

Aga Akbar was born a deaf-mute. The family, especially his mother, communicated with him in a simple sign language. A language that consisted of about a hundred signs. A language that worked best at home, with the family, though the neighbors also understood it to some extent. But the power of that language manifested itself most in the communication between Mother and Aga, and later between Aga and Ishmael.

Aga Akbar knew nothing of the world at large, though he did understand simple concepts. He knew that the sun shone and made him feel warm, but he didn't know, for example, that the sun was a ball of fire. Nor did he realise that without the sun there would be no life. Or that the sun would one day go out forever, like a lamp that had run out of oil.

He didn't understand why the moon was small, then gradually got bigger. He knew nothing about gravity, had never heard of Archimedes. He had no way of knowing that the Persian language consists of thirty-two letters: *alef, beh, peh, teh, seh, jeem, cheh, heh, kheh, daal, zaal, reh, zeh, zheh, seen, sheen, sad, zad, taa, zaa, eyn, gheyn, faa, qaf, kaf, gaf, lam, meen, noon, vaav, haa,* and *ye.* The *peh* as in *perestow* (swallow), the *kheh* as in *khorma* (date), the *taa* as in *talebi* (melon), and the *eyn* as in *eshq* (love).

His world was the world of his past, of things that had happened to him, of things he had learned, of his memories.

Weeks, months, and years were a mystery to him. When, for example, had he first seen that strange object in the sky? Time meant nothing to him.

· · ·

Aga Akbar's village was remote. Very little went on in Jirya. There wasn't a trace of the modern world: no bicycles, no sewing machines.

One day, when Aga Akbar was a little boy, he was standing in a grassy meadow helping his brother, who was a shepherd, tend a flock of sheep. Suddenly their dog leapt onto a rock and stared upwards.

It was the first time a plane had flown over the village. It may, in fact, have been the very first plane to fly over Persian airspace.

Later those silver objects appeared above the village often. The children then raced up to the roofs and chanted in unison:

Hey, odd-looking iron bird,
come sit in our almond tree
and perch in our village square.

"What are they chanting?" young Aga Akbar asked his mother.

"They're asking the iron bird to come sit in the tree."

"But it can't."

"Yes, they know that, but they're imagining it can."

"What does 'imagining' mean?"

"Just thinking. In their minds they see the iron bird sitting in the tree."

Aga Akbar knew that when his mother couldn't explain something, he should stop asking questions and simply accept it.

One day, when he was six or seven, his mother hid behind a tree and pointed to a man on a horse—a nobleman with a rifle slung over his shoulder.

"That's your father."

"Him?"

"Yes. He's your father."

"Then why doesn't he come home?"

Using their simple sign language, she placed a crown on her head, stuck out her chest, and said, "He's an aristocrat, a man of noble birth. A scholar. He has many books and a quill pen. He writes."

Aga Akbar's mother, Hajar, had been a servant in the nobleman's palace, where he lived with his wife and eleven children. He could see that Hajar was different, however, so he took her to his house on Lalehzar Mountain, where he kept his books and worked in his study.

She was the one who tidied the study, dusted the books, filled the inkpot and cleaned the quills. She cooked his lunch and made sure he had enough tobacco. She washed his coat and suit, and polished his shoes. When he had to go out, she handed him his hat and held the horse's reins until he was in the saddle.

"Hajar!" he called one day from his desk in the study, where he was writing.

"Yes, sire?"

"Bring me a glass of tea. I'd like to have a word with you."

She brought him a glass of tea on a silver tray. (That very same tray can still be seen on the mantel in the house of Aga Akbar's wife.)

"Sit down, Hajar," he said.

She continued to stand.

"Come now, Hajar, I've given you permission to sit, so take a seat."

She sat on the edge of a chair.

"I have a question for you, Hajar. Is there a man in your life?"

She didn't reply.

"Answer me. I asked you if there was a man in your life."

"No, sire."

"I'd like you to be my *sigeh* wife. Would you like that?"

It was an unexpected question.

"That's not for me to say, sire," she replied. "You'll have to ask my father."

"I'll ask your father in due course. But first I'd like to know what *you* think of the idea."

She thought for a moment, with her head bowed. Then she said clearly, "Yes, sire, I would."

That same evening, Hajar's father was taken to the nobleman's study by the village imam, who recited a short sura from the Holy Book and said, "*Ankahtu wa zawagtu,*" declaring Hajar to be the wife of Aga Hadi Mahmud Ghaznavi Khorasani.

Next the imam explained to her that she was allowed to have children, but that they couldn't have their father's name. Nor would they be able to inherit anything. Hajar's father was given an almond grove, the profits of which were to be shared with Hajar: one half for him, the other half for Hajar and any children she might bear. When her father died, the entire grove would belong to Hajar and her children.

Ten minutes later her father and the imam left. Hajar stayed.

She was wearing a blue-green dress that she'd inherited from her mother.

Early in the morning she'd gone to the village bathhouse and furtively removed her body hair. Then she'd dipped her toes in henna and her fingertips in the sap of the *runas*—a wild, reddish-purple flower—until it had dyed her fingers red.

"I'll be spending the night here, Hajar," the nobleman announced.

She made up the bed.

Then Aga Hadi Khorasani slipped into the bed beside her, and she received him.

· · ·

Hajar had seven children. Aga Akbar, the youngest, was born a deaf-mute.

She noticed it before he was even a month old. Though she saw that he didn't react normally, she didn't want to believe it. She kept him with her at all times, allowing others to see him only briefly. This went on for six months. Everyone realised that the baby was deaf, but nobody dared to say anything. Finally Kazem Khan, Hajar's oldest brother, decided that it was time to broach the subject. Kazem Khan, an unmarried man who rode through the mountains on horseback, was a poet. Though he lived by himself on a hill above the village, there were always women in his life. The villagers saw a succession of women silhouetted against his lighted window.

Nobody knew what he did or where he went on his horse.

When there was light in his house, people knew he was home. "The poet is at home," they then said to each other.

Nothing else was known about him. Yet when the village needed him, he was always ready to lend a helping hand. At such moments he was the voice of the village. If a flash flood suddenly turned the dry riverbed into a raging torrent and their houses filled with water, he immediately appeared on his horse and diverted the flow. If a number of children unexpectedly died and the other mothers feared for their children's lives, he galloped up on his horse with the doctor in tow. And all the village brides and grooms considered it an honor to have him as a guest at their wedding feast.

This same Kazem Khan rode his horse into the courtyard of Hajar's house and stopped in the shade of an old tree. "Hajar! My sister!" he called, still in the saddle.

She opened the window.

"Welcome, brother. Why don't you come in?"

"Could you come to my house tonight? I'd like to talk to you. Bring the baby with you."

Hajar knew he wanted to talk to her about her son. She realised she would no longer be able to hide her baby.

As evening fell, Hajar strapped her baby to her back and climbed the hill to the house that the villagers referred to as "a gem that had fallen among the walnut trees".

Kazem Khan smoked opium, a generally accepted practice in those days. It was even considered a sign of his poetic nobleness.

He had lit the coals in the brazier, laid his pipe in the warm ashes and put the thin slices of brownish-yellow opium on a plate. The samovar was bubbling.

"Sit down, Hajar. You can warm up your dinner in a moment. Let me hold the baby. What's his name? Akbar? Aga Akbar?"

She reluctantly handed the baby to her brother.

"How old is he? Seven or eight months? Go ahead and eat your dinner. I'd like some time alone with him."

Hajar felt a great weight bearing down on her. She couldn't eat. Instead, she burst into tears.

"Come now, Hajar, there's no need to cry. Don't feel so sorry for yourself. If you hide the baby, if you give up on him, you'll just make him backward. For the last six or seven months, he's seen nothing, done nothing, had no real contact with the world. Everywhere I go in the mountains, I see children who are deaf and dumb. You have to let people talk to him. All you need is a language, a sign language that we can invent ourselves. I'll help you. Starting tomorrow, let other people take care of him too. Let everyone try to communicate with him in his or her own way."

Hajar carried her child into the kitchen and again burst into tears. This time tears of relief.

Later, after Kazem Khan had smoked a few opium pipes and was feeling cheerful and light, he came in and sat down beside her.

"Listen, Hajar. I don't know why, but I have the feeling I should play a role in this child's life. I didn't feel this way about your other children, mostly because they were fathered by that nobleman, and I don't want to have anything to do with him. But before you leave, we need to talk about him and about your baby's future. It's high time that nobleman learned that Akbar has an uncle."

The next day Hajar took Akbar to the palace. Never before had she shown any of her children to their father. She knocked on the door of his study and entered with Akbar in her arms. She paused for a moment, then laid the baby down on the desk and said, "My child is deaf and dumb."

"Deaf and dumb? What can I do to help you?"

A few moments went by before Hajar could look him in the eye.

"Let my child bear your name."

"My name?" he asked, and fell silent.

"If you'll let him have your name, I promise never to bother you again," said Hajar.

The nobleman remained silent.

"You once said you liked me, and once or twice that you respected me. And you said I could always ask you for a favour. I've never asked for anything before, because I didn't need to, but now I beg you: let my child bear your name. Only that. I'm not asking you to make him an heir. Just to have Akbar's name recorded in an official document."

"The baby's crying," he said after a while. "Give him something to eat."

Then he stood up, opened the window, and called to his servant, "Go and get the imam. Hurry up, we haven't got all day!"

Before long, the imam arrived. Hajar was sent off to wait in another room while the two men discussed the matter behind closed doors. The imam wrote a few lines in a book, then drew up a document and had the nobleman sign it. The whole thing took only a few minutes. The imam rode back home on his mule.

"Here, Hajar, this is the document you wanted. But remember: keep it in a safe place and tell no one of its existence. Only after my death can it be shown to other people."

Hajar tucked the document in her clothes and tried to kiss his hand.

"There's no need for that, Hajar. You can go home now. But come and visit me often. I'll repeat what I've said before: I like you and I want to go on seeing you."

Hajar strapped her baby to her back and left. When she came down from the mountains, she knew she was carrying a child with a venerable name: Aga Akbar Mahmud Ghaznavi Khorasani.

The document turned out to be worthless. After the nobleman died, his heirs bribed the local imam and had Aga Akbar's name removed from the will. Since Hajar hadn't been expecting her child to inherit anything, it hardly mattered. She was satisfied with the name alone. Aga Akbar's parentage was known. His father had roots that could be traced back to the palace on Lalehzar Mountain.

Akbar grew up married and had children. And even though he was a simple carpet-weaver, he remained proud of his lineage. He kept with him at all times the document with his long name.

Akbar often talked about his father. He especially wanted his son Ishmael to know that his grandfather had been an important man, a nobleman on a horse with a rifle slung over his shoulder.

The nobleman was killed by a Russian. Just who the murderer was, nobody knew. A soldier? A gendarme? A Russian thief who sneaked over the border?

· · ·

The mountain range where Aga Akbar lived and where his forefathers had lived before him bordered on Russia, known in those days as the Soviet Union. The southern part of the range belonged to Iran; the northern part, with its permanent layer of snow, to Russia.

No one knew, however, what that Russian soldier, or the Russian army, had been looking for in the mountains.

All that was left of the murder was a story that lived on in Aga Akbar's memory.

When they were home by themselves, Akbar told the story to Ishmael, who was assigned the role of the nobleman on horseback. Akbar was the Russian soldier, wearing an army coat and a cap with a bold red insignia.

Ishmael, his wooden rifle slung over his shoulder, mounted a pillow. Aga Akbar put on his coat and cap and hid behind the cupboard, which served as a makeshift boulder.

Ishmael rode his horse—not too fast, not too slow, but sedately, as a nobleman should—past the cupboard. A head peeked out. The horseman went on riding for another few yards, then the soldier suddenly leapt out with a knife in his hand, took two or three giant steps and planted his knife in the horseman, who fell off his horse and died.

No doubt this story was largely a fantasy, but the death of Aga Akbar's mother was very real.

"How old were you when Hajar died?" Ishmael signed.

Aga Akbar had no concept of time.

"She died when a group of unknown black birds perched in our almond tree," he signed back.

"Unknown?"

"I'd never seen them before."

"How old were you when the black birds perched in the tree?" Ishmael signed.

"My hands were cold, the tree had no leaves and Hajar no longer spoke to me."

"No, I mean how old? How *old* were you when your mother died?"

"Me, Akbar. My head came up to Hajar's chest."

He had been about nine, Kazem Khan explained later. Hajar had been feeling ill, so she had gone to bed. Akbar had slipped in under the blankets and held his mother in his arms.

"Your mother died in your arms?" Ishmael signed.

"Yes, but how did you know?"

"Uncle Kazem Khan told me."

"I crawled under the blankets. When she was sick, she used to talk to me and hold my hand. But this time she stopped talking, and her hand no longer moved. I was scared, really scared, so I stayed under the blankets, not daring to come out. Then a hand reached under the blankets, grabbed me and tried to pull me out. I held on to Hajar's body, but Kazem Khan finally dragged me away. I cried."

The next day the oldest woman in the family wrapped Hajar in a white shroud. Then several men came with a coffin and carried her to the cemetery.

After the funeral Kazem Khan took little Akbar with him.

"I wanted him to understand what death was," he later told his nephew Ishmael. "So I rode over the mountains with him, in search of something that would show him that dying was part of life.

"I looked around in the snow, hoping to find a dead bird or a dead fox or maybe even a dead wolf. But on that cold winter day the birds flew more energetically than ever and the wolves bounded across the rocks. I stopped, sat him down on a boulder and pointed at the plants buried beneath the snow. 'Look! Those plants are dead, too.' But that wasn't a good example. I saw an old mountain goat who could barely leap from one rock to another. 'You see that goat?

He's going to die soon.' No, that wasn't a good example either.

"I was hoping that a bird would stop flying in mid-air and suddenly drop dead at our feet. But no birds dropped dead that day.

"I put Akbar back on the horse and we rode on.

"After a while, I saw the nobleman's palace in the distance. It had been empty since his death. I rode over to it."

"Why?"

"I had no idea. I just thought, Let's have a look. I led the horse around to the back. Aga Akbar didn't know what I was trying to do. 'Stand on the horse's back,' I gestured to him, 'and climb up onto the stone wall!'"

"'Why?' he signed.

"He didn't want to. So I went first. I climbed up onto the wall and lay there. 'Come on!' I said. 'Give me your hand.'

"I grabbed him, pulled him up and then helped him climb up onto the roof. We inched our way to the courtyard stairs.

"'Don't look so surprised,' I said when we reached them. He didn't want to go down the stairs.

"'What are we going to do?' he signed.

"'Nothing, just look around. Come on, this palace belongs to you, too.'

"We walked gingerly down the stairs. He briefly forgot his mother. I even noticed a smile on his face.

"We went into the courtyard. I'd never been inside the palace before. I thought the doors would be locked, but they were open. I thought the rooms would be empty, but no, the furniture was all in place. The courtyard door had been blown open by the wind and the snow had drifted halfway down the hall. We went in.

"There was dust everywhere. Even the expensive Persian carpets were covered in a fine layer of sand. We left footprints. You could see that a man and a little boy had walked through the rooms. 'Give me your hand,' I said to Akbar. 'Do you see that? That's what death is.'

"I looked for the nobleman's study, for his library. Akbar stared in amazement at everything—the chandeliers, the mirrors, the paintings. 'Go on, take a look,' I said. 'You see those portraits? Those are your ancestors. Take a good look at them. Oh, Allah, Allah, what a lot of books!'

"I had no idea there were so many books on Lalehzar Mountain. 'Hey, Akbar, come here. You see this book? It's been written by hand. Let me read it:

Khoda-ya, rast guyand fetna az to-ast
wali az tars na-tavanam chegidan
lab-o dandan-e torkan-e Khata-ra
beh een khubi na bayad afaridan.

"I took out a sheet of parchment on which a family tree had been drawn. 'Do you see those names? Each one of those men has written a book. You can also write one. A book of your very own.'

"'Write?' signed Akbar.

"'I'll teach you.' I rummaged around in the drawer in search of an empty notebook and found one. 'Here, take it. Put it in your pocket. Now hurry up, let's go.'"

They left the palace and rode home. Kazem Khan needed to smoke his opium pipe and drink a few cups of strong tea. "Where are you, Akbar? Come here, I've got a lump of sugar for you. Russia's finest sugar. Mmm, delicious. Have a sip of tea, Akbar. Now where's your book? Come sit by me. Opium is bad. You must never smoke opium. If I don't smoke my pipe in time, I get the shakes. When I do smoke it, though, I think up fantastic poems. Go get your book and write something in it."

"I can't write. I can't even read," Akbar signed.

"You don't have to read, but you do have to write. Just scribble something in your notebook. One page every day. Or maybe just a couple of sentences. Anyway, try it. Go upstairs, write something in your book, then come and show it to me."

When Kazem Khan had finished his pipe, he went upstairs.

"Where are you, Akbar? Haven't you written anything yet? It doesn't matter. I'll teach you. You see that bed? From now on, it's your bed. Open the window and look out at the mountains. That beautiful view is all yours. Open the cupboard. That's yours, too. You can keep your things in it. Here, this is the key to your room."

It was impossible to concentrate on reading or writing when you were sitting by the window in that room, Kazem Khan complained, because you would be mesmerised by the view, by nature. You had no choice but to lay down your book, put away your pen, go and get your pipe, chop up some opium, put a piece of it in your pipe, pick up a glowing coal with a pair of pincers, light the pipe, then puff, puff, puff on it, blow the smoke out the window and stare at the view.

The first thing you saw were the walnut trees, then the pomegranate trees and, beyond that, a strip of yellow wildflowers and a field dotted with opium-coloured bushes. The yellow flowers and the brownish-yellow bushes merged at the foot of Saffron Mountain, which rose majestically into the sky.

If you could climb to the top of Saffron Mountain, stand on its craggy peak and peer through a pair of binoculars, and if there happened to be no fog that day, you would be able to make out the contours of a customs shed and a handful of soldiers, because that's where the border is. Back when Aga Akbar and Kazem Khan were standing by the window, however, no villager could have reached that mountain peak.

Saffron Mountain is famous in Iran, not so much because

of its nearly inaccessible peak, but because of its historically important cave. Saffron Mountain is a familiar name in the world of archaeology. The cave, located halfway up the mountain, is extremely difficult to reach. Back in those days, wolves slept in it during the winter and gave birth to their cubs in it during the spring.

If you scaled the wall with ropes and spikes, like a mountain climber, you'd find bits of fur everywhere, along with the bones of mountain goats devoured by the wolves.

If you came in the spring, you might see the cubs at the mouth of the cave, calling to their mothers.

Deep inside the cave, on a dark southerly wall, is an ancient stone relief. More than 3,000 years ago, the first king of Persia ordered that a cuneiform inscription be chiselled into the rock, beyond the reach of sun, wind, rain and time. It has never been deciphered.

Sometimes when you looked out of Kazem Khan's window, you saw a cuneiform expert—an Englishman or a Frenchman or an American—riding into the cave on a mule, which meant that another attempt was being made to decipher the cuneiform.

"Come! Get the mules ready," Kazem Khan gestured to Akbar.

"Where are we going?"

"To the cave."

"Why?"

"To learn how to read. I'm going to teach you to read," signed Kazem Khan.

They put on warm clothes, mounted two strong mules and headed up Saffron Mountain. There was no path going up to the cave. The mules simply sniffed the ground, followed the tracks of the mountain goats and slowly climbed higher and higher. After three or four hours, they reached the entrance to the cave.

"Wait!" Kazem Khan signed. "First we have to scare off the wolves."

He took out his rifle and fired three shots into the air. The wolves fled.

They got down from their mules and entered the cave. Once inside, Kazem Khan lit an oil lamp. They walked deeper and deeper into the cave, with the mules trotting along behind.

"Come on, Akbar, follow me."

"Why are you going into the darkness?" Akbar signed.

"Be patient a bit longer. Come with me. Look! Up there!" Kazem Khan said, and he held up the lamp. "Can you see it?"

"See what?" Akbar signed. "I don't see anything."

"Wait, I'll go and look for a stick."

He hunted around in the cave for a stick, but didn't find one.

"Here, hold the reins."

Kazem Khan sat on top of the mule and held up the lamp again.

"Can you see it now? That thing on the wall, *in* the wall. Go and stand over there, so you can see it better. Wait, let me get down from the mule. Look carefully, Akbar. Do you know what that is? It's a letter. A letter written by a king. A great king.

"Back in the old days, people couldn't read or write. Paper hadn't been invented yet. So the king ordered that his words be chiselled into the wall of the cave. All those foreigners who come up here on mules actually want to read the king's letter, the king's story. Now get out your pen and notebook. I'm going to hold the mule against the wall and I want you to stand on its back. Yes, on the mule's back. Good. Are you comfortable? Look, there's a place for you to hang up the lamp, so you can see better. Now I want you to write down the text. Look carefully at all the symbols, at all those cuneiform words, and write them down on the paper, one by one. Go ahead! Don't be afraid. I'll hold the mule. Just write!"

Aga Akbar may or may not have understood what his uncle had in mind, but in any case he started copying the text. He stared at the cuneiform script and did his best to draw each character, one by one, in his notebook. Three whole pages.

"It's finished," he signed.

"Good. Now put it in your pocket and get down. Be careful."

That evening, when Kazem Khan was at home again, smoking his opium, he signed to Akbar, "Go and get your book and come sit here by the brazier. Now give me your pen and listen carefully. You copied the letter written by the king. Do you know what it says?"

"No."

"That letter is something that used to be inside the king's head. Nobody knows what it says, but it must say something. Now you, yes *you*, can also write a letter. Here, on the next page of your notebook. Some other time, you can write another letter on another page. You can write down what's inside your head, just like the king did. Go ahead and try it!"

Years later, when Ishmael, the son of Aga Akbar, was sixteen and living in the city, he went to visit his uncle in the mountains. "But Uncle Kazem Khan," he asked him one evening at dinner, "why didn't you teach my father the normal alphabet, so he could read and write like everyone else?"

"What do you mean 'like everyone else'? Nowadays you have to learn to read, but you didn't have to back then. Especially not here in the mountains. Even the village imam could barely write his name. Who could have taught the alphabet to a deaf-mute child? I wasn't the right man for the job. I simply didn't have the patience. I've never liked sitting around the house. I'm always on the go, always riding off somewhere on my horse.

"To teach a child like that, you need a capable father and a strong mother. I didn't want to teach him how to write, but I felt—or, rather, observed—that Aga Akbar was forming sentences in his head, that he was thinking up stories. Do you understand?

"Those sentences in his head, that storytelling talent, could have destroyed him. He had headaches all the time, and I was the only one who knew why. That's the reason I taught him to write in cuneiform. To write for the sake of writing. I didn't know if he'd be able to do it, or even if it would help. I was simply trying to solve a problem. Anyway, no one can read the king's cuneiform inscription. Maybe the puzzle will never be solved. But the king did write down his thoughts.

"Did I steer Akbar in the right direction or not? You're entitled to your opinion, but I think my method worked. Your father still writes, to this day. And cuneiform is a beautiful and mysterious script. Your father has his own language, his own written language. Do you ever look in his notebook?"

"No. I see him writing in it sometimes."

"Have you ever tried to read it?"

"I can't read a word of it."

"You could ask him to teach you how."

"What about you? Can you read it?"

"No, but I know what he's writing about. One time . . . God, how long ago was it? I went to his room and found him sitting at his desk, writing. I think he was about as old as you are now. Except that he was stronger. Big shoulders, dark hair, clear eyes. Anyway, I saw that he was writing. 'Show it to me,' I said. 'Tell me what you've written.'

"In those days he had quite a bit of contact with the foreigners who went to the cave, the ones who were trying to decipher the text. I think he'd learned something from those experts—something about other reliefs, or maybe even a likely translation. 'Explain to me what you've written,' I said.

At first he didn't want to. He was embarrassed, but I kept pressuring him. I wanted to know if my method had worked.

"So he read. I can still recite his words from memory. Listen, it's beautiful: *I, I, I am the son of the horseman, the horseman from the palace, the palace on the mountain, the mountain across from the cave. In that cave is a letter, a letter from a king, a letter carved in the rock, from the time when there were no pens, only hammers and chisels.*"

Later, when Aga Akbar was a young man, he became a guide. He led the cuneiform experts—the Americans, the British, the French and the Germans—up to the cave on mules. Then he stood on a mule and held up the oil lamp, so they could take pictures or copy the text for the umpteenth time.

Anyone interested in cuneiform or in decoding old inscriptions is sure to own books on the subject. And those books are sure to have a couple of pictures of the cuneiform inscription in the cave on Saffron Mountain. And one of those pictures is bound to show a youthful Aga Akbar, standing on a mule and holding up an oil lamp to illuminate the cuneiform relief.

The Train

We can't understand Aga Akbar's notes
without knowing about Shah Reza Khan.
We look at the background to the story,
at the details not given in the notebook.

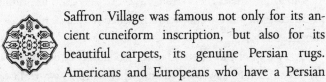 Saffron Village was famous not only for its ancient cuneiform inscription, but also for its beautiful carpets, its genuine Persian rugs. Americans and Europeans who have a Persian carpet in the living room don't realise that it might have been made in Saffron Village. You can tell by the pattern. If it has a strange bird with an odd-looking tail, it no doubt comes from the village where Aga Akbar grew up.

In the middle of winter, hundreds of strange birds suddenly flew in from the other side of Saffron Mountain, from the former Soviet Union. Since it was cold, the birds were hungry and thirsty. The villagers always knew when the birds were about to arrive: early in the morning, on one of the first days after the full moon had appeared to the left of the mountain peak. The women leaned their ladders against the walls in expectation.

At the first sign of the birds, the women climbed up onto the rooftops and set out bowls of warm water and bits of left-over food.

The strange birds landed on the roofs. The women and children watched from the windows and saw the birds walk across the roofs with their strange long tails, bobbing their heads in thanks. The birds rested for a few hours, then flew off. And the women, who spent the whole day, the whole month, the whole year, the whole of their lives in the village, weaving rugs, the women who never got a chance to leave Saffron Mountain, wove those birds into the patterns of the carpets.

Another motif that made its way into their carpets was the cuneiform script.

The illiterate women of Saffron Village used the secret language of the cave's relief to weave their hopes and longings into their carpets.

Sometimes the carpets depicted a foreigner in a hat riding to the cave on a mule and holding a sheet of paper filled with cuneiform.

At the end of the 1930s the women suddenly began weaving a completely new pattern into their carpets—a train. A train trailing smoke as it snaked its way up Saffron Mountain.

Nowadays the carpets show a bomber flying over the village, dropping its deadly cargo.

Though the women didn't realise it, the train and its trail of smoke symbolised a shift in power. In those days Reza Khan, the father of the last shah of Iran, had the country firmly in his grip. There was a centralised dictatorship. Reza Khan was a simple private who had worked his way up to general. What he lacked in education, he made up for in ambition.

In 1921 he staged a coup. Announcing that the Qajar dynasty had come to an end, he declared himself the new king of Persia. From then on, it was to be known as the Pahlavi kingdom.

Reza Shah wanted to weave the country into a new pattern. He wanted to transform the archaic kingdom of Persia into a modern nation oriented toward the West. That meant new businesses, modern schools, printing presses, theatres, steel bridges, roads, buses and taxis, not to mention radios and radio stations that would broadcast, for the first time in Persian history, the magical voice of a singer:

> *Yawash, yawash, yawash, yawash*
> *amadam dar khane-tan.*
> *Yek shakh-e gol dar dastam*
> *sar-e rahat benshastam.*
> *Be khoda' yadat narawad az nazram.*

> *Softly, softly, ever so softly,*
> *I walked past your house and*
> *Sat on the roadside with a flower*
> *In my hand as you passed by.*
> *God knows I shall never forget you.*

Reza Shah wanted more. He wanted to change women's lives overnight. From one day to the next, women were forbidden to wear chadors. Whenever they went out, they were expected to wear hats and coats instead.

He wanted everything to happen quickly, which is why he governed the country with an iron hand and stifled all opposition. On his orders, the poet Farokhi had his lips sewn shut because he'd recited a poem about women who stumbled and couldn't walk without their chadors. During Reza Shah's reign, many writers, intellectuals and political leaders were thrown in jail or murdered, and others simply disappeared.

According to the opposition, Reza Shah was a lackey of the British Embassy in Tehran and had been ordered to modernise the country for the benefit of the West. In the eyes of the imperialists, he was merely a soldier, a pawn to be used in the struggle against the Soviet Union.

Whether or not he was a British puppet, one thing is certain: he wanted things to change. In his own way, he was determined to radically reform the country, but he was a soldier, a brute. Everyone was terrified of him.

Reza Shah hoped that his most important projects would be finished before his son succeeded him.

The train was one of his pet projects.

During the twenty-five hundred years in which various kings, sultans and emirs had ruled the Persian Empire, no government official had ever come to the mountains to take a census of the inhabitants. Now that Reza Khan was shah, however, he wanted his subjects to carry identity cards.

Throughout the ages the imams had controlled the mountains and the countryside. Now the populace had to contend with a gendarme, a man in a military cap emblazoned with one of Reza Shah's slogans, a man who answered to no one but His Majesty.

Reza Shah needed an army that obeyed him unquestioningly. And that army needed soldiers whose names and dates of birth were listed on identity cards. So, for the first time in history, the exact number of boys in Saffron Village was recorded. The vital statistics were entered in a book, which the gendarme kept in his cupboard.

Thanks to Reza Shah, Aga Akbar also was issued with an identity card. At last, his full name was officially on record.

· · ·

To realise his great dream, Reza Shah ordered that a railroad be built from the southernmost part of the country to its northeastern border. Right up to the ear of the giant Russian bear, to be exact. He knew that the Europeans had the most to gain from this route, but he also knew that the rails would be left behind long after those Europeans were gone.

The railroad tracks crept through the desert, over the rivers, up the mountains, down the valleys and through the towns and villages until they finally reached Saffron Mountain.

The iron monster started to climb the mountain, but was forced to stop halfway, when it came to the historic cave with the cuneiform inscription. The building of the railroad had disturbed the cave's eternal rest. More importantly, the engineers were afraid that if they blasted through the rock with dynamite, the cave would collapse.

The cuneiform inscription, their ancient cultural heirloom, was in danger. The engineers feared it would crack. They panicked. The chief engineer didn't know what to do. He didn't dare take a single risk. He knew the shah would have him beheaded if anything went wrong.

With trembling hands, he sent a telegram to the capital: CANNOT PROCEED WITH RAILS. CUNEIFORM BLOCKING ROUTE.

The shah read the telegram, hopped into his jeep and had himself driven to Saffron Mountain. After a long night's drive, the jeep stopped at the foot of the mountain. The local gendarme offered the shah a mule, but he refused. He wanted to climb the mountain himself. Early in the morning, before the sun had struck the mountain peak, Reza Shah stood at the entrance to the cave. Wearing a military tunic and carrying a field marshal's baton under his arm, he checked on the progress of his dream.

. . .

"What's the problem?" he asked.

"Your Majesty—" the chief engineer began, trembling. He didn't dare go any further.

"Explain it to me!"

"Th-th-th-the rails have to go past here. I'm afraid that . . . that . . . that . . ."

"Yes?"

"I-I-I would like Your Majesty's permission to . . . to . . . to relocate the cuneiform relief."

"Relocate it? Shut up, you stupid engineer! Find another solution!"

"We've done all the cal-cal-cal-culations, checked out all the options. No matter how we do it, the dynamite could destroy the cave."

"Find another route!"

"We've explored every alternative. This is the best route. The others are virtually impossible. We could make a huge detour, but . . ."

"But what?"

"It'll take longer."

"How much longer?"

"A number of months, Your Majesty. Six or seven months."

"We haven't got that much time. We can't lose a day. Or even an hour. As for you—get out of my sight, you idiot! 'Impossible'—is that the only word you engineers know? Six or seven months? You must be joking!"

Furious, the shah marched into the dark cave. Outside, no one dared to move. After a while he came out again. He looked down at the hordes of peasants—young men who'd climbed up the mountain to catch a glimpse of Reza Shah. When they saw him emerge from the cave, they leapt onto the rocks and began to shout, "*Jawid shah! Jawid shah! Jawid shah!*"

The shah thrust his field marshal's baton under his arm and slowly made his way down the mountain. Just as the gendarmes were about to chase away the peasants at the bottom, a group of elders from the surrounding villages appeared. Dressed in their most festive garments, they walked toward Reza Shah, carrying a bowl of water, a mirror and the Koran. When they were a hundred yards away, the oldest man threw the water in the direction of the shah and the other men bowed their heads.

"*Salaam*, sultan of Persia!" the man exclaimed. "*Salaam*, God's earthly shadow!"

He knelt and kissed the ground.

"Come forward!" commanded the shah, pointing his baton at the place where he wanted the old man to stand.

"Listen, graybeard! I don't need your prayers. Use your head and give me some advice. That idiot of an engineer doesn't know how to route the railroad track. How can I get the train past the cave without doing any permanent damage?"

The old man turned and went back to confer with the others.

After a while he came back.

"Well?"

"For centuries our fathers have built houses here on Saffron Mountain, using only a pick-axe and spikes. No one has ever damaged the mountain. They chipped away the rock only in places where it was absolutely necessary. If Your Majesty wishes, I will call together all of the young men in the village. They will clear a path for your train."

A look of relief spread over the shah's face. Then it clouded over again.

"No, it'll take too long. I don't have that much time. I want it done fast."

"As Your Majesty wishes. In that case, I will call all of the young men on Saffron Mountain and, if necessary, all of the young men from the neighbouring mountains. We have experience, we know the mountain. Give our men the opportunity to prove themselves."

The shah was silent.

"Give us the strongest pick-axes in the country."

"And then?"

"Then we will clear a path, so the train can go around the cave and reach the other side of the mountain."

That evening the muezzins from all the villages called from the roofs of their mosques, "*Allahu akbar. La ilaha illa Allah.* In the name of Allah, our forefathers and Reza Shah, we call on all strong men. Hurry, hurry, hurry to the mosque. Whatever you're doing, stop right now and hurry to the mosque."

All evening and all night young men from the neighbouring villages poured into the mosque in Saffron Village.

Early the next morning hundreds of men walked behind the village elder and stood in the designated spot at the foot of the mountain. One of those men was the seventeen-year-old Aga Akbar. He didn't have the faintest idea who Reza Shah was or what he had in mind, much less what his plans for the country were. Like the other men, he had no idea why the railroad tracks had to reach the other side of the mountain so quickly. All he knew was that a train had to go around the cave and that it was their job to save the cuneiform inscription.

Reza Shah stood high on a rock and looked down at the men. The villagers had heard the legends about the shah.

In those days the people in the towns and villages thought of him as a saviour. A powerful man. A champion of the poor. A reformer who wanted to give the country a face-lift.

But his reputation in Tehran was very different. There he was known for his brutal treatment of the opposition.

The shah had ordered that all the opium, tea and sugar be removed from the house of an important mullah, and had kept him under house arrest for three weeks. To the mullah this was tantamount to the death penalty. The shah had ordered the imams to remove their turbans and appear in public with their heads bare. His policemen went through the streets plucking chadors off the women who were still wearing them. When the imams in the holy city of Qom rose up in revolt, Reza Shah ordered that a cannon be placed at the gates of the golden mosque. Then he taunted the leader of the Shiites: "Come out of your hole, you black rat!"

A rat? A black rat? What did he mean by that? He just called our great spiritual leader a black rat! Suddenly hundreds of young imams with rifles appeared on the roof of the golden mosque.

"Fire!" the shah screamed at his officers.

Dozens of imams were killed and dozens arrested. The sacred shrine was partially destroyed. A wave of shock ran through the Islamic world. Shopkeepers turned off their lights. The bazaar closed. People wore black. But the shah wouldn't listen to reason.

"Are there any more out there?"

No, not a soul was left on the streets and rooftops. Everyone was sitting inside, behind locked doors.

Aga Akbar knew none of these stories. He thought the shah was simply a high-ranking military officer. A general in a strange-looking tunic, with a stick under his arm.

The village elder walked over to the shah, bowed and said, "The men are prepared to sacrifice themselves to realise Your Majesty's dream."

Reza Shah didn't answer. He looked at the peasants. His face was filled with doubt. Would they really be able to solve his problem?

Just then a pair of armoured cars drove up and stopped

near the men. Two generals leapt out and raced over to the shah, each holding his cap in one hand and his rifle in the other.

"Everything is ready, Your Majesty!" called one of the generals.

"Unload them!" ordered the shah.

The generals hurried back to the armoured cars.

The soldiers threw open the doors and unloaded hundreds of English pick-axes.

"You!" the shah yelled at the village elder standing before him. "Here are the pick-axes you asked for! If any of your men are lazy, I'll put a bullet through your head!"

He wheeled around. "Don't just stand there," he said to the chief engineer. "Get started!"

The shah headed for his jeep. Suddenly he stopped, as if he'd forgotten something. He returned to his elevated position on the rock and beckoned one of the generals with his baton. In turn, the general beckoned seven soldiers, who were lined up with seven bulging bags in their arms. The soldiers marched over to the shah, deposited the bags on the ground in front of him and snapped back to attention.

"Open them!" he commanded one of the soldiers.

The soldier opened the bags, one by one. The shah took out a handful of brand-new bills.

He turned to the peasants. "Start smashing those rocks!" he ordered. "This money will be your reward. I'll be back next week!"

"*Jawid shah* . . . Long live the shah!" the men shouted three times.

The shah climbed down again and went over to his jeep.

The engineer quickly led the peasants, each equipped with a pick-axe, to the place where the work on the tracks had come to a halt. The peasants made jokes, flexed their muscles and swore they would reduce even the hardest rocks on Saffron Mountain to rubble. They had no idea what was in store.

Years later, a faded black-and-white photograph proudly displayed on Aga Akbar's mantle showed him with a pick-axe resting on his right shoulder and a spike—as thick as a tent stake—between the thumb and forefinger of his left hand.

Akbar is turned at a slight angle. The photographer had focused on the pick-axe and spike, but the young Aga Akbar had flexed his muscles, so that your eye is drawn to his bulging biceps rather than to the tools.

When Ishmael was little, Aga Akbar told him a long story about the picture. A story that was actually about his biceps and about the money—the large sum of money—he had earned.

"Come here!" he gestured to his son. "Tell me! Who's the man in the picture?"

And he launched into a story. "I, Akbar, was very strong. I—and only I—could break that rock with the pick-axe. Can you see the rock? There, in the background. No, you can't see it, the picture's no good, it's old. But there, behind me. Sure you can't see it? Never mind. That rock had to go, all the rocks had to go. They couldn't use those exploding things. They were bad for the cuneiform inscription.

"One day I'll take you to the cave. Wait a minute. Don't you have a . . . where's your schoolbook? Have you ever seen a picture in your schoolbook of an officer, a man in a military tunic with a crown on his head? Isn't there one in your schoolbook? . . . Seven, yes, seven potato sacks full of money. And that money was for us. Because of the train."

Did Ishmael understand what his father was talking about in his rudimentary sign language?

One thing little Ishmael did know was that his life was interwoven with that of his father. Everyone—his mother, his uncles, his aunts, the village imam, the neighbours, the children—made him sit, stand and walk beside his father. His job was to be his father's mouthpiece.

Later the missing bits of information would be supplied by his aunts and uncles, or by the old men of Saffron Mountain. Or he himself would look up the facts in history books and novels.

More often, however, he would go and visit his father's elderly uncle. He would sit down by Kazem Khan and listen as he filled in the missing parts of the stories. "Your father was strong. I told him that a railroad track was being built. Personally, I've never cared for aristocrats and generals and shahs, but I'd heard a lot about Reza Shah. Though I was hoping to catch a glimpse of the man, I didn't see him."

"Why not?"

"Because I was stubborn. I rode over there on my horse, but the gendarmes wouldn't let me through."

"Why not?"

"Because people weren't allowed to approach the shah on horseback. You were supposed to go on foot, to grovel on your hands and knees. I refused to do that. I turned around and went home, but I came back the next day, because I wanted to see what the men of Saffron Mountain were doing."

"Did you go on foot or on horseback?"

"Nobody's ever seen me go anywhere on foot. I looked at the men from a distance. They were working in shifts, around the clock, smashing the rocks and clearing a road for the train."

"Did the men manage all right with the pick-axes? I mean, did they finish the road on time?"

"Oh, no. Or, actually, they did. At first everything was going fine. They were banging away with all their might, and you could see the road taking shape. Then, just below the southern wall of the cave, they ran into a rock that was unusually hard. The men pounded at it—first one shift, then another—but hardly made a dent. The work had gone well the first two weeks. After that, their strength was gone. The men were thin and worn, exhausted, barely recognisable. The engineers were so terrified of the shah that they hadn't realised the men were broken. They panicked. Reza Shah would be arriving soon and the men would still be banging away at that one rock.

"The shah wasn't an educated man, nor did he come from a family of book readers, but he was smart, especially when it came to ordinary people. He took one look at the workers and knew what the problem was. He fired the chief engineer. 'Go and pack your bags, bookworm. You don't know what work is. All you can do is read, read, read.'

"Reza Shah ordered ten big kettles to be brought from the army barracks. He knew that a worker needed more than bread and goat cheese if he was to smash rocks for weeks at a time. So ten fat cooks came running up with ten big kettles. The soldiers were ordered to shoot five mountain goats and hand them over to the cooks.

"Work was suspended for the day. All that the men had to do was eat, drink, smoke and rest.

"That same evening the shah returned with a new engineer. He was determined not to go back to Tehran until the railroad tracks had reached the other side of the cave.

"Early the next morning, even before the sun was up, the shah climbed up to the cave. A soldier, carrying a bag of money, trotted along behind.

"The men were lined up with their pick-axes resting on their shoulders. They waited for the shah to reveal his new plan.

"The shah took off his tunic, grabbed a handful of money and positioned himself on top of a rock. He pointed his baton at one of the men.

"'You!'

"The man stepped forward.

"'And you—'

"'No, not you, the man next to you.'

"The other man stepped forward. It was your father. Of course, he hadn't heard the shah, but his fellow workers had tapped him on the shoulder.

"The shah selected eleven strong men.

"'Listen!' the shah said. 'After today, I don't want to see this rock ever again. Every time you chip off a piece, I'll give you one of these bills. Who wants to go first?'

"Of course, your father didn't know what the shah was saying, so he couldn't be first. But the first man brought the pick-axe down with all his might and chipped off a piece. 'Here's your money,' the shah said. 'Now you!' He pointed at your father. Only then did your father understand what was going on. He slammed his pick-axe down so hard that a huge chunk of rock flew off. The shah smiled.

"'Here, young man, I'm giving you two bills. Next!'

"And so it went. The rock was smashed to pieces, and those eleven men went home utterly broken and exhausted. But that night, everyone in the village knew that Reza Shah had tucked a wad of bills into your father's pocket. And that Aga Akbar had then collapsed.

"There was a newspaper photographer, whose job it was to record the work on the railroad. The shah pointed at your father, lying there on the ground. The moment he saw the shah point, your father grabbed his pick-axe and leapt to his feet.

"'Put the pick-axe on your shoulder,' the photographer instructed him. 'Hold up one of those spikes. Right, that's good. Now don't move.' But your father turned and angled himself slightly so that his biceps showed up better in the picture.

"The whole village was talking about it and laughing that

night. Everyone in Saffron Village was proud of having a picture in the newspaper.

"Those eleven men became the richest men on Saffron Mountain. They built new houses out of stone, just like the houses in the city. Everyone wanted to give their daughters to those men. They married the most beautiful girls in the village.

"But we couldn't find a girl, a suitable girl, for your father. Not then, at any rate. Life is like that, my boy, though it's also full of surprises."

"You know, Uncle, I've heard a lot of bad things about Reza Shah. The building of the railroad has been heavily criticised. What do you think?"

"Listen, my boy, didn't I just finish saying that I don't know anything about politics? Don't ask me. I've never been much of a one for reading newspapers, either, especially not back then. I only read my own books, or old books, poetry, history. I know nothing about criticism. What I do know is that Saffron Mountain is no ordinary mountain. It's not simply a pile of rocks, it's our country's spiritual legacy. Our roots can be found in its boulders and crevices. And I'm not just referring to the cave, because there's more on Saffron Mountain. The sacred well, for example. The mountain lives and breathes. Go into the cave and stand still. You'll hear it. Kneel down by the sacred well and listen. You'll hear Saffron Mountain's heart beating. And to think they suddenly started blasting our mountain with dynamite and pounding it with English pick-axes."

"Why did you send my father off to work there?"

"I didn't. I simply explained what was happening. Besides, he never listened to what I said. He always did whatever the other boys his age were doing.

"Looking back on it, though, I see that things have worked out all right. I was afraid that the mountain wouldn't survive. Now, after so many years, I can see that the mountain has recovered. Bushes and flowers have sprung up on the slopes and covered up the scars. Mountain goats graze between the rails and the baby goats leap from one railroad tie to another. The mountain has accepted the railroad and assimilated it. You can hardly see the traces.

"The train will be here soon. It doesn't make much noise, and that's good. Our ancient Saffron Mountain has acquired something new, something modern. A train with little red cars that chug up the mountain. Life is like that, my boy. That's just the way things are."

A Wife

*We suspect that Aga Akbar wrote
about his friends in this section.
And about his wife.*

 All the birds had started making their nests, all except Aga Akbar. He had no mate. No wife.

By then the other strong men, who had also built stone houses, already had children. Aga Akbar's house, however, was still empty.

In those days he came into frequent contact with prostitutes. That was because of his work: he called on customers and mended their carpets.

Back when Aga Akbar was twelve, Kazem Khan had taken him to see an old friend in another village. Uwsa Gholam had a small business up in the mountains. He made natural dyes out of the roots and flowers of plants that grew on Saffron Mountain. People came to him from all over the country to match the original colours in their carpets.

In fact, Uwsa Gholam made a living out of mending carpets. Old and expensive carpets were always getting damaged. If the hole or tear wasn't mended, the rest of the weave would gradually come unravelled, too. Not everyone, though, can mend a carpet. In unskilled hands, a mend will forever be a fresh wound in the old weave. Uwsa Gholam was one of the best carpet-menders in the country, but he was getting old. His eyes weren't as good as they used to be. He could no longer do his work.

Kazem Khan knew that Aga Akbar would make a poor farmer. He wasn't suited to a life of plowing fields or tending sheep. He needed to do work that required him to use both his hands and his head. That's why Kazem Khan had brought him to Uwsa Gholam.

"*Salaam aleikum,* Uwsa! Here's the boy I've been telling you about. Akbar, shake Uwsa's hand."

The old man reached into his pocket and pulled out a single purple thread from an old carpet. "Akbar, go find some flowers that match the colour of this thread!"

This is how Aga Akbar got started in his career, in the work that he continued to do until the day he died.

For three years he went to Uwsa's early every morning and rode home again at dusk. Then Uwsa died, but by that time Akbar had learned enough to mend carpets and produce natural dyes on his own.

Though no one could take Uwsa's place, Akbar had already made a name for himself in the region. The villagers liked him. They trusted him and would rather have him than a stranger in their homes. And so he rode his horse from one village to another. It was during this period that he came into contact with prostitutes.

. . .

Kazem Khan was very choosy when it came to finding a wife for Aga Akbar. He didn't want a woman with only one eye, or a farm girl who wove carpets. No, he wanted a strong woman with a good head on her shoulders, a woman who could organise things, a woman who understood the man whose children she would bear.

"No, not just any woman," he used to say. "I'll wait, I want him to have just the right one. He can hold out for a few more years. It won't kill him."

But the other men in the family said to him, "You shouldn't compare him to yourself, Kazem Khan. You have women all over Saffron Mountain, but that boy doesn't. If you don't let him marry, he's bound to go astray."

"He can get married tomorrow if he likes, but not to a woman who's deaf, lame or blind."

Unfortunately, there were no strong, healthy, intelligent women on Saffron Mountain who would agree to marry Akbar.

So he turned to prostitutes for warmth and they provided it willingly. "Hello, Aga Akbar, come in. Take a look at my carpet. Do you think you can mend it? Come sit by me. You're tired, your arms ache, your back aches. Here, have a cup of tea. There's no need to stare, I'll come sit beside you. Let me hold your hand. Now doesn't that feel nice?"

If you want to hear the story of Aga Akbar's relationships with prostitutes, you should ask his childhood friend *Sayyid* Shoja.

Shoja was blind. He'd been blind from birth, yet he was famous for his keen sense of hearing—he could hear as well as a dog. He had a sharp tongue, which he didn't hesitate to use. The men tried to stay out of his way, since they knew he heard everything they said.

Sayyid Shoja knew all of the prostitutes on Saffron Mountain and called them by their first names. He also knew which men went to see them. He recognised them instantly by their footsteps. "Hey, little man, you're tiptoeing past. Are you trying to avoid me? What for? Have you been doing naughty things again with that poker in your pants? Come on, shake my hand, say hello, you don't need to be afraid. Your secret is safe with me."

As evening fell, he used to sit by the side of the road and lean against the old tree. The girls came back from the spring with their jugs of water, and he always recognised the footsteps of the girl he loved. "*Salaam aleikum,* my little moon. Let me carry your bucket for you."

The girls laughed at him and he teased them.

"You there," he'd say. "Yes, you with the big butt. Don't sit on the ground, you'll leave a hole in the dirt!"

He didn't have any money, but he didn't need any, because Aga Akbar paid his bills.

The men who didn't like him and feared his sharp tongue sometimes chided him: "You're a leech, Shoja, sucking Akbar dry."

The *sayyid* was too high-minded to worry about such unimportant things.

There was another man who shared his secrets with Akbar and Shoja: Jafar the Spider.

Jafar was crippled. He couldn't walk or stand upright. He was skinny and had a tiny head. The way he scuttled over the ground with his muscular arms and legs made you think of a spider. Yet he owed his nickname not so much to his spidery crawl, but to the fact that he climbed trees like a real spider. People would see him in places a normal person couldn't go. Suddenly he'd be hanging from a branch or crawling up the dome of a mosque. One of his favourite pastimes was peeking through the window of the bathhouse and spying on the naked women.

Jafar saw what the blind Shoja couldn't see.

And since Jafar was Shoja's friend, he was Aga Akbar's friend, too. They formed a tight-knit threesome, and they could do many things together that they were unable to do alone.

They even went to the prostitutes together. That was the agreement. Jafar would crawl onto the back of the blind Shoja, who would then take hold of Aga Akbar's arm, and in this way the three of them would make their way up Saffron Mountain.

They needed Jafar because he was the expert. They never went straight into the prostitute's house. They let Jafar check it out first. He was the one who had to give the OK. Jafar would point his finger at Akbar and say, "Never go in there without me! You might catch a disease! Then you won't be able to pee, and it'll hurt like hell!"

That's how they did things and it had always gone well.

Then, one night, Jafar climbed up on the roof of the outhouse and heard a strange noise. He put his ear to the hole, so he could hear better. He knew instantly what Aga Akbar's problem was. He hurried back to *Sayyid* Shoja. "Shoja," he said, "help me!"

"What's wrong? How can I help you?"

"That idiot's sitting in the outhouse, crying his eyes out."

"What? Who's crying?"

"Akbar. He can't pee."

The two of them went over and stood by the outhouse door.

"You hear that? He's crying."

"I'll be damned, he is. But maybe he's crying about something else."

"Of course not. You don't go to an outhouse to cry about something else."

"Give me a minute to think about it."

"There's nothing to think about, man. It's clear as a bell. We have to look at Akbar's thingy. Then we'll know for sure. We've got to nab him as soon as he comes out."

They hid behind a wall and waited for Akbar.

He came out and Jafar beckoned to him.

Though it was dark, Akbar knew immediately what his friends were up to. His first impulse was to flee, but Jafar was too quick, hurling himself in front of Akbar and grabbing his foot so that he tripped and fell. Shoja rushed over and pinned him to the ground. "Don't run away, asshole! Come with us."

They dragged him into the barn.

"Hold him!" Jafar yelled.

He shimmied up a pole and lit an oil lamp.

Then he pulled down Akbar's pants and inspected his penis. "Let the bastard go. He's sick."

Early the next morning they went to the city in search of a doctor.

Several months later, after Aga Akbar had been cured, Shoja and Jafar had a little talk. Akbar was gradually distancing himself from them and they knew why. As true friends, they felt obliged to inform his uncle. So, one evening, Jafar picked up a lantern and climbed up on Shoja's back.

They went to Kazem Khan's house.

"Good evening," Shoja said. "May we come in?"

"Of course, *Sayyid* Shoja. You two are always welcome. Have a seat. Can I get you some tea?"

"No, thanks. We don't want to be here when Akbar gets home. We've come here to tell you something. We're Akbar's best friends, but some secrets need to be brought out into the open. We've come here to say that we're worried about him."

"Why?"

"You know that the three of us go out together sometimes.

Strange things happen every once in a while, though it usually turns out all right. But this time it's different. This time Akbar has gone too far."

"What do you mean, 'too far'? What's he done now?"

"I may be blind, but I do have two good ears. Besides, there's nothing wrong with Jafar's sight. Maybe I better let Jafar tell you what he's seen."

"Tell me, Jafar. What have you seen?"

"How shall I put it? It's like this: Akbar goes out sometimes . . . well, almost every night, to sleep with a prostitute. I-I-I think he's in love with her. That isn't necessarily bad. She's . . . well, she's young and . . . very friendly. I get the impression that she's fond of Akbar.

"But we think he's gone too far this time. Right, Shoja? Anyway, that's what we wanted to tell you. There's nothing wrong with the woman. She's young and healthy. But we thought you ought to know. Right, Shoja?"

"Right," Shoja said. "Well, that's it. Come on, let's go before Akbar gets home."

Kazem Khan knew that he had to do something for Akbar and that there wasn't much time. If he didn't act soon, no one would want their daughter to marry Akbar.

He had to admit that he'd failed to find the ideal wife for his nephew. So he turned the job over to the old women in the family.

The women rolled up their sleeves and got to work. Before long, however, their enthusiasm dwindled. None of the prospects they came up with fitted into the family. One had a father who was a beggar, another had brothers who were thieves, the third had no breasts, the fourth was so shy she didn't dare show herself.

No, the women of the family weren't able to find a wife for Aga Akbar, either.

Only one more door was open to them. The door to the house of Zeinab *Khatun,* Saffron Mountain's aging match-maker. She always had a ready supply of brides.

Zeinab would be sure to find a good one for Akbar, be-cause she was an opium addict. The women in the family merely had to take her a roll of Kazem Khan's yellow opium and she would arrange the whole thing.

Zeinab lived outside the village, in a house at the foot of the mountain. Her customers were usually single men in search of a wife. "Zeinab *Khatun,* have you got a girl for me? A virtuous woman who can bear me healthy children?"

"No, I don't have a girl—or a woman—for you, virtuous or otherwise. I know you—you're a wife-beater. I still haven't forgotten the last one. Get out of here, go ask your mother to find you a wife."

"Why don't we step inside? I've brought you half a roll of yellow opium. Now what do you have to say?"

"Come right in. You need to smile more often and re-member to shave. With that stubble of yours and those awful yellow teeth, I'll never be able to find you a wife."

Sometimes an elderly mother knocked on her door. "I'm old now, Zeinab *Khatun,* and I don't have any grandchildren. Do something for my son. I'll give you a pretty chador, a real one from Mecca."

"People promise me all kinds of things, but as soon as their sons have a wife, they disappear. Bring me the chador first. In the meantime, I'll think it over. It won't be easy, you know. Few women want to marry a man who drools. But I'll find someone for your son. If I die tonight, I'd hate to be car-ried to my grave in my old, worn-out chador. So go and get it. I'll wait."

The men of the family were opposed to the plan. But the women stuck a roll of opium into the bag of an elderly aunt, put on their chadors and went to Zeinab's house.

The men thought it was beneath the family's dignity to ask the matchmaker for a bride. Of course, they wanted Akbar to have a wife. But what they really wanted for him was a son. An Ishmael who would bear Akbar's burden.

Since they didn't want the child's mother to be a prostitute, they resigned themselves to letting the women use a matchmaker.

Giggling, the women knocked on Zeinab's door.

"Welcome! Please sit down."

While they were still in the hall, the elderly aunt awkwardly pressed the opium into Zeinab's hands. "I don't know the first thing about this," she said. "It's from Kazem Khan."

She was impatient. "I won't beat around the bush, Zeinab *Khatun*. We're looking for a good girl, a sensible woman, for our Akbar. That's all there is to it. Do you have one for us or not?"

The women laughed. They got a kick out of the elderly aunt.

"Do I have one?" said the experienced Zeinab *Khatun*. "I'll find one for you, even if I have to scour this entire mountain. If I can't find a bride for Aga Akbar, who can I find one for? Sit down. Let's drink some tea first."

She brought in a tray with glasses and a teapot. "Let me think. A good girl, a sensible woman. Yes, I know of one. She's very pretty, but—"

Auntie cut her off. "No buts! I don't want half a woman for my nephew. I want a whole one, with all her working parts in order."

"Allah, Allah, why don't you let me finish? God will be angry to hear us talking about one of His creations with such disrespect. The woman I'm referring to is beautiful and in perfect health. It's just that one leg is shorter than the other."

"Oh, that doesn't matter, as long as she can walk," the women said.

"Walk? Can she walk? She leaps like a gazelle. But all right, I can't ask God why He made one leg shorter than the other. He must have had His reasons. Still, I have another woman, but she's slightly deaf."

"No, we don't want a deaf woman for Akbar," said the elderly aunt.

"She's not deaf, just a little hard of hearing. She's good and she's also beautiful, trust me. Come to think of it, this one's even better than the other one. Aga Akbar needs a wife who can walk, who can stand firmly on her own two feet. It doesn't matter if she's deaf. Aga Akbar won't be talking to her anyway."

"No, Akbar won't, but their children will."

"Good heavens, what am I hearing tonight! How can you say such things when you have a deaf-mute in your home? God will be angry. All right, I have another woman. She has a beautiful face, beautiful arms, a neck the colour of milk, a broad pelvis and firm buttocks. Take this woman. God will be pleased with your choice."

The next day the women went to admire Aga Akbar's future bride. She lived in another village on Saffron Mountain. It was a short visit. Zeinab *Khatun* was right—the girl was beautiful. But she looked a bit ill.

"A bit ill?" said the matchmaker. "Maybe she had a slight cold. Or maybe it's that time of the month, you know what I mean, don't you, ladies? Don't worry, she'll be as right as rain by the time the wedding rolls around."

She dazzled them with her words and sent them home happy.

A week later, as twilight fell, the men escorted the bridegroom from the village bathhouse to his home.

Aga Akbar looked strong and healthy in his suit. The blind *Sayyid* Shoja was his best man. He sat on a horse with Jafar the Spider in front of him, holding the reins. They climbed the hill to the house, where the women were to bring the bride and seven mules.

Everyone stood around outside, waiting and watching for the procession.

Before long, seven mules came into sight. The women let out cries of joy and a group of local musicians began to play. Aga Akbar helped his bride to dismount. He offered her his arm and escorted her, as tradition dictated, to the courtyard. Then he shut the door.

The only person who knows exactly what took place behind those closed doors was the old woman who was hiding in the bridal chamber so she could later testify that the marriage had been consummated.

As soon as the groom disappeared with his bride, the guests left. The old men sat around Kazem Khan's and smoked until the old woman came and announced, "It's over. He did it!"

The men all shouted in chorus, "*Allahom salla 'ala Mohammad wa ahl-e Mohammad* [Peace be upon Muhammad and all of his descendants]."

Since Ishmael was Aga Akbar's son, he was allowed to hear the story in greater detail. By then, several older family members, including Kazem Khan, had died. On one of his visits to Saffron Mountain, his elderly aunt invited him in.

How old had he been? Fifteen? Sixteen? At that time, he'd been making frequent visits to his father's village. He'd spent the entire summer there, in his family's summerhouse. He wanted to know more about his father's past.

"Ishmael, my boy," his elderly aunt said as he stepped into the hall, "give me your hand. Come in, my boy."

She squeezed his hand and stared at him with unseeing eyes, as she expressed her admiration for her nephew's son by uttering God's words, "*Fa tabaraka Allah al-husn al-khaleqan*

[And God was pleased with the beauty of the one he had created]." (According to the Holy Book, God fell in love with his own creation.)

Ishmael was not just a son, but the son the whole family had been waiting for. They'd prayed that he would be big and healthy enough for his father to lean on. He'd been a godsend, exactly what everyone had been hoping for. Surely it had been Allah's will.

Auntie took Ishmael into the courtyard.

"Before I die, I have something to tell you about your father's wedding. Come, let's and go and sit over there. I've spread out a carpet in the shade of the old walnut tree."

She leaned back against the trunk and said, "What happened is this, my boy. I stuck a roll of yellow opium in my bag and went off to the matchmaker's with the other women to find a wife for your father. That was wrong. I shouldn't have done that."

"Why not?"

"We failed to carry out the job properly, which is why we were punished by God."

"Punished! Why?"

"Because we forgot that God was watching over your father. We insisted that he get married. We were behaving as if we didn't believe in God, as if we didn't trust Him, as if He had forsaken your father. And we were punished for that reason."

"I don't understand you."

"The women escorted the bride and her seven mules from the village of Saruq to your father's house. I placed her hand in your father's hand and led them to the bedroom. I was the woman who was hiding behind the curtains."

"Hiding behind the curtains?"

"It was the custom back then. I was supposed to watch in secret and see if everything went all right. To see if the woman . . . Oh, never mind, my boy. If only someone else had stood behind those curtains instead of me!

"I listened and sensed that something was wrong. Though I didn't know what the problem was, I had the feeling that God was somehow displeased.

"Your father went to bed with his bride. He was strong, he had such broad shoulders. I could hear *him,* but not her. No movement, no words, not even a sigh, a moan, a cry of pain, nothing, absolutely nothing.

"But the marriage had been consummated, so I tiptoed out and went over to the other house, where I signalled to Kazem Khan that the celebration could begin.

"Everyone cheered, everyone smoked and ate, and we celebrated for seven days. But we knew that God was displeased with us. And that was my fault.

"I was the oldest, I should have known better. I should have kept my eyes open and bided my time. I should have told everyone not to be in such a hurry."

"How come?"

"I was worried. I don't know why. I hadn't seen any sign of the bride. After all, she's supposed to show herself. To stand by the window or smile or open the curtains. But no, she didn't do a thing."

"Why are you telling me all of this? Are you talking about my mother?"

"No, my boy. Let me finish. On the seventh night, your father went to bed with his bride as usual. I was asleep in another room, since I was supposed to stay near them for the first seven nights. In the middle of the night, I heard loud footsteps. Your father burst into the room. It was dark, so I couldn't see his face. He uttered a few choked sounds. I didn't know what he was trying to say, but I knew it was serious. I got out of bed and led your father into the courtyard, into the moonlight. What's happening? 'Cold,' he gestured. 'The bride is cold.' I raced into the bedroom and held up the oil lamp so I could see her face. She was as cold as marble, my boy. She was dead."

"Really?" Ishmael said in surprise. "So my mother wasn't Father's first wife?"

"No."

"Why didn't anyone ever tell me this?"

"I'm telling you now, my boy. There was no point in telling you before."

Years later, Ishmael came home one night from Tehran and said to his father, "Come! I want to show you something." He took a picture of a young woman out of his bag and handed it to Aga Akbar.

"Who is she?" his father signed.

"Don't tell anyone," Ishmael said, "but I might marry her some day."

Aga Akbar studied the picture. He smiled and gestured: "Very pretty. But be careful! Check her out. Listen to her lungs. Make sure they're working all right, make sure she breathes properly. I, I can't hear, but you can, you have good ears. Healthy lungs are important."

"Don't worry. I've listened. She has healthy lungs."

"And her chest? Does she have pain in her chest?"

"No, her chest is fine, there's no pain."

"Her arms?"

"Fine."

His father smiled. "Check out her stomach, too."

That evening was the first time Aga Akbar had ever talked to Ishmael about his first wife. He told him that the bride had had aches and pains all over. She'd had some kind of disease in her chest, in her lungs. He still didn't know exactly what. "A woman's breasts should feel warm, my boy, not cold. No, they should never feel cold."

The Well

Persians are always waiting for someone.
In Persian songs, they sing about the Messiah,
the one who will come and set them free.
They wait in their poetry. They wait in their stories.
But in this chapter, the one they wait for is in a well.

 If you face the cave, you can see Saffron Mountain's peak to the right and a long range of brownish-yellow mountains to the left. There's also an odd-looking spot that immediately catches your eye. Particularly if this is the first time you've climbed Saffron Mountain, you'll notice it the moment you look in that direction.

It's almost impossible to reach this spot. If you're standing beneath it, the sun is so bright that all you can see is a craggy rock face. Rain, snow and frost have given it a miraculous shape. "Miraculous" and "sacred" are the words you automatically associate with this spot. At the bottom of this mysterious rock face is a natural well, a deep depression probably created by an erupting volcano.

This well is of special significance to Muslims.

For centuries, Shiite Muslims have been waiting for a Messiah, for the Mahdi, since he is a *naji,* a liberator. On this point, the Shiites differ greatly from the Sunnis. The Shiites believe that the Prophet Muhammad was followed by twelve imams. The twelfth successor—and, according to the Shiites, the last of the pure ones—was called Mahdi. To be precise, he was called Mahdi ibn Hassan Askari.

Mahdi was the son of Hassan, and Hassan was the son of Hadi, and Hadi the son of Taqi, Taqi the son of Reza, Reza the son of Kazem, Kazem the son of Sadeq, Sadeq the son of Baqir, Baqir the son of Zayn al-'Abidin, Zayn al-'Abidin the son of Hussein, Hussein the brother of Hassan, and Hassan the son of Ali. And Ali was the son-in-law of the Prophet Muhammad.

Fourteen centuries ago, Muhammad called his followers together after a great victory. According to tradition, Muhammad stood on a camel, lifted his son-in-law Ali by the belt and cried, "Whoever loves me, must also love Ali. Ali is my soul, my spirit and my successor."

The Sunnis think the Persians made this story up. That's why the Persians and the Arabs are always squabbling and why there's constant war and bloodshed.

Ali himself was killed with a sword while praying in the mosque.

His son and successor Hassan was kept under house arrest for the rest of his life. Hussein, the third successor, was beheaded. His head was stuck on a pole and displayed on the town gate. Zayn al-'Abidin, the fourth successor, lived a life of seclusion. Baqir recorded large numbers of traditions. Sadeq had his freedom severely curtailed: he wasn't allowed to show himself in public during the day, or to walk past a mosque. Kazem died in prison. Reza was poisoned by purple grapes. His grave has become one of the holiest places in Iran.

Little is known about Hassan, the eleventh successor. But Mahdi, the twelfth and last successor, escaped an attempt on his life and sought refuge in Persia.

Since then Mahdi has occupied a special place in the hearts, as well as in the literature and religion, of the Persians.

The following story cannot be found in the Holy Book, or in any other book, and yet the villagers on Saffron Mountain believe it and tell it to their children:

The night the Arabs tried to kill Mahdi, he fled to our country, where the majority of his followers lived.

He sought refuge in the east, which is where we live.

He climbed up our mountain—first on horseback, then on a mule and finally on foot—until he reached the cave. There he spent several nights.

If you take an oil lamp and go into the cave, all the way to the very back, you will still see, even today, the ashes of his fire.

Mahdi wanted to stay in the cave even longer, but the Arabs following him had managed to track him down.

So he climbed even higher, until he reached that miraculous rock face. There he realised that he was going to be Muhammad's last successor and that he had to hide in the well and wait until he was called.

Many centuries have gone by since then. He's still waiting in the well. In the well of Mahdi ibn Hassan Askari.

Thus it became a sacred place.

Every year thousands of pilgrims climbed up Saffron

Mountain. They rode mules halfway up the mountain, to about 8,000 feet. There they spread their carpets out on the rocks and sat down, drank some tea, cooked some food and talked until deep into the night. The moment the moon went down behind the mountain peak, they all fell silent. In that great silence, they stared at the sacred well until a wondrous light struck the rock face, a light that seemed to come from a lamp inside the well. It shone briefly, then disappeared. The watching pilgrims all knelt in prayer.

The pilgrims believed the story and told each other that the light was the reflection of the oil lamp by which Mahdi read his book.

Yes, the Messiah sat in the well, reading and waiting for the day when he would be allowed to leave.

The well itself was inaccessible to ordinary mortals. It was also off-limits to foreigners, especially those who wanted to climb up to it with ropes and spikes.

Some of the villagers were able to reach it by jumping from ledge to ledge on the narrow mountain paths like nimble-footed mountain goats. Only a handful of the men in Saffron Village had ever accomplished this feat. Aga Akbar was one of them.

When Aga Akbar was little, his mother often talked about Mahdi.

"Does he really live in the well?" he asked her.

"Yes, he really does. God is in the sky and the holy man is in the well."

"Have you seen him in there?"

"Me? Heavens, no, I can't climb up there. Only a few men have ever reached the well. They looked into it and saw the holy man."

"Who? Which men?"

"The men who wear a green scarf around their necks. Haven't

you ever noticed? They walk through the village with their heads held high."

"Will I be able to climb up to the well some day?"

"You have to have strong legs. But you also have to be clever and daring."

He'd attempted the climb a few times, but had always turned back halfway. At a certain point the narrow paths were so unsafe that you didn't dare take another step. Perhaps the paths could be crossed only once, perhaps they'd collapse behind you. How would you get back if there was no path?

You couldn't think about that as you climbed, or you'd never reach the well. How could anyone dare to go to a place from which he might never return?

That was the secret. It wasn't just a matter of strong legs and quick wits, but also of necessity. You had to be prepared to leave your life behind, to say goodbye, to bid your life farewell. Only then could you reach the well.

Aga Akbar was prepared. After his wife's death, he'd reached a point where he wanted to go to the well and never come back again. He needed the holy man. He needed to kneel at the well and admit that he was afraid, that he no longer dared to live.

Just when his bride was being placed in her coffin so she could be carried to her grave, he slipped out through the back door. He started up the mountain in order to forget life.

People looked all over for him. The entire village was waiting at the cemetery, wondering where he could have gone.

Kazem Khan decided to go look for him in the mountains. He thought he knew where his nephew was headed, but he was afraid that Akbar wouldn't be able to reach the well, that he'd fall and no one would be able to rescue him.

He saddled up his mule, grabbed his binoculars and

climbed the mountain. He rode until the animal refused, or perhaps didn't dare, to go any farther. He stood on a rock and peered at the sacred spot through his binoculars. No Akbar in sight.

He looked again to see if . . . Wait a minute, someone was kneeling down, touching his forehead to the ground, or, rather, looking into the well. No, he was sitting on his knees and writing.

"What a clever boy!" Kazem Khan said and laughed aloud. Akbar had reached the well!

What could he do to help him? Nothing, no one could do a thing.

Kazem Khan laughed again. The mountain echoed his laughter. "He's reached the well!" he shouted. "My Akbar! Hurrah! Hurrah for him! Hurrah for me! Let him weep! Let him write! Ha, ha, ha. I wish I had my pipe. Oh, God, I wish I'd brought my opium. Then I'd sit on this rock and watch him and quietly smoke my pipe."

How would Akbar get back down the mountain? Don't worry. Anyone who could make it up to the well ought to be able to get back down. Clever mountain goats always find their way home again.

What should he do? Wait for Aga Akbar here or go home?

He retraced his steps, for now he had a reason to celebrate, a reason to sit on his pipe-smoker's carpet. Maybe it wasn't quite the thing to do, he thought, given that Akbar's wife had just been buried, but her family should have mentioned their daughter's illness. We're not going to mourn, we're going to celebrate! We have to help Akbar get over her death. We'll hold a party, first thing in the morning. No, we'll hold it now, tonight, in the dark. I'm going to say to everyone I see, "Hurry! Hurry! Go up onto your roof! Salute my nephew! He's reached the well!"

Kazem Khan went straight to the house of his oldest sister.

"Where are you? Go get a green scarf for Akbar! What a man! Our Akbar has reached the sacred spot. At this very moment, he's standing at the edge of the well! Here, take the binoculars! Hurry! Go up onto the roof! Look! He's still standing there!"

Then he rode over to the mosque, where people were mourning the bride. He got down from his mule and raced inside. "Men! Allah! Allah! Look, a green scarf! Here, take my binoculars! Go up onto the roof and look before it gets dark! Akbar has reached the well!"

In the middle of the night, when everyone had begun to fear that he'd never be seen again, a dark figure strode into the town square. Akbar.

Kazem Khan wrapped a green scarf around his neck and wept.

Back before the railroad had been built, in the days before the train, the area around the well had been shrouded in mystery. It was said that even the birds muffled their wing beats and bowed their heads when they flew over the well.

The train changed all that. The well used to be synonymous with inaccessibility, but that was no longer true. It was hard to know whether the railroad had desecrated the site or made it even holier.

For the first two years after the train began running past the cave, the sacred well was still inaccessible.

The mountain-dwellers took no notice of the train. It was as though that newfangled thing snaking its way up to the border had nothing to do with them. After all, it was Reza Shah's train, not theirs. Gradually, however, they got used to the steel tracks cutting through the rock to the top of Saffron Mountain.

As time went by, more and more pilgrims climbed the mountain by walking up the rails.

"Look! A road! A divine road, ready and waiting!"

Why take the treacherous mountain paths when there was a railroad track? It even brought you a bit closer to the sacred well. (Did Aga Akbar use this route? It's impossible to tell from his notes.)

Now that people had discovered this holy path, they wanted to teach the mules to climb up the railroad track. But the mules refused. They were frightened by the rails, which reeked of oil, and didn't dare place their hooves between the wooden ties. The older and more experienced mules, in particular, were terrified. They fled.

So, they tried younger mules. People spent days, even weeks, teaching young mules to step between the railroad ties.

And so, an entire generation of mules growing up on Saffron Mountain went and stood on the tracks the moment you smeared a bit of oil on their muzzles. Then the pilgrims mounted the mules and the animals gingerly made their way up the mountain, one railroad tie at a time.

The pilgrims, especially the older ones, were hesitant at first. But before long, you saw even little old ladies in chadors, giggling as their mules climbed up the tracks.

The stream of pilgrims quickly swelled. Men came to Saffron Mountain from all over the country, carrying sick children, crazed wives and ailing mothers and fathers on their backs. They hired mules to take them up the mountain.

The boom didn't last long. On Friday evenings, when the train tooted its horn, the animals panicked. They shook off their mounts and raced back to the village and their stables. One of the mules invariably broke its leg, or even its neck. Others got their hooves caught between the rails. An old woman was sure to snag her chador on a railroad bolt.

Then, one day, a couple of trucks drove up. They were loaded with fencing materials and barbed wire. Dozens of labourers from the city fenced-off the tracks and strung barbed wire over the top. Not even a snake could crawl onto the rails now.

But people discovered another route, another way to reach the sacred well. Not everyone was cut out for it. You had to be young, clever and strong.

In the past only a handful of men had been able to reach the well. In the meantime their numbers had grown. Young men and boys now risked everything to obtain the coveted green scarf. It was a great challenge. A supreme test. Perhaps the most difficult test they would ever face.

They climbed up the mountain to the place where the barbed wire came to an end. Then they waited in the dark for the train and jumped on its roof as it went by.

That part was fairly easy. It could be accomplished by almost anyone who dared to jump on top of a moving train. The decisive moment came after about fifteen minutes, when the train made a sharp turn. You had to run across the roof as fast as you could, then leap onto a rock.

To land on exactly the right rock, you needed perfect timing, agility and courage. If you missed it, your broken or dead body would be loaded on a mule the next day.

Anyone who managed to land the jump and keep his balance, gripping the rock with his toes, like a tiger, was supposed to signal his success to the villagers down below, who were watching anxiously from their rooftops. The moment someone waved from the rock, an archer would light a torch and fire it into the air.

The rest of the trip was relatively easy. To reach the sacred well, all you had to do was scale seven tricky mountain walls. Almost everyone could manage that.

Early the next morning, when you made your way back down the mountain, girls and boys and old men climbed up part of the way to greet you. They all wanted to embrace you and to touch your eyes, because you had seen the well and the holy man in the well, reading his book by the light of an oil lamp.

The situation had got out of control. As we have seen, Reza Shah was determined to modernise the country. After he banned the use of chadors in public, his agents began snatching veiled women off the streets of Tehran and throwing them in prison. He had thousands of hats sent from Paris.

His dream had been realised: the Trans-Iranian Railroad now stretched from one end of the country to the other, from north to south and from east to west. Reza Shah had no doubt. The time had finally come to do away with the imams, with all that superstitious nonsense, with all those holy men in wells reading books.

"Get rid of the well!" he ordered. "Cover it up! Fill it in and send the pilgrims packing!"

Who would dare to do such a thing? To destroy the sacred well and send the pilgrims home? No one. If you so much as lifted a finger against the pilgrims, someone would set your house on fire.

But the shah insisted. No pilgrim would be allowed to climb the mountain ever again.

The pilgrims didn't listen. They kept coming, carrying the sick and the lame to the sacred spot, where they prayed.

Then, one day, a couple of armoured cars drove up. Dozens of gendarmes leapt out with their rifles cocked.

"Go home!" they ordered.

No one moved.

"If even one mule starts up that path, I'm going to shoot. Go home!" screamed a gendarme.

An old man began to climb. The gendarme aimed his rifle at him and fired over his head.

"*La ilaha illa Allah*," someone shouted.

"*La ilaha illa Allah*," hundreds of pilgrims shouted in response. Then they set off towards the well.

The gendarme fired a few more shots into the air.

The pilgrims kept climbing. Finally, another gendarme dared to fire on the crowd. Two men fell to the ground. At that point the crowd turned on the gendarmes and the terrified men raced back to their armoured cars and roared off.

The next day the holy city of Qom was in an uproar. The ayatollahs who had been thrown in jail ordered the Muslims to close the bazaars and go on strike.

Reza Shah was furious.

"Plug up that well with cement!" he ordered.

Who would dare to carry out his orders?

No one.

"Then I'll do it myself!" he said.

Early in the morning the whistle of a special railroad car rang out over Saffron Mountain. Everyone knew immediately that something unusual was happening. No one had ever seen such an odd-looking train before. They all went up to the rooftops to see what was going on. The funny little train slowly wound its way up the mountain and stopped at the familiar curve where the young men always jumped off the train. Reza Shah got out and, with some assistance, climbed up to the sacred well. Five trained mountain climbers plodded up after him, carrying shovels, water and cement. He took off his army muffler, laid it down on a rock and went and stood with his boots planted firmly on the edge of the well. In the thirteen centuries since Mahdi had hidden in the well, no one had ever done such a thing.

"Bring me that big stone!" he said. "Set it down right here!"

The five climbers picked up the stone and, with trembling hands, laid it over the opening of the well.

Then they plugged it up with cement.

The shah declared the area a military zone. From then on, only the royal mountain goats would be allowed in.

That same evening he flew to the holy city of Qom, arriving in the middle of the night. The striking shopkeepers had gathered in the golden mosque, where a young imam was delivering a speech against the shah. When the shah heard his inflammatory words, he issued an order: "Arrest that man."

Everyone was arrested. Everyone, that is, except the clever young imam, who was named Khomeini. He managed to escape over the roof.

At that moment, not even the devil himself could have suspected that, fifty years later, that very same imam would destroy Reza Shah's kingdom.

During the second World War, the Allies forced Reza Shah to leave the country. He was sent to Cairo and there he died.

Then those same Western governments helped his son (who would later be known as the shah of Iran) onto the throne.

While all this was going on, Aga Akbar was living in Saffron Village. Several years had gone by since the death of his young bride, but no one had been able to find him a suitable wife. He went back to sleeping with the young prostitute. Kazem Khan didn't like it, but he couldn't stop him. Then he came up with the idea of sending Aga Akbar to Isfahan.

Isfahan

We go to Isfahan with Akbar, where
we weave carpets. That and nothing more.
When night-time comes, we sit on the roof
of the Jomah Mosque and stare at the sky.

 The Dutch poet P. N. van Eyck (1887–1954) believed that life was good and beautiful because it
was filled with mystery and sorrow. One of his
well-known poems is "Death and The Gardener":

A Persian Nobleman:
One morning, pale with fright, my gardener
Rushed in and cried, "I beg your pardon, Sir!

"Just now, down where the roses bloom, I swear
I turned around and saw Death standing there.

"Though not another moment did I linger,
Before I fled, he raised a threatening finger.

"O Sir, lend me your horse, and if I can,
By nightfall I shall ride to Isfahan!"

Later that day, long after he had gone,
I found Death by the cedars on the lawn.

Breaking his silence in the fading light,
I asked, "Why give my gardener such a fright?"

Death smiled at me and said, "I meant no harm
This morning when I caused him such alarm.

"Imagine my surprise to see the man
I'm meant to meet tonight in Isfahan!"

A sombre poem. A sombre story. A sombre Akbar rode on horseback with Kazem Khan to a deserted station, where he left for Isfahan.

His uncle wanted him to leave Saffron Village for a few months, or even a few years. He had arranged for Akbar to stay with a friend of his in Isfahan.

Kazem Khan wanted to free him from the isolation of the village, which he thought was a suitable place to live only if you happened to be old or ill or an opium addict. It was time for Akbar to move on and meet other people. But where was the best place to send him?

Being an opium addict wasn't easy. No matter where you were, you had to have a pipe, a fire in a brazier, a teapot, a special tea glass, sugar, a clean spoon, a carpet, and a safe but quiet place looking out over trees and mountains or some other pretty landscape.

That's why the opium addicts needed each other. That's why they kept in touch. All over the country they had friends and acquaintances with whom they were always welcome to smoke a pipe.

Kazem had many friends, especially poets and famous carpet designers. Men with high social standing. One of these men lived in Isfahan.

The train came in and Aga Akbar climbed on board. It was his first train ride. In his pocket he had all the information he needed: the name and address of his contact in Isfahan, his own address in Saffron Village and even the telegraph number of the sergeant in charge of the local gendarmerie.

Imagine leaving your birthplace for the first time and going directly to Isfahan, the city referred to as "half the world". The city containing Persia's oldest mosques. Centuries ago the builders had covered these mosques with beautiful azure tiles. The mysterious designs, numbering in the thousands, are so mesmerising that when you look upon them you no longer know where you are or what you're doing there.

Behind the magical Naqsh-e-Jahan Square is an ancient cemetery, with tombstones dating back to the time of the Sassanids. This is the burial place of the Persian gardener, the one mentioned by the Dutch poet. On his tombstone, it is written: "Here lies the gardener, the man who momentarily escaped Death's clutches."

If you look to the left when you're standing by the grave, you can see a tall cedar off in the distance. If you walk toward it, over an ancient stone path that meanders through a rose garden, you'll eventually come out near a bazaar—the oldest in the country and the most beautiful in the Islamic world. That's where you can see the most amazing Persian rugs. Hundreds of them are piled high in every store. In the rear there's always a workshop, where an old, experienced weaver plies his trade.

He doesn't weave new carpets, but mends old ones. Expensive rugs are for sale in the bazaar. Sometimes these unique works of art get damaged, so there's always an experienced carpet-mender—a craftsman—on the premises who can perform wonders with a needle and a few coloured threads.

In one of those stores there was a well-known carpet-mender named Behzad ibn Shamsololama. He had pure magic in his fingers. He also happened to be the man waiting for Aga Akbar at the station in Isfahan.

After twenty-three hours the train finally reached its destination.

Aga Akbar got out.

"When you get off the train," his uncle had told him, "don't go anywhere. Wait right there until an old man with glasses and a cane comes to get you."

And that's what must have happened, because years later a black-and-white photograph of a bespectacled man with a cane stood on the mantel in Aga Akbar's living room. If you examined the picture closely, you could see faint traces of the word "Isfahan" on the wall behind him.

Aga Akbar lived in Isfahan for a year and a half. He worked from sunrise to sunset in the workshop at the rear of the store. When the store closed, he went to his sleeping place on the roof.

Isfahan made a lasting impression on him. In the years that followed he never missed an opportunity to broach the subject. If he happened to see an Isfahan carpet, he would say, "Look, this carpet comes from Isfahan. Have you ever been there?"

Or he would talk about the mosques. He would point up at the sky to describe the blue tiles of the Sheikh Lotfallah Mosque. A dome located defiantly opposite the dome of the universe.

To express his admiration for the ancient Jomah Mosque, he would pick up a brick, then drop it. This was his way of saying that the tiles used in the mosque had come from heaven.

When he talked about the bazaar, he would put his hand over his mouth and look around in astonishment. What he meant was that the magic carpets unfurled by the shopkeepers made your jaw drop in amazement.

But how could he explain Isfahan in his simple sign language? Nobody understood what he was trying to say. He needed a son, an Ishmael, to turn his words into a language people could understand.

"What else did you do in Isfahan? I mean, in the evenings and on the Fridays you had off? Tell me what you did when you weren't mending rugs."

"On Fridays I went to the mosque to pray. There were lots of people."

"And afterwards?"

"I stayed there until it got dark."

"And then?"

"And then I went up to the roof to look at the sky."

"What else did you do?"

"When?"

"On the other nights? What did you do on the other nights?"

"I looked."

"What do you mean? Did you spend every evening on the roof looking at the sky?"

"You see, here in my chest, on the left side, I felt something. I don't know what, a kind of pain. No, not a pain. Something else. A feeling . . . how can I explain it? I wanted to go home."

And at last he was allowed to go home.

"I got sick. I couldn't mend carpets anymore. My head hurt. I used the wrong threads. Green instead of blue. That was bad. I went to the old man, laid my forehead on the back of his hand and wept."

The old man brought Akbar to the station and sent him home. After a long trip the train stopped in the middle of the night at the station on Saffron Mountain. The conductor tapped Akbar's shoulder to let him know he'd reached his stop. He got out and climbed up the mountain to begin a new life.

He started to go home, then suddenly took another path. After an hour of walking up steep mountains and down into deep valleys, he arrived at the house of the prostitute.

He knocked on her door. She didn't open it. She was afraid it might be a drunk. He knocked again. Still she wouldn't open the door. He called to her, "Aayaa yayayaya aaayaya ya ya aya aya ya."

"Is that you, Akbar?" she called from above. She opened the door, threw her arms around him and led him inside. He spent the night with her and all of the next day. Only when evening came did he finally go home.

The next morning Aga Akbar stood in the town square and talked to the men about Isfahan. They stared at his fingers. The dyes that had discoloured his fingertips were very different from the ones they used. Isfahan's blue had taken on the colour of its sky, its yellow had been borrowed from its ancient stones and its green was not at all like the grassy green of Saffron Mountain. Everyone realised that Akbar had learned new techniques, that he'd picked up Isfahan's styles.

Later he applied these techniques to his business. People now welcomed him into their homes more than ever.

Had an ember fallen on your rug? No problem, Aga Akbar will mend it, he'll work his magic and make the hole disappear. Had a rat gnawed its way through the bride's dowry carpet? Don't worry, don't cry, we'll go and get Aga Akbar!

People received him in their homes as if he were an aristocrat. He behaved like a true craftsman, a man who was proud of his work. He never went anywhere without his leather satchel, the one he'd brought with him from Isfahan. He rode with it slung over his shoulder. When he went into someone's house, he tucked it under his arm, exactly as old Shamsolo-lama had always done, threw back his shoulders and gestured, "Where's the carpet?"

One time Ishmael asked Kazem Khan, "Why did you make my father learn that particular craft?"

"You see, my boy, carpet-weaving wasn't actually a suitable occupation for us. Even the women in our household didn't weave. It was the kind of thing that ordinary villagers did, farmers who had nothing else to do on long winter nights. I thought it would be the right job for him, but I soon realised it would make him miserable. He had to be free, he had to be able to get away. He wasn't the kind of man who could spend years working on a single rug. He needed a job that could be done in a few hours, so that he could just get up and leave. That's how I hit upon the idea of having him become a carpet-mender. It's not boring work. In fact, it's quite interesting. You have to use your head. You have to be an artist. Do you know what I mean? And I knew that your father had an artistic mind."

"An artistic mind?"

"Yes, that of an artist, or a designer, or a . . . How can I explain it? People didn't think in such terms in those days. You were supposed to work, weave, mow, plow, earn a living. What would you have done if you'd been in my position? Carpet-mending, my boy, that was the best kind of work he could do. There's always a damaged carpet somewhere. He got to travel all over the place. It allowed him to earn a living and to express himself as an artist: to weave, dye, embellish and design. He could work his thoughts into the carpet.

"Your father was an illiterate, deaf-mute poet. I've told you that before. He needed to channel his thoughts into something, whether it was a cuneiform notebook or a hole in a carpet."

. . .

And so, with his notebook in his pocket and his satchel on his back, Akbar rode from one village to another.

No one knew when he wrote in his notebook, or what he wrote about. He and his notebook were inseparable. It had become part of him, like his heart, which went on beating though no one paid any attention to that, either. Only Ishmael knew when his father was writing in his notebook. He knew that his father needed to write about the things he didn't understand or wasn't able to explain in sign language. Inaccessible, incomprehensible, intangible things that suddenly struck him and caused him to stare helplessly, or to stand transfixed, or to sit down and ponder. Death, for example, or the moon, or the rain, or the sacred well, or love, that indescribable process going on in your heart. Or else incidents that had marked him for life. One of these incidents had taken place when he rode into the village of Sawoj-Bolagh.

Aga Akbar often told the story to Ishmael, who had a vague idea of what it was about. But he still couldn't figure out exactly what had happened.

One time, when he was about ten or twelve, his father took him along on one of his walks.

"Where are we going?"

"Hurry up," his father signed. "A friend of mine lives up there. He can tell you the story. He knows all about it."

"Which story?"

"The story about my military service. You know the one I mean. Hurry up, the faster you walk the sooner we'll get there."

To tell you the truth, Ishmael didn't really want to climb the mountain. After an hour and a half, they reached a village, but Akbar kept going. Darkness was falling and the villagers were starting to light their lanterns.

"Now where are we going?" Ishmael moaned.

"Hurry up. We're going to that farm. Can you see it? Over there, where that light is."

Akbar hadn't realised that the climb might be too difficult for Ishmael. That a city boy might not be as good a hiker as a village boy.

"Hurry up! We're nearly there!"

After walking uphill for another half an hour, they finally reached the farm, which was guarded by a big, black, barking dog.

A farmer came to meet them with an oil lamp in his hand.

"Who's there?"

Aga Akbar began shouting in his deaf-mute voice: "Aka, Aka, Akba, Akba, Is, Isma, Isma."

"Is that you, Akbar? *Salaam aleikum!* Hello, young man, what's your name? Come this way. Stop barking, dog, shoo! Come in."

The dog disappeared into the darkness. They went inside.

"So, you're Aga Akbar's son, Ishmael. Allah, Allah, that's good. I knew Aga Akbar had a son, but I didn't know he had such a bright, decent-looking boy. It's an honour to welcome you to my humble farm. Come on in, my boy. Yes, this is a real honour."

He called to his wife, "Where are you? Come and look who's here!"

The farmer's wife came in. She looked in surprise at Aga Akbar, who had thrown his arm around Ishmael's shoulder.

"So, that's your son?" she signed. "Allah, Allah, who could have imagined that Aga Akbar would have such a fine son?"

She planted a kiss on Ishmael's forehead.

"Welcome, my boy. We never had children, so you're like a son. Welcome to our humble abode. Make yourself at home. We're friends of your father. Go on into the living room and sit down on that rug over there."

A while later the farmer's wife came in with a big brass tray of food on her head.

They ate and talked about the past. Ishmael didn't need to interpret, since the three adults all understood each other. Then it was time for Ishmael to ask the farmer about his father's story.

"Haven't you heard that one before, my boy? Oh, of course not, how could you if I never told it to you?"

Aga Akbar kept his eyes on the farmer's mouth and followed every word of the story, as if he could actually hear it being told. "Do you know who Reza Khan is?" the farmer began. "Reza Shah? Have you ever heard of him? Or read anything about him?"

"Of course. There's a picture of him in our schoolbook. A man in a military tunic with a field marshal's baton under his arm."

"That's the one! Allah, today's children. They know everything! Yes, he was the father of our present shah. Before Reza Khan, we didn't have compulsory military service. When he became shah, he ordered all young men to serve in the military for two years. But we didn't want to go. Who would work the soil and plough the fields and mow the hay? After two years, we wouldn't have a farm to come home to. So, whenever we saw a gendarme, we ran and hid on a roof or in a haystack.

"Sometimes, though, dozens of gendarmes swept down on the village and seized all the young men.

"Can you believe that, my boy? They just grabbed you, pushed you into a truck and took you away. And two years went by before you saw your family again. He was hard as nails, that Reza Shah."

"Did you get picked up by the gendarmes?"

"Yes, they found me and beat me up. One day a truck pulled into the village and gendarmes hopped out. The young men made a run for it, scattering in all directions. They hid up on the roofs, down in the wells, up in the trees, you name it. Soon there wasn't a single young man to be seen in the entire village. The gendarmes started shooting in the air. Just then your father rode into the town square on his horse, on his way to a customer."

"Where were you? I thought you said you were hiding."

"Clever boy! You're a good listener. I was lying on the roof of the mosque and watching the whole thing from there."

Aga Akbar laughed.

"Do you remember?" the farmer signed to him. "Akbar, do you remember when the gendarmes starting shooting in the air and . . . no, of course not, you couldn't hear the shots."

"No, I didn't hear the shots," Aga Akbar signed to Ishmael.

"Anyway, he rode into the square, sitting straight and tall in the saddle. Then he noticed a couple of gendarmes with rifles. He stopped and looked at them for a moment, then calmly rode on. 'Stop!' yelled one of the gendarmes. But Akbar didn't hear him. 'Stop, I said!' There was no one in the square to tell the gendarme that Aga Akbar was a deaf-mute. 'Stop!' the gendarme yelled for the third time. 'Stop, or I'll shoot.' Allah, what a moment. I lay on the roof and watched."

"Then what happened?"

"Well, I had a tough decision to make. Actually, it wasn't all that tough. All I had to do was stand up and say, 'Stop! Don't shoot.'"

"And did you?"

"Of course I did. I stood up then and there, put my hands in the air and shouted, 'He's deaf! Don't shoot, he's deaf!'"

"And then?"

"The gendarme pointed his gun at me and yelled, 'Get down here!'"

"And my father?"

"He hadn't heard a thing. He didn't realise what was happening, so he just went on."

"Now the gendarme was after me. 'Jump!' he yelled. And I had to jump down from that high roof. Did you happen to notice the mosque in our town square?"

"No, we didn't come through your village."

"Well, it has a high roof. I jumped from it. The heel of my right foot still acts up from time to time. Anyway, the gendarmes tied my hands together with a rope and shoved me into the truck. Then they went after your father. They didn't believe he was a deaf-mute."

"Why not?"

"They just didn't. Your father was sitting up so straight and tall in the saddle and riding with such self-confidence that they had a hard time believing he couldn't hear or talk."

"And so they arrested him?"

"Yes. They grabbed the horse's reins and beat your father up. Then they tied his hands behind his back and threw him into the truck next to me. And that's how I wound up spending two years in the military."

"And my father?"

"It's a long story. Let's have some tea first."

The farmer's wife came in with a cup of tea for Aga Akbar and her husband, and some hot cinnamon rolls for Ishmael.

"Haven't you heard this story before?" she asked.

"Not really. My father's tried to tell it to me many times, but I had no idea it went like this."

"I must have heard it a hundred times. Your father used to visit us often, and the moment those two men sat down, they started in again on the gendarmes and the military service."

The farmer drank his tea and continued his story.

"I swore up and down that Akbar was a deaf-mute. But the gendarmes wouldn't listen. They took us to the army barracks in the city. The thing was, all kinds of people were trying to avoid the draft by pretending to be deaf and dumb, or blind.

Some of the draftees even chopped off their forefingers so they couldn't shoot a rifle. The gendarmes thought your father was faking it, so they locked him up."

"In a prison cell?"

"Yes."

"What'd my father do?"

"I don't know. He probably didn't have the faintest idea what was happening."

"Why not? He must have been able to work it out. Didn't he know what military service was?"

"I don't think so. I wasn't really sure myself. The whole idea scared me, it scared us all. The girls in the village wept when we left. They thought we'd never come back."

"Why'd they put him in a cell?"

"They always locked up the men pretending to be deaf-mutes. They didn't give them anything to eat or drink. After a while the men opened their mouths and begged, 'Water, water! Please, I'm thirsty! Can you hear me? I'm not a deaf-mute. Water, please!'

"I was afraid that Akbar would get dehydrated. I had to do something."

"Couldn't you have reported it to the general or one of the officers?" Ishmael asked.

"No, they wouldn't talk to the likes of me. Besides, I wouldn't have dared. I'd never lived anywhere but in our village. I'd never been to the city before. I'd never even seen an officer or a general.

"Then things went from bad to worse. They found a book, a strange little book, in the pocket of your father's coat."

"What kind of book?" Ishmael asked.

"How would I know? I didn't even know your father had a book. Anyway, the gendarmes got together to discuss it: What is it? How did this man get hold of a book written in cuneiform?

"Things were looking bad. I was called into the office. The chief gendarme asked me, 'Do you know anything about this book?'

"'Me? No.'

"I looked at it. I didn't know how to read, but I flipped through it and saw that it wasn't an ordinary book. It was written in a funny kind of writing. Hundreds of little wedges and spikes that looked like they'd been drawn by a child.

"They brought your father into the office. He'd lost a lot of weight. He was nothing but skin and bones. 'What's this?' they asked.

"'It's mine,' he signed.

"'How did you get hold of it?'

"'Me, Akbar, I wrote it,'" he signed.

"'You? You wrote this book?'

"'Yes.'

"'What did you write about?'

"'The things in my head,' he signed.

"The gendarmes didn't understand him and they certainly didn't believe him."

"And you? Did you believe him?"

"I knew your father, but I didn't always understand him, either. To be honest, I had my doubts. I was afraid he'd stolen the book from one of those foreigners, one of those cuneiform experts.

"'My uncle,' Akbar suddenly gestured. 'My uncle knows all about it. He told me to write down the things in my head.'

"'Come with me,' the gendarme gestured. 'We'll go and see the general!'

"So, they took us to see the general. The gendarme put the book on the general's desk.

"'A book? In cuneiform?' the general exclaimed. 'Where did you get this?'

"'I found it in his pocket,' the gendarme replied. 'He claims he's deaf and dumb.'

"Only God could help him now.

"'Mine. It's mine,' Aga Akbar gestured. 'Uncle. My uncle knows about it. I think, then I write in the book.'

"'Do you know this man?' the general asked me.

"'Yes, he's a friend, uh, I mean an acquaintance. He's a craftsman, the best carpet-mender in the whole region. He lives with his uncle in Saffron Village.'

"'Do you know how he got hold of this book?'

"'No.'

"'OK, you're dismissed.'

"I had no idea what they were going to do with him.

"An hour later I heard someone shout, 'Look, it's Aga Akbar!' I went out to see what was going on. The gendarmes had taken off his clothes and thrown him into a freezing pond."

Ishmael looked at his father in surprise. Aga Akbar, who was following every word of the story, nodded and smiled.

The farmer's wife sat down next to Ishmael and put her arm around his shoulder. "Now, thank God, Aga Akbar has a son to help him."

The farmer continued. "I couldn't be sure that Akbar was telling the truth. It was hard to believe he'd written those things. But I was the only one who could do anything and after a while I couldn't bear to watch any longer. I ran over to the general, who was standing by the pond. I knelt at his feet and said that Akbar was telling the truth, that he was a good man and that they should send for his uncle Kazem Khan."

"Did that help?" Ishmael asked.

"It did, thank God. They hauled him out of the pond, draped a blanket over his shoulders and took him back inside. Do you remember, Akbar?"

Aga Akbar nodded. "Yes, I remember. I haven't forgotten."

"Three days later Kazem Khan turned up at the army barracks with the imam from Saffron Village. The imam placed the Holy Book on top of the general's desk and swore that Akbar's book was nothing more than a deaf-mute's attempt to imitate cuneiform writing, that they were just Aga Akbar's meaningless scribbles."

. . .

Many years later, after Aga Akbar's death, the mail-carrier handed Ishmael a package.

By then Ishmael was the same age his father had been when captured by the gendarmes. He opened the package. It was a book. The notebook with Aga Akbar's scribbles.

Ishmael sat down at his desk, thumbed through the pages and thought: How will I ever discover the secrets contained in these pages? How can I let the book tell its own story? How can I translate it into a readable language?

A New Wife

We've talked quite a bit about Ishmael,
though we haven't yet described his birth.
Soon we'll encounter a woman in the snow.
Kazem Khan will pick up the tale from here.

 Sometimes you have to be patient. If whatever it is you're doing doesn't seem to be working out, leave it for a while. That way you give life a chance to sort itself out.

Kazem Khan was away on a trip. He couldn't go home because the snow was nearly three feet deep. It would take a few days to clear the road.

So he rode around in search of a fellow opium smoker. Just as it was getting dark, he came to the village of Khomein.

"Good evening!" he called to an old man clearing the road.

"Good evening, stranger. Can I help you?"

"I'm looking for the hunter."

"Which one? Everyone in this village is a hunter."

"Er . . . the one who hunts mountain goats."

"Ah, yes, I know who you mean. He used to hunt mountain goats, but he'd be lucky to hit a farm goat these days. Anyway, go down the road I've just cleared until you see an old oak tree. Take the path to your left and keep going up the hill through the snow. In the distance you'll see a house with a long stone wall and a large pair of goat horns above the gate. That's where your hunter lives."

Kazem Khan rode up the hill through the snow to the house, but it looked deserted. From his horse, he called out, "Hello, is anyone home?"

No answer.

He knocked on the door with his riding crop. "Hunter! Are you there?"

"Hold on!" came the voice of a young woman, "I have to clear the snow."

Had the voice come from the courtyard or the roof? He couldn't tell.

"*Salaam*, stranger!" the woman called.

Kazem Khan looked over his shoulder.

"Here, I'm up here. Who do you want to talk to?"

"Oh, up there! Hello. I'm looking for the hunter."

"He's asleep."

"So early?"

"Yes," she said and vanished.

Kazem Khan needed a place to sit down and smoke his pipe. It was his usual time and he was already beginning to get the shakes. So he called out again, "Yoo-hoo, young lady, where are you?"

Again no answer.

"What on earth are you doing up there?"

"Clearing the snow, so the roof won't fall down on the head of your hunter."

"Come on down. This is urgent. I need—"

"I know what you need," she said. "But you won't get it here. Goodbye."

"Please wake up the hunter and say that Kazem Khan is here. Did you hear me? Kazem Khan."

"No, I won't wake him up. I refuse to have any more strangers in the house. Goodnight, sir!"

"I'm not a stranger, I'm Kazem Khan."

"I don't care who you are, you aren't getting anything from me. No opium, no fire, no tea. Pleasant journey!"

"God, what a difficult woman! Listen to me! I need to smoke my pipe this instant. If I don't, I'll drop dead here on your doorstep."

"That's what they all say."

"This is different."

"Your name means nothing to me, so go ahead and drop dead on my doorstep. But smoke a pipe? No, not in my house, not any more. Who do you think will have to make the fire? Me. And who will have to make the tea? Me! Do you understand what I'm saying? I'm never going to do those things for anyone ever again!"

"Then go get the hunter!"

"The hunter is dead. Now are you happy?"

"Do you want me to beg? Do you want this old man to go down on his knees? Look at me, I'm practically falling off my horse."

She ignored his pleas.

He thought about it, then tried another tack.

"I understand what you're saying. You're absolutely right. But I'm not your average opium smoker. I'm the most famous man on Saffron Mountain. I read books and I know hundreds of poems by heart. I also write them. If you open the door, I'll write a poem especially for you."

No answer.

"Who are you anyway?" he called angrily. "His new wife?"

"Me? The hunter's wife? Don't be ridiculous! After that re-mark, you can be sure I won't open the door."

Discouraged, he rode off.

"Stranger! Wait a moment," she called and came down-stairs.

She opened the gate. Kazem Khan rode inside.

Just then he was struck by an idea: maybe she was the woman they'd been looking for. But the idea disappeared as quickly as it had come.

He got down from his horse. The woman led him into the opium room, where the hunter, his pipe in his hand, had fallen asleep beside the cold brazier.

She lit a few dry almond twigs and got a fire going. Then she transferred the glowing twigs into a clean brass brazier, placed a few chunks of pure yellow opium on a porcelain plate and fetched a bowl of fresh dates. "Here, these are for you," she said and disappeared.

Kazem Khan was speechless. He'd been smoking opium since he was a young man, but in all that time no one had ever presented him with such a clean opium kit.

"What's your name?"

"Tina," she said from the adjoining room.

"What?"

"Tina."

"Is that a Persian name? Or is it a name from the other side of the mountains, from Russia?"

She didn't know. Kazem Khan smoked and thought: no, it probably wouldn't work. Even if he promised her a mountain of gold, she wouldn't agree to marry Akbar.

He smoked and blew the smoke out through the shutters and into the cold night air. Something will eventually unfold, he thought. Life, a miracle, a secret. Or maybe it won't, maybe I'm mistaken.

"Tina," he called again. "Where are you? Your name *is* Tina, isn't it? Come here, I have something for you."

She appeared with a fresh pot of tea and a bowl of brown sugar, which had come from far, far away.

"Is this the hunter's house or is it paradise? Thank you. I have a turquoise ring for you. I have no children—no sons or daughters—but you could be my daughter. Go ahead, put it on your finger. Why don't you come and sit by me?"

Tina warily sat down across from him and tried on the ring, which had a beautiful turquoise stone. Then, apparently having decided that the old man wasn't serious, she started to get up.

"Please don't go. You're the hunter's daughter, aren't you? Good, may I ask you a question? Do you live here with your father, or are you just visiting?"

He saw the sudden fear in her eyes. She handed him back the ring and ran out of the room.

Just then the hunter woke up.

"My God, look who's here! Is this a dream, or are you real?"

"It's a dream," Kazem Khan said. "As for me, I'm in paradise. Your daughter let me in. Come sit over here. The fire is as red as a ruby. That Tina of yours is worth her weight in gold."

"I'm at your service. It's an honour to have Kazem Khan as my guest," the hunter replied. "Tina," he called, "prepare a meal for this gentleman."

Kazem Khan took out his wallet and tucked a few bills under the carpet on which the hunter was sitting.

"Heavens, no. You're my guest. You're welcome in my house."

"I insist, hunter, but thank you. Anyway, you're lucky to have such a nice daughter."

"Nice? She's a shrew."

"A shrew?"

Kazem Khan passed him the pipe. After the hunter had taken a few puffs and relaxed, he continued. "She sits up on the roof like a tiger and won't let anyone through the gate."

"Does she live here with you? I mean, is she married?"

"Married? She's been married three times. She hates men. If you even mention the subject, she screams, and the women in the neighbouring houses go running up to their roofs and shake their brooms. They think I'm trying to sell her to some old opium addict. Hey, Tina, where are you?"

While millions of stars twinkled in the sky, Tina served the aging poet a delicious meal. She treated him with such extraordinary kindness that her father was amazed.

When the hunter fell asleep again, Kazem Khan called to her.

"Tina? Please sit down. Here, take the ring, it's yours. I'd like to talk to you. I have a problem and you may be the only person who can help me."

"What kind of problem?"

"Listen, child. I'm going to ask you a few questions. You can answer or not, as you please. I'm going to spend the night here, then go back home in the morning. Who knows? Maybe it was fate that brought me to this house. Maybe you're the one we've been looking for. I have a son . . . well, actually he's my nephew. A strong, handsome young man from a good family. But we have a problem."

"What's the problem?"

"He's a deaf-mute. And we still haven't found him a wife. We're looking for an intelligent woman. Do you understand me?"

They talked until deep in the night.

The next morning, as soon as the sun's first rays hit the snow, Kazem Khan mounted his horse. Though it still wasn't safe to travel, he rode through the snow to Saffron Village.

"Where's Akbar?"

He went from house to house in search of his nephew, and finally found him at a customer's.

"Come with me, Akbar! No, leave that. I want you to go to the bathhouse, then put on your Isfahan suit and comb your hair with brilliantine. Here, take the fastest horse. Don't forget to put some dried rose petals in your pockets. Hurry, Akbar! Now ride with me. Here's a necklace. As soon as she opens the door, throw back your shoulders and hold your head high! Then take the necklace out of your pocket and give it to her."

They reached the hunter's house at nightfall. Kazem Khan knocked on the door. Tina opened it.

"Here he is," Kazem Khan said aloud and he pointed at Aga Akbar, dressed in his good black suit and looking down at Tina from his horse. Neither of them knew what to do next. Even the experienced Kazem Khan was at a loss for words.

"Come in," Tina said. She turned to Aga Akbar and welcomed him with a gesture.

Kazem Khan's eyes filled with tears.

"Excellent. You're an excellent woman. Come, Akbar, get down from your horse. Stop staring. We're going into the house. But first, Tina, my daughter, I have something to say to you. Tomorrow our family will be coming to pick you up and soon you'll be our bride. We'll take you home and give you a hearth of your own. But I warn you that your life may be hard. Or maybe it won't be. There's no way of knowing in advance. I do know, however, that it won't be easy, especially not in the beginning. Now you've seen your future husband. Take your time, you can still change your mind. Go stroll by the cedars and think it over. I'll wait for you."

But Tina didn't need to take a stroll. She walked up to Aga

Akbar and gestured, "Go inside. My father will be here shortly."

"Oh, my God, oh, merciful God, what a moment, what a wonderful woman! Where are you, hunter? Roll out the carpets and stoke up the fire."

The horses arrived the following day. The family brought gold, silver, clothes, cloth, walnuts, bread, meat, sheep, chickens, eggs and honey. All for the hunter. They dressed Tina in a flowery white chador and helped her mount the horse. No party, no songs, no guests—just a bride on a horse. It was as if they were afraid to celebrate, to express their feelings.

Don't say a word, just go, you read in their eyes. Nevertheless, the imam recited a short melodious sura: "*Ar-rahman, alam al-Qur'an, Khalaqa al-insan, 'allamahu al-bayan. Ashshams wa al-qamaru be-husbanin, wa as-sama'a rafa 'ha wa waza'a al-mizan.*"

The bride was taken to Akbar's house. "Here's your home, your husband, your bed."

This time there was no old woman behind the curtains. "Here's the frying pan, the bread, the tea, the cheese. We'll leave you to it, Tina," they said and left.

They let matters take their own course.

It had been ordained by fate, by life itself. And Tina became pregnant.

One cold night in November, Tina lay under the blankets by the tiled stove, a special stove that people slept beside during particularly cold winters. She pressed her foot against Akbar's back and woke him up. He knew the baby was due, so he leapt out of bed and lit the oil lamp.

"Are you in pain?"

"Hurry," Tina signed, "go get the midwife."

The men of the family arrived even before the women did. Someone brought a large samovar. Someone else a large brazier. Kazem Khan brought his yellow opium. Who knew? Maybe they'd have something to celebrate.

Kazem Khan was sure they would, since he had consulted the Koran. The answer had come in the sura of Mary:

Wa azkur fi al-kitab maryam eze antabazat min ahleha makanan sharqyan . . .

When Mary went away from her family to an Eastern-looking place and took a veil to hide herself from their eyes, Allah sent her his Spirit in the form of a perfect man. She said: "I seek my refuge in Allah. Leave me." He said: "I am only a messenger of the Lord. You are to bear a son."

The men sat in a circle in the guest room and waited in silence. It took so long that the fire almost went out. The men all looked at Kazem Khan, who had lit the brazier so he'd be able to reach for his pipe the moment the baby was born. There was an ominous silence, then suddenly they heard the wail of an infant from the next room.

According to family tradition, no one was allowed to break the silence yet. So the midwife gestured: "A son."

Kazem Khan smiled so broadly that his gold tooth gleamed. A while later the oldest woman in the house took Ishmael in her arms and brought him into the guest room. No one spoke, because the first word, the first sentence to reach the baby's unspoiled mind had to be a poem—an ancient melodic verse. Not a word uttered by a midwife or an aunt's joyful cry, not an everyday word from the mouth of a neighbour, but a poem by Hafez, the medieval master of Persian poetry.

Kazem Khan stood up, took the volume of Hafez, closed his eyes and opened the book. At the top of the page, on the right-hand side, was the proper poem to be chanted into the child's ear. Kazem Khan brought his opium-scented mouth to Ishmael's ear and whispered:

Bolboli barg-e gol-i khosh-rang dar menqar dasht
wa andar-an barg o nava khush nalaha-ye zar dasht.
Goftam-ash, "dar 'ayn-e wasl in nala o faryad chist?"
Goft, "mar-ra jilva-ye ma'shuq dar in kar dasht."

A nightingale once sat with a bright petal in its beak,
But this memento of its loved one merely made it weep.
"Why bewail this token of your heart's desire?" I cried.
"It makes me long for her all the more," the songbird sighed.

The first words to reach Ishmael's brain were about love, sadness and the longing for a loved one.

Then Kazem Khan handed the child to Aga Akbar. "Here, your son!"

The women uttered a cry of joy.

Kazem Khan's voice was the first voice Ishmael heard. Or so he thought. Years later, when he was trying to decipher his father's notebook, he discovered that things hadn't happened quite that way.

Ishmael had always had trouble with his left ear. His father knew why. He'd tried to tell his son something about the midwife and the book and the ear and the stupidity of a new father, but Ishmael hadn't understood.

What actually happened (according to Aga Akbar's notes) was this:

I was sitting with the men. I didn't know if the baby had been born yet. Suddenly I saw Kazem Khan's gold tooth gleam. I knew then that the baby had been born. My aunt came in with the baby in her arms. I was afraid the baby would be a deaf-mute like me, and I wanted to see if he was deaf. I know it was wrong, but suddenly I stood up, ran over to my aunt, took the baby from her, put my mouth to his ear and spoke into it. The baby screamed and turned blue. Kazem Khan snatched him from me and shoved me out of the house. I went and stood at the window. Everyone frowned at me. I had shouted into the baby's ear. Everyone said it would be damaged for good. It was stupid of me, stupid. Akbar is stupid.

Damaged? No, not really, but whenever Ishmael was sick, or under stress, or feeling discouraged, whenever he fell down and had to stand up again, a voice shouted in his ear. His father's voice. Aga Akbar was always inside him.

BOOK II

New Ground

New Ground

Ishmael is in doubt. He isn't sure he can
get his father's story down on paper.
After long hesitation, he picks up his pen.

 A well-known Dutch classic begins like this:

I am a coffee broker, and I live at No. 37 Lauriergracht, Amsterdam. I am not in the habit of writing novels or things of that sort, and so I have been a long time making up my mind to buy a few extra reams of paper and start on the work which you, dear reader, have just taken up, and which you must read if you are a coffee broker, or if you are anything else. Not only have I never written anything that resembled a novel, I don't even like reading such things, because I'm a businessman. For years I've been asking myself what is the use of them, and I am amazed at the impudence with which a poet or story-teller dares to palm off on you something that never happened, and usually never could happen. If I, in my line—I am a coffee broker, and I live at 37 Lauriergracht—gave a statement to a principal—a principal's someone who sells coffee—which contained only a small portion of the untruths that form the greater part of all poems and all novels, he would transfer his business to Busselinck & Waterman at once. They're coffee brokers, too, but you don't need to know their address. So, then . . . I take good care not to write any novels, or make any other false statements. And I may say I have always noticed that people who go in for such things generally come to a bad end. I am forty-three years old, I've been on 'Change for twenty years, so I can come forward if anyone's called for who has experience. I've seen a good many firms go down! And usually, when I looked for the reasons, it seemed to me that they had to be sought in the wrong course most of the people had taken in their youth.

Truth and common sense—that's what I say, and I'm sticking to it. Naturally I make an exception for the Holy Scripture. . . .

Nothing but lies! . . .

Mind you, I've no objection to verses in themselves. If you want words to form fours, it's all right with me! But don't say anything that isn't true. "The air is raw, the clock strikes four." I'll let that pass, if it really is raw, and if it really is four o'clock. But if it's a quarter to three, then I, who don't range my words in line, will say, "The air is raw, and it is a quarter to three." But the versifier is bound to four o'clock by the rawness of the first line. For him, it has to be exactly four o'clock, or else the air mustn't be raw. And so he starts tampering with the truth. Either the weather has to be changed, or the time. And in that case, one of the two is false. . . .

Nothing but lies, I tell you!

And then, this business about virtue rewarded! Oh, oh, oh! I've been a coffee broker for seventeen years—37 Lauriergracht— so I've seen quite a bit in my time; but I can't help always getting *frightfully annoyed when I see God's precious truth so shamefully distorted. Virtue rewarded? If it was, wouldn't that make virtue an article of commerce? Things just aren't like that in the world, and it's a good thing they're not. For what merit would there be in virtue if it was rewarded? So why do people have to invent such infamous lies? . . .*

All lies, abominable lies!

I'm virtuous myself, but do I ask a reward for it? . . . And the fact that I am virtuous can be seen from my love of truth. That is my strongest characteristic, after my devotion to the Faith. And I should like you to be convinced of this, reader, because it is my excuse for writing this book. . . . I am, let me say, a coffee broker, 37 Lauriergracht. Well then, reader, it is my unimpeachable love of truth, and my enthusiasm for business, that you have to thank for these pages.

Reader! I've included this passage from Multatuli's *Max Havelaar* because what that coffee broker says has parallels to my story. Multatuli writes about a Mr Droogstoppel, a coffee broker living at No. 37 Lauriergracht. That same Mr Droogstoppel tells us, in turn, the story of Max Havelaar. And that's how you end up reading a book about both a coffee broker and a man named Max Havelaar.

In the novel, Mr Droogstoppel is given a package—the writings of Max Havelaar. He uses it to write a book.

A few months ago, I, too, received a package—my father's notebook. I've never written a book before, but I'd like to try and write one now, because, if it's at all possible, I'd like to put my father's writings into a readable form.

"Nothing but lies," says the coffee broker. "All nonsense and lies."

I admit that I've set about my work in the same way. I'm not a coffee broker and I've never been involved in the coffee trade. I'm a foreigner who's been living in Holland for several years.

My name is Ishmael, Ishmael Mahmud Ghaznavi Khorasani. I don't live at 37 Lauriergracht, but at 21 Nieuwgracht. And I don't live in Amsterdam, but in the Flevopolder—the reclaimed ground that the Dutch have wrested from the sea.

I'm sitting at my desk in the attic, staring out the window. Everything in the Flevopolder is new: the soil still smells of fish, the trees are young and the birds build their nests with fresh twigs. There are no ancient words, no ancient love stories, no ancient feuds.

Everything in my father's notebook is old: the mountains, the well, the cave, the cuneiform relief, even the railroad. That's why I don't dare put pen to paper. I can't imagine writing a novel on this new ground.

I look at the dyke and see the sea. At least the sea is old, though, to be honest, it isn't actually the sea anymore, but just a small part of it that's been dyked-in by the Dutch. Much as I, a little patch of ancient Persian culture, have been surrounded by a Dutch dyke.

Maybe this ex-sea can help me.

The city in which I live is new, but the remains of ancient habitation are all around me. That's exactly what I need.

Just as Holland invented this ground, this landscape, I can use my father's cuneiform writings to invent something new.

There are poets in this polder and I know a number of them. We meet once a month in a new café and read our work to each other.

Here are a few poems from a collection titled *Flevoland*. Annemarie wrote:

Above this landscape
the wind breathes like a father
caresses the waves from time to time
and buttresses the voices in the land.

Tineke penned these lines:

Man and his machines have come.
There where wind and waves
played their powerful games
the tide was turned.
The sea bed has been laid bare.

And Margryt wrote this poem:

No language. No ancient tale that you can
fall back on. Land stretching into infinity.
A map, plotting a railroad track, and bridges
connecting one blank space to another. Not a word
to assure us that this will be a safe place to live.

I'm writing my story in Dutch—the language of the Dutch classics and thus of the following long-dead writers and poets: the anonymous author of the miracle play *Mariken van Nieumeghen*, Carel van Mander, Alfred Hegenscheidt, Willem van Hildegaersberch, Agathan Marius Courier, Dubekart, Antonie van der Woordt, Dirck Raphaëlsz Camphuysen, Caspar van Baerle, also known as Barlaeus, and, in more recent centuries, Louis Couperus and Eduard Douwes Dekker, also known as Multatuli.

I write in my new language because that's what refugees do.

I begin:

Every one of the blind men in the village had a son. A coincidence? I don't know, but I suspect it's nature's way of making up the balance.

The sons became their fathers' eyes. The moment the baby started to crawl, the blind father placed the palm of his left hand on the baby's shoulder and showed him how to be his guide. The child soon realised that he was an extension of his father.

The sons of the deaf-mutes had an even more difficult task, since they had to serve as the mouths, minds and memories of their fathers. The families and the other villagers did their best to teach these boys the language of adults. The imams even taught them how to read the Holy Book at a very young age. They had little contact with other children, since they were always with the men. They were expected to fulfil family obligations and to be present at both feasts and funerals.

In the deepest darkness of my memory, a baby crawls over the floor. A hand appears, takes hold of its head from behind and gently turns it upwards and to the right. This is followed by the words "*Negah kon. Negah kon. An-ja negah kon*"— "Look, look up here."

The baby looks up at a mouth, at a man, at the father who smiles.

Another scene hangs like a black-and-white photograph in the strong-room of my memory. I'm sitting on my knees on a carpet beneath an old almond tree, with my head bent over a book. An aged hand appears and points to a verse in the book. I can't see which poem it is, but the smell of opium suddenly fills my nostrils, and I recall the love poem of the medieval Persian poet Hafez:

Gar che sad rud ast az chesh-e man rawan.
Yad-e rud zendeh-kar an yad bad.

Tears of longing roll down my cheeks like a hundred rivers,
And remind me of the river flowing through my home town.

Otherwise I remember very little. But in the next chapter

our belongings are being loaded into a covered wagon. We're moving. I was only seven or eight years old, and yet the scene stands out clearly in my memory. I see my mother running to the house of Kazem Khan. I hear her call: "Uncle! Help! Akbar's gone mad!"

Then I hear the clatter of hooves as Kazem Khan's horse gallops into our courtyard.

"Where's Akbar?"

Moving

Aga Akbar suddenly decides to move.
Why? No one knows.

 Life in Saffron Village went on as usual. My mother, Tina, had three other children—three girls. Aga Akbar was, therefore, the father of four healthy children, who not only could hear well but could also express themselves extremely well in both Farsi and sign language.

Akbar worked as hard as he always had and gave all of his earnings to Tina, leaving household matters and the raising of the children to her. He still travelled a lot. Sometimes he was gone for a week or even longer.

"Where's Akbar?"

"Working."

"Where?"

"On the other side of the mountain."

"He has enough customers here. What's he doing on the other side of the mountain?"

No one knew exactly where he went. Or who he slept with. (There's no reference to this in his notebook.)

I don't really know what Tina was doing in those days or how she dealt with Akbar. Nor do I know what the first few months of her marriage were like. She never discussed it.

"Mother, how did you learn sign language?"

"Oh, I don't know. It was so long ago, I've forgotten."

"Wasn't it hard, suddenly having to live with a man you couldn't talk to?"

"I don't know, it was all so long ago."

She never mentioned her own mother and father. It was as though she didn't have any family, as though she were an orphan, nobody's daughter. Everything I knew about her I had learned from Kazem Khan.

"Was your father a hunter?"

"Yes."

"What about your mother? I don't know anything about her."

"I don't, either. She died when I was very young."

In fact, her childhood, youth and first years of marriage had been neatly tied into a bundle and tucked away. "I don't know" was her standard reply.

I stopped asking questions. But now that I live in the polder and take walks along the dyke, these questions occur more often.

I don't want to get bogged down in the past, but until you've come to terms with it, you can't really settle into a new culture.

That's why I've become so engrossed in my father's notebook. After all, his story is also my story. If I can transform his writing into Dutch, I'll be able to adjust to my new culture more easily.

During yesterday's walk, I thought back to that first meeting between Tina and Kazem Khan. To the scene in which

Kazem Khan rides around in search of the hunter so he can smoke opium and Tina clears snow from the roof.

I now wonder how much of that story is true. Perhaps Kazem Khan made it up, since the Tina in the story bears little resemblance to my mother.

Perhaps he exaggerated a bit and turned Tina into his dream woman.

Tina was a good mother and she had a strong personality, but she was definitely not the Tina on the roof.

She got fed up with Akbar sometimes and buckled under the weight on her shoulders. One incident stands out clearly in my mind:

Kazem Khan came into our house. Tina screamed, "I can't stand it! I can't live with that man one day longer!" Then she began to beat herself over the head and kept it up until she fainted.

Kazem Khan grabbed her by the shoulders and dragged her to bed.

"The Holy Book," Kazem Khan murmured.

I took the Koran down from the mantel and handed it to him. He knelt in front of Tina's bed and read from it softly: "*Eqra: be-asme rabbeka alazi khalaqa. Khalaqa al-ensana min allaqin. Eqra: wa rabbok al-akram, alazi allama be el-qalam.*"

As I walked along the dyke, I recalled another scene from that same period:

A covered wagon creaked into view. My father was at the reins. He drove through the gate of our house, said nothing to Tina, but signed to me, "Come! I need your help!"

He unhitched the horse and led it to the stall. Then he pushed the covered wagon into the barn, where he spent the entire evening. Tina was restless. She knew that something was about to happen, but she also knew she was powerless to prevent it.

"What's your father doing?" Tina called.

"I don't know. The door's locked from the inside."

He stayed in the barn until late that night.

Early the next morning I woke to the sound of an angry voice in the courtyard.

"What do you think you're doing?" Tina screamed at Akbar.

I leapt out of bed and looked out the window. My father had crammed all of our carpets, blankets, buckets and pots and pans into the covered wagon and was now going inside to get my sisters, who were still in bed.

"Help, Ishmael! Go and get—" Tina called.

I raced downstairs and ran all the way to Kazem Khan's house in my bare feet. "Come quickly, Uncle," I shouted. "My father's gone mad."

Here in the polder I hear the hoofbeats of Kazem Khan's horse as it galloped into our courtyard.

"Where's Akbar?" called Kazem Khan.

My father had laid my still-sleepy sisters in the wagon and covered them with a blanket. Kazem Khan swiftly dismounted and gestured to my father with his crop, "Come here!"

My father didn't budge.

"What on earth are you doing?"

He didn't answer.

"What's going on in that head of yours?"

"We're moving to the city," my father signed.

"Have you discussed this with Tina?"

No response.

"Why didn't you tell me?"

No response.

Kazem Khan pointed to the wagon. "Unload it! Take everything out!"

Tina took me inside so I wouldn't have to watch.

"You've got four children now," I heard Kazem Khan say angrily. "But you still do stupid things! Unload this wagon!"

I thought my father would start lugging carpets and blankets back inside, but he didn't.

"Unload it, I said!"

I peeked out from behind the curtain.

Akbar signed to Kazem Khan that he was going to move to the city no matter what and that he had no intention of unloading our things.

Kazem Khan stood helplessly beside the wagon. Then he stuck his crop under his arm and strode over to his horse. He grabbed the reins and led the horse to the gate.

"Kazem Khan is leaving," I said to Tina.

She pushed aside the curtain. She looked miserable.

Kazem Khan paused by the gate. His head was bowed. Then he turned and called, "Ishmael!"

I ran out to him.

"Here," he said, handing me the reins. "Take the horse to its stall. I'm old. Your father will no longer listen to me. I've lost whatever hold I had on him."

I took the horse to its stall and raced back outside.

"Listen, your father wants to move to the city and I can't stop him. I'm going into the house to talk to your mother. Keep an eye on your father."

"Tina," Kazem Khan called, "how about a cup of tea?" And he went in.

"Akbar's determined to move to the city," I heard him say. "You mustn't be so weak. There's no need to cry and scream and beat yourself over the head every time something happens. Give me a cup of tea, my throat's dry. Ishmael, go and get your father!"

Kazem Khan sat down. Tina set a cup of tea in front of him. I brought my father into the house and stood beside him.

"Ask him why he wants to live in the city," Kazem Khan said to me.

"Why the city?" I signed. "Why do you want to go there?"

"Me, Akbar," he signed, "I want to go where there are cars and—"

"Cars!" Kazem Khan exclaimed. "He's been bewitched by cars!"

"And schools," my father signed. "A school for Ishmael. And for the girls. The girls need to go to school."

"Schools?" Kazem Khan said in surprise. That wasn't the answer he'd expected. "Cars. Schools. You want them to go to school? To move to the city? A deaf man with four children in the middle of a strange city with all those cars?"

"I'm deaf," my father signed, "but Ishmael isn't deaf. The girls aren't deaf. And Tina isn't deaf either."

Kazem Khan was silent.

"Did you see that?" he said to Tina. "You shouldn't come running to me before you find out what's going on. Your husband wants to send your children to school. Don't look so unhappy. Stand up straight! Support your husband! He may be deaf, but he's not stupid. At least he thinks about things. Give me another cup of tea. This one is cold."

Then he turned back to me. "Ask him if he's arranged for a house to live in."

"Not a house, but a room," my father replied.

"Ask him what he plans to do in the city. Tell him that everything's different there, that nobody knows Akbar, that he's not automatically welcome everywhere. Here in the mountains he's Aga Akbar the magician, but there in the city he's a nobody, a deaf-and-dumb carpet-weaver. He needs to know that. Make sure he understands!"

I told him. I made sure he understood.

"We'll see," my father said.

"OK. I have nothing more to say to him. Have a safe trip.

You can tell him that from me," Kazem Khan said, and he stood up. "Forget the tea, Tina. I'm going."

He went into the courtyard. "Ishmael!" he called. "Would you come here for a moment?"

I followed him as he walked past the cedar trees. He didn't look at me as he talked. I've forgotten his exact words, though I have a vivid memory of the scene: I was walking behind Kazem Khan, not looking at his face but at his hands, clasped behind his back. In his hands he held a crop. The sun shone down through the trees and struck his shoulders. He walked, I followed. He talked, I listened. At some point, he turned, held out his hand and said, "Have a safe trip, my boy."

Then the scene suddenly shifted again: the covered wagon creaked down the road. I was sitting beside my father. A stricken Tina sat in the back and stared vacantly into space with my youngest sister on her lap. My other two sisters were delighted at the unexpected journey. They giggled as the wagon bounced and swayed down the treacherous mountain road.

I was worried about Tina, afraid she'd go into hysterics again. Despite my age, I was now the man of the house. That's what Kazem Khan had wanted to tell me before we left. My job, he said, would be to look after Tina and the girls.

This was the first time my father had assumed responsibility for his family and we were now on our own. I could feel the weight of this enormous responsibility on my shoulders, too. My throat was so tight I could barely swallow. I was scared, but I was also determined not to let anyone see the fear in my eyes.

After about three hours, we had left behind the mountains, the mountain goats, the foxes and the wild red tulips, and descended into a plain. We travelled the same roads as the cars and buses.

We hadn't eaten breakfast and apparently we weren't going to get any lunch, either.

"Stop," I signed. "We've got to eat."

In all those hours I hadn't said a word to my father, or even looked at him. Was I angry? I don't remember. No, probably not, because I didn't think of myself as a separate individual. How can I explain it? I was him, or he was me; in any case, we were one. I couldn't be angry with him. And even if I were, my anger would have been directed not so much at him as at myself, because I—or, rather, my father and I—had embarked on the same great adventure. We didn't know if we could survive in the city, but we wanted to try. The city called to us and we couldn't refuse.

He stopped the wagon and we got out to rest.

"Don't look so gloomy," I signed. "Talk to Tina, so she doesn't start acting crazy again."

Only then did he seem to realise what was going on. He took some bread and cheese out of a cotton bag and gave it to Tina. Then he patted my sister, the one sitting on Tina's lap. I saw his hand graze Tina's breast.

We rode on. After an hour we came to the outskirts of the city. To my surprise, there were no cars and no schools. Off in the distance we saw three tall blocks of flats. My father headed the horse in that direction and soon we pulled up in front of the ugliest one. Apparently our rented room wasn't in the city itself, but in an outlying industrial area.

We were excited anyway, because we'd never seen a building that was four stories high.

We carried our things up to a flat on the top floor: one large room plus a dark storeroom. If you looked out the window you could see the mountains, including the peak of

Saffron Mountain, which rose up above the entire range. The city was off to the right, though you couldn't see it from our apartment.

Tina unrolled the carpets and put the kitchen things in the storeroom. She started to make soup, the traditional meal of Saffron Village, and as she cooked, she pondered her new situation.

"We'll see," she said and placed a bowl of soup before me. She hadn't said a word all day.

And with those two short words, our life in the city began.

Early in the morning, my father went off to work. A carpet-weaver he met in the bazaar had promised him a job.

"What kind of a job?" I asked. (Tina was actually the one who wanted to know.)

"I'm not sure. It's in a big building. The boss is rich. He's the one who lent me the covered wagon. I'm not sure . . . I think I'll be sewing numbers on carpets."

"Sewing numbers," Tina sighed.

"Why sewing numbers?" I gestured.

"I don't know. A lot of people in the shop sew numbers on carpets. Then they load the carpets into a truck and take them to the train. And the train brings them to . . . I don't know . . . far, far away."

"May Allah protect us," Tina said. "Aga Akbar, the magician, has become a seamstress!" She went into the storeroom and locked the door.

A week later I started school. The arrangements had been made by one of the men my father worked with. The school was on the other side of town, about three or four miles away. Because no buses went that way, I had to walk, like all the other children.

As soon as school was finished, I went straight home. I was

worried about Tina. Kazem Khan had told me to keep an eye on her, because there was a wild animal inside her—a wolf.

One afternoon I came home to find my sisters playing quietly. Tina was nowhere to be seen. I don't know why, but suddenly I sensed the presence of the wolf.

"Where's Tina?" I asked.

They didn't know. I opened the door to the storeroom and peered into the darkness. There was no sign of Tina. I ran over to the neighbours.

"Hello, is Tina here?"

No, she wasn't. So far, she'd had little contact with the neighbours. I raced home and went back to the storeroom. I stood in the dark for a while, but I still couldn't see her. Then I listened intently and heard a sound. It was Tina. Or not really Tina. The gleaming eyes of the wolf stared back at me from the darkest corner of the storeroom. God help me, I didn't know what to do. If we'd been in the village, I would have jumped on the horse, ridden straight to Kazem Khan's and cried, "Come quick! The wolf is back!"

But we weren't in the village and Kazem Khan wasn't here.

So I took a step backwards, as I had seen Kazem Khan do, and called softly to my sister, "Go get the Holy Book!" She snatched the book off the mantel and handed it to me.

I knelt by the storeroom door, turned to the wild beast, kissed the cover, closed my eyes, opened the book to a page and began to chant:

Wa az-zoha, wa az-zoha.
Wa al-layl eza saja.
Wa al-layl: ma waddaka, waddaka,
ma waddaka rabboka, rabboka
Wa az-zoha wa al-layl,
Wa al-akhiratu khayrun lakka
Rabboka Allah, rabboka zaha rabboka.

I swear by the dawning light
And the night when all is still.
I swear by the darkest night
That God has not forsaken you.
I swear by both morning and night
That your life will soon be better.

As I recited the sura, I quietly took one step forward, then another. Reciting all the while, I held out my hand to her and saw the light go out in the wolf's eyes. I went on until I felt Tina's hand seek mine in the darkness. "Come, Tina, come!" I whispered. "Let's go eat." She struggled to her feet and then walked into the living room.

I look out my window and I see the wolf running through the Dutch polder.

Let it run, let it go, let the wolf lose its way on this new ground, so it will never be able to find its way back to Tina.

A Woman in a Hat

*It's not the schools and buses
that have cast their spell on Akbar,
but something else.*

 I'm sitting in my attic again, but it's hot, almost too hot to work. I read . . . no, that's not really the right word . . . I run my pencil along the words, the phrases, in my father's notebook, then feed them—or, rather, whatever fragments of text I can understand—into my computer. It's not an easy job. I'm forced to base my story on the frequently indecipherable and incomprehensible thoughts of another person. Usually I keep working until a headache forces me to stop.

The attic is my office. I sit up here nearly all day. My daughter goes to school and my wife works part-time in Lelystad. On her off days I go to my classes in Dutch literature at the University of Utrecht.

I get headaches because I don't know how to proceed with the story. A couple of times I've thought about quitting, but in the end I always go on.

I hear children playing in the schoolyard. They're giggling and shouting, "Stop, stop!" I go over to the window and see the teacher spraying the kids with a hose. They grab the hose and turn it on her, until she's soaking wet. She runs, laughs and takes off her shoes. The kids chase after her. She runs, laughs and takes off her wet blouse.

It's hot. Everyone's sitting in the shade of an umbrella or under a tree. Trailers are parked up and down the street, since everyone has just got back from their holidays.

I didn't go on holiday this year, though my wife and daughter spent a few weeks in Germany with friends. I chose to spend my time working on the book. I need to find the right form for the story before the autumn semester begins.

I go outside and do something no one else is doing in this heat: I run a few laps. To hell with the computer and Aga Akbar's notebook.

I run to get away from the story, but, as it turns out, I meet it head-on. I run down a path that used to be the bottom of the sea, then climb to the top of the dyke. Off in the distance are becalmed sailboats. I run to the end of the dyke, with beads of sweat dripping from my forehead. My headache has finally disappeared. I know how the story should continue.

I sit on the couch and watch the news. Prince Claus, the husband of the Dutch queen, was giving a speech at an award ceremony, when he suddenly took off his tie, urged men to liberate themselves from "the snake around their necks" and tossed it into the air. The camera shows the tie in slow motion, sailing up in a high arc, then fluttering gently to the floor.

Prince Claus is right—ties are a thing of the past. You can see it in clothing stores. Men's ties are always on sale—first 50 per cent off, then 75 per cent off, and finally marked down so much that you can buy a good green silk tie for only a guilder.

A few months before the student association's party at the university, I bought myself a tie. On the big night, I put it on and went to the party. One second after I entered the room, I put my hand over the knot and headed for the gents'. Everyone was dressed in jeans and T-shirts. I was the only one in a suit and tie.

It was my first time to wear a tie as an adult, but the second time in my life to furtively take one off and stuff it in my pocket. The earlier occasion had been in my childhood, soon after we moved to the city.

One evening my father came home with two ties: a grassy green one for me and a bright red one for himself.

First he knotted mine, then he went over to the mirror to tie his own.

"Why do we have to wear these ties?" I signed.

"I want to take you into town."

"Why with a tie?"

"All the men in town wear a tie," he signed back.

Tina wasn't home. She and my sisters were visiting a woman who'd recently moved to the city. Clearly, my father didn't want Tina to know about the ties. That wouldn't be a problem—from the day I was born, my father had been teaching me not to divulge his secrets.

We walked to the heart of the city, to a street I'd never heard of. Men were strolling around a square, lit by multicoloured electric lights. There were a few women, too, though none wearing a chador. Everything was different—the people, the cars, the newspaper boys shouting, "The latest news! Read all about it!"

A couple of men with a record player were selling records. The magical voice of a Persian singer rang out over the square.

Whose voice did I hear that evening? What song were the record salesmen playing? I don't remember the lyrics and there aren't any Iranians in my area who might know. So I close my eyes and open my ears. No, I can't hear the words, my memory has erased the lyrics, but I do hear an old melody: *baradam, baradam, baradam,* which seems to go with the following song:

Be rahi didam barg-e khazan
Oftadeh ze bidad-e zaman.
Ay barg-e payizi,
Az man to chera be gerizi?

In my travels I saw a falling leaf,
Tossed about on the winds of time.
Tell me, autumn leaf,
Why are you fleeing from me?

There were men selling ice-cream cones and walnuts, and there were men wearing ties. Most of them walked around with a newspaper or stopped beneath a lamppost to read. My dear father, who couldn't read a word, suddenly pulled a rumpled newspaper out from under his suit, tucked it under his right arm and started strolling around the square like all the other men. I followed him, curious as to what he would do next, but he didn't do anything special. He walked around for a while, then stopped beside a lamppost, unfolded his newspaper, held it up to the light and pretended to read. I thought he'd gone mad again. Kazem Khan was right: my father was crazy, my father was a fool.

After a while he tucked the newspaper back under his arm and continued his stroll.

How could I have known that my father was head over heels in love?

If I'd been in his place, I think I'd have fallen for one of those women, too.

The women in the square were not at all like the women we were used to. I'd never seen women do anything but work. Women wove carpets and cooked and prayed; women had children and cried and got sick and had a wolf inside. Now I saw women prancing around in high heels.

At a certain moment a young woman wearing a hat walked into the square from a side street. My father's eyes lit up. He walked over to her, gestured, then pointed at me with his newspaper: "My son. He can talk, he can hear, he can even read a newspaper."

"What a clever boy!" the young woman exclaimed and leaned closer. "What's your name?"

"Ishmael," I said, instantly on my guard.

Did my father actually know what love was? Was he aware that he was "in love"? I mean, was he capable of knowing that he'd entered the domain of love? Would he be able to explain his longing? His desire to be with her, to hold her hand, to smell her hair, to possess her?

Unless you've read about it, heard about it, or talked about it, you have no way of knowing what's happening to you.

An old Persian classic describes the travels of a man named Hodjah Nasreddin. To understand the meaning of life, he travels through the world on foot. At the gate to Hamadan, he sees a crowd—men, women, children, camels, donkeys, horses, goats, chickens—all racing after a young man. The young man dances, weeps, mutters, flings himself to the ground, gets back up again, weeps some more, laughs, runs and pours a handful of dirt over his head.

Nasreddin stops an old man. "Please, brother, what's gotten into that young man?"

"He's in love. We've all come to watch, so we can learn what love is."

My father took me to the square every evening. The woman in the hat usually arrived later on and the three of us would go sit on a bench, with me in the middle, to act as their interpreter.

Who was she? How had they met? I had no idea.

My poor father had trouble concentrating on his work. He sewed wrong numbers on the carpets and created chaos in the account books and warehouses. One of the employees dropped by to warn Tina: "I don't know what's wrong with him, but if he doesn't snap out of it, he'll be fired."

He didn't snap out of it and he was fired.

He was absent-minded at home, too. He stared out the window, or tried to find a quiet place where he could write in his notebook. Tina warned the family, "Help! Akbar has fallen into disgrace!"

As a Persian, you don't actually need to have been in love yourself. You can read about it in Persian stories, in Persian myths and even in the Koran. Like every Persian, Tina must have known the story of the sheikh and the tarsa (Christian).

The sheikh, an elderly Sufi leader, sets out on foot for Mecca, together with thousands of his followers. Months go by. Then, in one of those foreign cities, the sheikh sees a beautiful tarsa in the bazaar and immediately falls in love with her. It couldn't get any worse—to be headed for Mecca and to fall in love with a Christian! The sheikh abandons his plan and sets off, barefoot, in search of the beautiful tarsa.

The entire Muslim world is horrified. "The sheikh has fallen into disgrace!" they cry.

My father and I had donned our ties again. We were sitting on a bench in the square, beside the woman in the hat, when suddenly, off in the distance, I thought I saw two of our horses. How could that be? How could the horses we left behind in Saffron Village now be trotting towards the square? Then I recognised our wagon and, moments later, heard the voice of my oldest aunt as she talked to my other aunts and uncles.

The horses stopped in the glow of a nearby streetlamp.

My oldest aunt got out and marched over to my father. She grabbed hold of his tie and dragged him over to the wagon, like a cow.

My aunts held him down, while my uncles undid my father's red tie and tossed it to the ground. Then my oldest aunt bustled over, grabbed me by the ear and dragged me over to the wagon, too. "A fine job you did, my boy!" she exclaimed. "A fine job of looking after your father!"

We all got in and the horses trotted off.

I could hear my father crying. I couldn't see him very well, however, since he was sitting behind my aunts, with his head bowed and his hands over his face.

I looked back at the square. The woman was still there, standing in the lamplight and clutching her hat as if there were a strong wind. She watched us go.

The next day my aunts and uncles loaded our belongings into the wagon and brought us to another city—Senejan. I have no idea how they did it, but the arrangements had already been made. We had a flat and my father had a job in a textile mill.

He spent all day walking up and down a row of looms and reconnecting broken threads. He wasn't allowed to move away from the machines, not even for a minute.

. . .

I no longer saw my father in the daylight hours, since he left home before sunrise and got back after sunset. Tina immediately gave him his dinner. He ate in silence, sat for a while, held his daughters in his lap, drank one last cup of tea and went to bed.

When I think back to him at that time, I always picture him asleep.

Sometimes he didn't even bother to take off his work clothes. He'd lie down for a short rest, then fall into a deep sleep from which we couldn't wake him.

"Ishmael, pull the covers up over your father," Tina used to say. Another memory from that time. I knew I was supposed to cover him up, but I always waited for Tina to ask me. Maybe that's why this particular phrase has stuck in my memory.

The woman in the hat had arrived to split my father's life in two. She ended one phase of his life and ushered in another. Otherwise she had nothing to do with us and we had nothing to do with her. She came, did her job, and left.

Aga Akbar had once been a highly respected carpet-mender, who had galloped on his horse from one village to another with his head held high. His hair had been black and his white teeth had glowed in the dark. After our move to Senejan, his hair turned grey and he looked ill. All he did was work, work, work.

I leaf through my father's notebook with hopes of finding out more about that time. Since the pages don't have numbers, I pencil them in on the lower right-hand corner of every page. On page 134 I see a few tiny sketches. I assume they represent the phases of the moon: a new moon, a quarter moon, a half moon, a three-quarter moon, a full moon, and then suddenly a dark moon and a red moon.

He clung to a habit he'd acquired during the first period of his life: no matter where he was or where he went, he always came home by full moon. When night fell and everyone was asleep, he would set the ladder against the wall and climb up onto the roof. He'd sit on our roof, stare at the moon and hum.

Hum?

What on earth could he hum if he didn't know any lyrics or melodies? If he didn't know the songs of the lovesick medieval poet Baba Taher and had never heard this famous Sufi leader's love poems?

His enchantment with the full moon was a throwback to his life in Isfahan. The nights there had been full of stars. The moon had hung above the magical mosques like a heavenly lamp.

If you stood in Naqsh-e-Jahan Square on a clear night, you could pluck the moon right out of the sky. It's what the ancient Persian poets did with their poetry.

Aga Akbar was mesmerised by the sky. During the lonely nights, he would steal up to the roof of the Jomah Mosque, sit down, lean back against the dome, wrap his arms around his knees and stare into the night. The night brought him closer to the inexplicable, to Allah, to love. Perhaps the best way to describe this is to quote two verses of a very long, old song:

Az nayestan ta ma-ra be-b'ridand
dar nafir-am mard o zan nalidand
sineh khwah-am sharheh sharheh az firaq
ta be-goy-am sharh-e dard-e ishtiyaq.

Every Persian knows this song, or at least these two verses. You hum them when you're in love. Even though Aga Akbar had never heard the words, he would still hum that song.

It's about a reed that stood in a field of reeds. Someone cut it down to make a flute. The reed then laments:

From the moment I was cut down they all
Played me and poured out their longings.
I seek an aching heart, torn by loneliness,
So I can pour out my own painful yearnings.

One time I borrowed a projector. When the full moon rose that night and my father was about to lean the ladder against the wall and climb up on the roof, I tugged his sleeve: "Come, there's something I want you to see."

He didn't want to come with me, he wanted to see his moon.

"Listen, you don't have to go up on the roof. I have a moon for you, right in your own living room."

He didn't understand.

"The moon," I signed. "I've put the moon into that machine. Especially for you. Come look!"

He smiled, the usual bland smile he wore whenever he didn't understand something. I pulled up a chair for him and closed the curtains.

"Sit down!" I signed and turned off the light.

He hesitantly sat down and stared at the blank screen.

I switched on the projector. First there were some words in English, then suddenly a young man. My father didn't react, just sat quietly and watched. Gradually a quarter moon appeared, then a half moon and finally a full moon. He turned around, looking for me behind the projector.

This wasn't the moon of Isfahan, but the moon of the United States. An inaccessible moon in a dark blue sky. After that the screen filled with a picture of *Apollo 11*.

• • •

Was my father able to make the connection between the moon and the spacecraft?

A few minutes later *Apollo 11* landed, and for the first time man set foot on the moon. I turned off the projector and the moon vanished. My father sat in his chair with his hands on his thighs, almost as if he were praying. I didn't switch on the light, but let him sit in the darkness for a while. I looked at my aging father. All I could see of him was his silhouette and the moonlit glow of his grey hair.

Mossadegh

*Since Aga Akbar wrote nothing about
an important period in Iran's history,
I have to get that information
from another source.*

 Yesterday I took a quick look at the first part of this book. That's when I noticed that an important period in the political life of my country was missing.

How could Aga Akbar write about an event if he didn't even know it had taken place?

I'd prefer not to discuss politics in this book, but sometimes it can't be helped. I have to include the highlights, for the simple reason that the most important changes in Akbar's life were the result of radical changes in the country's political agenda.

My father's move to the city, for example, was prompted

by a major shift in Iranian politics: the CIA-backed coup that restored the young shah to the throne.

I had to say something about Mossadegh, but where would I find the necessary historical facts?

Though the university library undoubtedly had enough material, I didn't want an overly historical approach that would make me stray too far from my father's notebook. I wanted to sketch a clear portrait of Mossadegh, in a few simple lines. But how could I do that?

Then it occurred to me to phone Igor.

"Good morning, Igor. It's Ishmael."

"Good morning, Ishmael. What can I do for you so early in the morning?"

"Early? It's not that early. You usually get up at six-thirty. Don't tell me you're still in bed?"

"Today I am, for a change. I don't feel like getting up. Chalk it up to old age. That means no newspapers, no pens and no writing pads for me today. So, tell me, what can I do for you?"

"Nothing much. Just one question, which you don't need to answer right away. I'll drop by later on. I'd like to know something about Mossadegh."

"Mossadagh? Refresh my memory . . . where or who is Mossadagh?"

"No, Mossadegh. You must have come across his name before—the prime minister of Iran after the fall of Reza Khan Pahlavi . . ."

Igor, a former journalist, is a friend of mine. He used to live in Amsterdam, in an old house on a canal. It was so full of books and records that he had no room for more, so when he retired, he decided to sell his small house and move to the peace and quiet of the polder.

The first time I met him was on the day he moved. It was

hot and I was out running. Opposite the dyke, just past the new cemetery, was a beautiful house with a lovely view of the sea. It had been empty for a while, but now there was a moving van parked outside. An old man in a hat was pointing at dozens of book boxes and admonishing the movers. "Gently, please. Be careful . . . those are my files!"

Suddenly he began to shout, "Oh, God, they're ruining my books!"

I stopped and watched for a while. Fascinating, an old man in a hat with so many boxes of books.

"What are you looking at?" he asked me. "Help me! I've got to let my cats out."

I helped him carry a huge box containing seven miaowing cats into the house. We've been friends ever since.

Igor lives alone with his seven cats. For the last fifty years he's spent every morning cutting "important" articles out of the newspaper—with the same old scissors—and filing them in his archives, which consist of hundreds of files.

I was certain he had a file on Mossadegh. The question was whether I could find it.

I went over to his house. As usual, he didn't come down to open the front door. Instead, he stuck his head out of the window to see who was there, then tugged on a rope that ran from the top of the stairs to the door.

"You could buy yourself an electronic door opener, you know," I called up to him. "It beats having to use a rope." I say that every time I come for a visit.

"Phooey! Come on up, young man!"

The moment I walked in, seven cats started crawling up my arms and legs.

"Are you sick, Igor? Were you really in bed or—"

"Anyone who's got out of bed every morning at six-thirty

for the past fifty years also gets up every morning at six-thirty to die. Come in, I'm not sick and I'm not in bed, either. I'm just old, that's all. But, uh . . . you wanted to know something about Mossadegh. Why Mossadegh, all of a sudden?"

I was about to explain why I needed the information, but as usual he went on talking. Besides, I hadn't told him about the notebook. I knew I'd have to tell him some day, but I didn't yet dare.

"You know," he said, "I became addicted to newspapers at a very young age. When I was about ten, I read about a statesman in your country who wept when he was forced to resign. You probably know your history better than I do, but what I do know is that he wanted to nationalise the Anglo-Iranian Oil Company, which, by the way, seemed to me a very sensible thing to do.

"Help yourself to some coffee, my boy. I've put out a nice cup for you, one that comes from the Middle East. I bought it at a flea market. No, wait, at a rummage sale in Amsterdam. Anyway, the coffee tastes better in that cup.

"That man, that Mossadegh . . . I don't know all that much about him. I have a file, though I'm not sure where it is. The shah wanted to get rid of him, I think, and threw him in jail. I don't know if Mossadegh always wept in public, or if that was the only time. We didn't have television in those days, but movie theatres used to show a newsreel before the movie began. Mossadegh's tears struck me as a breath of fresh air. At last, a statesman who showed his emotions in public.

"In the post-war years the Netherlands had a greatly respected prime minister by the name of Willem Drees. Still, you never saw him laugh, much less cry. He might have shed an occasional tear in the privacy of his own home, but the general public didn't know that. Dutch men aren't supposed to show their emotions, they're supposed to suppress their tears.

"What did I tell you? The coffee does taste better in that

cup! Have a biscuit, the biscuit tin's over there, by the . . . oh, I forgot, I hid it from the cats. They like to bat it around, and the biscuits get broken. I might have stuck it behind those files . . .

"It's OK to cry at a funeral, that's acceptable. As for me, I cry whenever I feel like it. Come to think of it, I don't know whether I got that from my mother or from Mossadegh . . . Anyway, the shah didn't have Mossadegh killed. Wasn't that nice of him? I had a pretty low opinion of the shah in those days, because he was a friend of our prince Bernhard. You know who Prince Bernhard is, don't you? The husband of our former Queen Juliana and the father of our present Queen Beatrix. He's known for keeping bad company. My analyses are often based on emotions, so the way I looked at it, the shah was bad and Mossadegh was good. Now, where's that biscuit tin?"

Igor had nothing more to say about Mossadegh, but he did point me in the general direction of the clippings.

I sat on the floor for a couple of hours, poring over his files. And this is what I found:

From 1921 to 1925 Mossadegh served as minister of justice, then of finance and finally of foreign affairs. He was elected to Parliament in 1944. He founded the National Front Party in 1950 and became prime minister in 1951, at which point he nationalised the Anglo-Iranian Oil Company. The country was plunged into a direct conflict with Great Britain. Mossadegh was forced to resign in 1952, but was reinstated three months later, as a result of popular riots. He promptly curtailed the power of the shah—the son of Reza Khan—and began to lean heavily on the support of leftist factions. The shah fled the country. Backed by the United States, however, he returned. The national government fell and Mossadegh was arrested.

When Churchill learned that Mossadegh had been placed under permanent house arrest, he raised his glass and said, "He was mad . . . a dangerous man."

Mossadegh was far from "dangerous". He was our pride and joy.

Thousands of his followers were arrested. Many of them were executed and hundreds fled the country. The majority of the refugees were members of a left-wing Russian-oriented party that was opposed to the shah as well as to American interference.

Because of its popularity, the party had assumed it would soon be in power. Its adherents had been dissatisfied with Mossadegh, because they believed he made too many concessions to the imperialists. So, when the shah returned to power, they failed to support Mossadegh until it was too late. When he fell, the party fell apart. Some of its followers were executed, some went underground and some escaped.

Many of them fled to Saffron Mountain, in hope of crossing the border into the Soviet Union. It wasn't all that easy. Gendarmes chased them from one mountain to another in their American-made jeeps. Hungry and desperate, they sought refuge among the villagers.

My father probably didn't know the first thing about Communism, but he did know something about people on the run.

Once, when he and I were in Saffron Village, he took me to our almond grove. He thrust a hunk of bread into my hands, tiptoed through the trees and hid behind a tree trunk.

"What are you doing?" I asked.

"Come here. Give me the bread," he signed.

"What are you talking about?"

He snatched the bread from me and walked off hurriedly in the direction of the mountains.

"In the old days," he signed, "lots of men used to sneak through my almond grove. I gave them bread. After that they went into the mountains."

A year after Mossadegh's arrest, a long train whistle rang out over the mountains. The train stopped in Saffron Village, which it had never done before.

"What are we in for now?" people said to each other.

The answer was sugar. American sugar. Sacks of sugar with an English word stamped on the front: sugar.

The old Persian word *qand* had to make way for "sugar". It was the first English word to reach Saffron Mountain. It was followed by another word: "cigarette". The traditional pipes gradually made way for cigarettes.

The age-old word *kad-khoda,* for the headman of a village, disappeared and was replaced by another word: *bakhsh-dar.* The *bakhsh-dar* was a man in a tie who drove up and down the village in a jeep.

One day the *bakhsh-dar,* accompanied by the local imam and the village elders, stood on a chair and nailed a picture of the shah to the wall of the mosque.

That's what happened and that's how the son of Reza Khan came to be the shah of Persia.

In school, we learned nothing about Mossadegh, but everything about the shah. We learned that he was the son of Reza Khan, who was the son of an earlier shah, who was the son of an even earlier shah, and so on through 2,500 years of history, all the way back to Cyrus—the first king in Persian history, the man whose story is chiselled in cuneiform in the cave on Saffron Mountain: *My name is Cyrus. I am the king of kings.*

The Tuti

The shah has a son.
A dead parrot falls out of a tree.
These two events alter
the course of the story.

 Sometimes I think I'm writing this book out of guilt. The guilt of a son who failed his given task, who escaped halfway through the job and left his father to his fate. Maybe that's why my father comes to me so often in my dreams, why he never looks at me, but avoids my glance and averts his head.

Now that he's dead, I can't turn back the clock, I can't make it up to him. I can only hope that he's forgiven me and that the next time he appears in my dreams, he'll look me in the face.

I'm writing this book mostly for my father, but also to convince myself of the inevitability of my escape. To assure myself that events caught up with me, that I was no longer in control, that . . . how shall I say it? . . . that *he* was the reason I fled the country.

I can't explain it, other than to say that I'm sitting here now, struggling with another language, precisely because I'm the son of Aga Akbar.

Despite the fact that I later used my father to achieve my own goals, I've always served him faithfully.

For example, even now, when I'm writing this story, it's *his* book I'm trying to decipher and *his* words I'm trying to put into a readable form. I'm not complaining. I accept it as my fate. I have no choice—the story must go on.

The son of Reza Khan divorced his first two wives because they failed to produce an heir. The third one finally bore him a son, a crown prince. His dream had come true.

I was about ten or eleven, I think, when the crown prince had his third or fourth birthday. In the larger cities it was celebrated with great joy, but in our smaller, more conservative city it mostly escaped notice. In the schools of Tehran, bare-legged girls performed a dance. There was singing and everyone was given a banana as a special treat. Where I lived, nobody had even seen a picture of a banana.

The National Archives in Tehran have a collection of newspapers from that era, with photographs of schoolgirls slipping on banana peels. There's also a picture of the queen and her son visiting one of the injured girls in the hospital.

The mayor of our city did his best to promote the crown prince's birthday. He ordered our school, which occupied a forlorn and forgotten building on the outskirts of town, to organise a celebration. The mayor was to bring an "important" guest and the principal saw an opportunity to climb a rung or two up the bureaucratic ladder.

The principal would no doubt have loved to ask a Tehran

girl to dance bare-legged for the mayor, but even he knew that that was beyond the realm of possibility.

"Ishmael!" the principal tapped me on the shoulder one day. "Come with me. I want to talk to you."

In his office—normally off-limits to students—he offered me a biscuit and even showed me a skinny little banana. He started talking about the shah and then about our ancient Persian kingdom and its first king, Cyrus, the king of kings. Then he moved on to our present-day country, which was rapidly becoming a modern society. You could see progress everywhere, he said, except in our backward town, which was in the clutches of the clerics. And now, with the mayor and an important guest coming to our school, the principal needed my help.

"Me? Help you?"

"Yes, Ishmael, you have to help me."

Just thinking back to that day makes me cover my face in shame. Why me? Why me, of all people?

The principal leaned forward and said that I wasn't like all the other students. That I read books and knew a lot about the world. That the others were farm boys who didn't know the first thing about modernisation. Then, in strict confidence, he explained what he wanted.

I didn't have to do anything out of the ordinary on the crown prince's birthday, he assured me. All I had to do was show that I was every bit as cultured as a schoolboy in Tehran and just as modern as a boy in Paris.

The red-letter day arrived. The mayor ushered in his important guest and the two of them sat in reserved seats in the front row. I peeked out from behind the curtain to get a good look at the important guest and the crowded auditorium. When the curtain went up, I would dance. I would dazzle the mayor and the students and show them that we, too, were modern. No man in my family—from Adam to Ishmael—had ever done such a thing before.

When the curtain went up, I would lift my arms in the air, move my hips a bit, bend over and straighten up again, exactly as the mayor had taught me.

Just before I was about to go on, however, the principal suddenly appeared with a dancing-girl's costume and a wig. "Here, put these on!"

Only God and the principal knew that the costume and the wig hadn't been part of the bargain. All I was supposed to do was dance like a Parisian schoolboy. That in itself was a huge step, a giant leap forward, in this ultra-conservative town.

"Quick! Take off your pants!" the principal said.

"What?"

"Put this on!"

The principal would never have dared to pull such a dirty trick on any other schoolboy. He knew that the boy's family would kill him. He'd picked me because he figured that my disabled father wouldn't be a threat.

I fought them off, but the principal held me down while the vice-principal pulled off my trousers and shoved on the skirt. Then he jammed the wig on my head, applied red lipstick to my mouth and pushed me out onto the stage.

The musicians burst into loud song.

I stood on stage, not moving.

"Dance!" the principal hissed at me from behind the curtain.

I looked at the audience. The students were astonished, but nobody recognised me. The mayor smiled and clapped his hands. The musicians played even louder.

"Dance!" the principal hissed again.

I began to dance.

Even now the thought of it makes me break out in cold

sweat. I look out the window at the sea, at the pent-up sea banging its fists against the dyke.

My short skirt billowed up to reveal my white cotton underpants. There were laughs, cheers, and catcalls. The mayor slapped his knees in delight.

Suddenly I saw my father striding towards the stage. The policemen were hard on his heels, hoping to stop him. Even though he was sick, he pushed everyone aside and climbed onto the stage. He picked me up, threw me over his shoulder, and leapt to the floor. Then he lost his balance and the two of us fell. The policemen pounced on my father and beat him with their clubs.

Out of respect for my father, I'm not going to tell the rest of the story. Only this: imagine me standing bare-legged, with a trace of lipstick on my mouth, behind the door to the examining room, while a doctor and his assistant stitched up my father's head wounds.

This, too, shall pass, as does everything. The Persian kingdom no longer exists, nor does the shah. And where's his crown prince now?

One night I caught sight of him on TV. When Princess Diana died, all kinds of famous people came to her funeral: Hollywood stars, musicians, politicians, and princes and princesses galore.

Dozens of BBC cameras focused on the guests. One of them zoomed in on the face of a muscular young man staring into the lens with the military bearing of a solider. Who was he? Where did I know him from? And then I recognised him.

He, too, was a refugee, just like me.

For years I'd managed to block out this entire episode, then this morning it came flooding back to me.

What had brought my father to school that day? Where

had he suddenly come from? How had he known that his Ishmael was in trouble? Was it all a coincidence?

It couldn't have been. He couldn't have recognised me with that wig on. Somebody must have told him. But who? Who could have known what the principal was up to?

Maybe the janitor, the pious old janitor. It must have been him. In my imagination I now see him running to our house. "Allah! Hurry!"

My father just happened to be at home. No, it wasn't that much of a coincidence: he was sick a lot back then, so sick that he sometimes spent a week in bed.

That day changed my life and my father's life completely. For years afterwards, the boys in my neighborhood never gave us a moment's peace. They even chased me in my dreams. I ran away from them, panting, but they always caught me and beat me to a pulp. I couldn't fight back because I had to hold my belt with all my might to keep them from pulling down my trousers. They wanted another look at my bare legs. Whenever they ran into my father, they pointed at the scars on his head and unbuckled their belts. He tried to catch them and they threw stones at him.

These scenes are too painful to remember, much less write about.

Those were the years in which we took a detour on our way home to avoid running into the boys. Those years of humiliation for me and my father were golden years for the shah and his crown prince. That crown prince is now living in exile, too, and both of us have lost our fathers.

Later he and his father suffered countless humiliations, especially when the son could find nowhere for his father to die and after that nowhere to bury him.

He finally found a grave for his father in Egypt.

· · ·

I resigned myself to my fate. As soon as school was over, I raced home and sought refuge in books. In novels from the West.

I don't know what that thin, worn book was doing in our house or who had left it there. Maybe my father had found it somewhere and brought it home. At any rate, it was a real eye-opener. It wasn't like any book I'd ever read. What was it about? I've forgotten, but if I go for a walk and think back to that time, I should be able to remember.

I discovered a bookseller in our area, an old man who not only sold newspapers and magazines but also had a bookcase full of well-thumbed mysteries. I borrowed a few every time I went there and read them at night under the blankets. Then one day he had no more books for me and I thought I'd read all the books in the world.

My father started bringing books home.

"Here! For you!" he'd gesture.

I'd take them from him, flip through them and set them halfheartedly in my bookcase. They weren't books you'd read for fun. One old book he'd found at work, for example, was about cotton and thread. Another was filled with numbers and tables.

In the beginning it wasn't a problem: he'd bring me a book and I'd put it in the bookcase. But later he started asking me if I'd read it. "No, not yet, I'll read it later," I'd say.

Once he brought home an old company manual and wanted to know what it was about. "Numbers," I explained. "It's about one, two, three, four. And about angles and circles."

"So, it's good for you?" he said. "Yes, thank you," I said and slipped it onto the shelf beside the other books.

Sometimes he sat a few feet away from me, not doing anything or saying anything, just quietly watching me read. He was fascinated by books and reading. He wanted to know what it felt like to sit or lie so still and read a book.

Now that I'm working on his notebook, I can see that his life consisted of several phases. We've now landed in the book phase, which lasted for almost two years.

"Where do you get those books?" I once asked him.

"I buy them," he said.

"You shouldn't do that. You can't buy just any old book. If I need a book, I'll buy it myself."

He didn't listen to me and went on buying more and more books. One night Tina cried so long and hard that she fainted.

"Are you happy now?" I shouted at him. "Why can't you listen?" It didn't help.

Meanwhile the boys in our neighbourhood had discovered a new game. As soon as they saw my father coming home with a couple of books under his arm or in his coat pocket, they crept up behind him, snatched one of his books and ran off. He chased after them but the boys just tossed it back and forth.

The turning point came when he arrived home with torn trousers and a stack of mud-splattered books.

"What's this?" I asked angrily.

"Nothing. Those boys in our street," he signed and smiled.

"I don't want any more books," I screamed.

"No? No more books?"

I yanked one of the books out from under his arm and threw it against the wall.

"No books! You understand that? No more books!"

Afterwards I realised that I'd done a very mean and ugly thing. How old had I been at the time—twelve or thirteen? And yet I felt as if I were sixteen or seventeen, because in those two years I'd suddenly grown more than the other boys my age.

Then I did something even meaner. My father leaned over to pick up the book, but I beat him to it. I snatched it up and threw it and the rest of the books onto the roof, one by one. "Finished!" I signed angrily. "They're all gone! Now go inside!"

My father didn't say a word. He went inside and went to bed. (Oh, what a terrible, awful thing for me to do!)

That evening I felt like crying, but I couldn't. How could I make it up to him? What could I possibly do?

After a while, I had a flash of insight. I finally realised why he bought those books. I lit an oil lamp and woke him up.

"Come with me!" I signed.

"Where to?"

"Up onto the roof!"

At first he thought there was a full moon, that he'd forgotten. He looked out the window, but no, there was a new moon.

I was his Ishmael, he had to listen to me, so he got up and followed me.

With the oil lamp in one hand, I climbed the ladder.

"You, too! Climb up here!"

My father hesitantly climbed up onto the roof.

I handed him the oil lamp and started collecting the scattered books.

"Give me the lamp and come over here," I signed, then sat down by the chimney.

"Pick up one of those books. We're going to read together."

He picked up one of the books and sat down beside me.

He didn't know what I had in mind. I didn't really know myself.

He picked up the biggest book and handed it to me. It was *The Rose Garden* by the medieval poet Sa'di. The beauty and power of the Persian language leaps off its every page. Its stories, or *hekayas*, are a testimony to Sa'di's virtuosity.

Translating the master's rich poetic text into my father's

simple sign language would be quite a feat, but I had to attempt it, because he and I were perfectly attuned to each other: I immediately understood what he said and he immediately understood what I said. I was almost capable of reducing the big wide world to a few small gestures. We communicated not only by signs, but also by using our eyes, lips and bodies. In addition, we had a little help from my father's god—the god of deaf-mutes.

I flipped through the book in search of a short *hekaya*.

"What . . . what kind of book is it?" he signed, which I took to be a conciliatory gesture.

"How can I explain it? You see, it's a . . . uh . . ."

"Does it also come from up above?" he asked.

"No, this isn't a holy book, it's different. It's about . . . well . . . youth . . . and old age. About kings. About the heart, love, death and . . . yes, it's about love, kissing a woman, holding her, touching her, looking at her, or . . . wait, here's a *hekaya* about a centipede."

"A what?"

"A centipede, you know, the insect, the little insect with lots of legs that crawls so fast . . . hold on, I'll bring the oil lamp a bit closer."

I drew a centipede in the dust with a stick and made a rapid movement with my finger.

"I'm going to read it slowly, so you can lip-read the words, then I'll explain it to you. Watch carefully:

"'*Dast o pa-ye berideh-i, hezar pa-i be-kosht*'. In other words, 'A man whose arms and legs had been chopped off swatted a centipede to death.' Did you get that?"

"Didn't you say the man had no arms and legs?" Akbar signed.

"That's right, they'd been chopped off. Now listen: 'Praise be to Allah. Not even with a hundred legs could the centipede escape a man with no hands or feet when its hour of death had come.' This is going to be hard. I can't explain it, because I don't really understand it myself. You'll have to work it out on your own."

"How can he swat an insect if he doesn't have any arms or legs?" my father signed.

"Exactly. In order to swat something, you have to have at least one hand or one foot. You don't understand it and I don't understand it, but the man did kill the centipede. Maybe that's why the story's so beautiful. It's about death. When death comes, nobody can escape it. The centipede's time had come, so he had to die, his life was over, and if his life was over, even an armless and legless man could swat him to death. Do you have any other ideas?"

My father was silent. Then he laughed. "Clever," he tapped the side of his head. "That was clever of the writer. Can you read me another story?"

"Another one?"

I don't know why, but a well-known Persian story popped into my head. I thought it was one of Sa'di's, yet I hunted through the book for a long time without finding it. Apparently this particular story had been written by someone else.

"What are you looking for?" my father asked.

"For a story about a *tuti*."

"A *tuti*?"

"Yes, a beautiful, brightly coloured bird with a curved beak that can talk—a parrot."

"A bird? That can talk?"

"Well, not really talk. It imitates what you say. But I can't find the story in this book. It doesn't matter, I learned it at school, I know it by heart.

"A long, long time ago there was a Persian spice merchant who had a parrot in a cage. It came from India, a land that's far, far away. The bird longed for home. He was forever weeping and chirping: 'Home, home, home.'

"One day, when the merchant was about to leave for India on business, he went to his parrot and asked him if he had a message for the parrots in India. 'No, not really,' said the parrot. 'Just give them my regards and tell them I miss them.'

"Deep in an Indian forest, the merchant saw a parrot sitting in a tree. 'My parrot sends you his regards,' the merchant said. 'He misses his fellow parrots very much.'

"Suddenly the parrot fell out of the tree and died."

"It died?" my father asked.

"Hold on. The merchant came back from his trip and the parrot asked him if he had a message from the parrots in India. 'No, no message,' the merchant said. 'I did speak to a parrot, but when I gave him your regards and told him you missed your fellow parrots, he suddenly fell out of the tree and died.' 'It died?' said the parrot, and he also dropped dead."

"That one, too?" my father asked in surprise.

"Yes, the merchant's parrot also dropped dead."

"How did that happen?"

"Hold on. The man clutched his head. 'Oh, my parrot, my poor parrot. I shouldn't have told him.' But there was nothing he could do, the parrot was dead. He took the lifeless body out of its cage and threw it on the rubbish heap. Suddenly the parrot began to move, and then it flew off. 'Where are you going?' the merchant cried. 'Back home, back home, back home,' the parrot replied."

My father looked at me in surprise. At first he was silent, then he laughed out loud and signed, "Clever. The two parrots were very clever. A beautiful story. Beautiful."

We stayed on the roof a bit longer. While I leafed through the books, he sat beside me, lost in thought.

"The looms," he suddenly signed. "The looms in the factory are always going through my head, even in my sleep.

I . . . I don't know, but I wish I could . . . that I didn't have to . . . the work gives me a headache, you know, and upsets my stomach."

That was the first time he'd complained to me so clearly about his work. I could tell by his eyes that it wasn't a foolish complaint but a cry for help.

"My throat hurts and is always swollen," he continued. "Sometimes I can't breathe, I suddenly have to gasp for air. I . . . I don't want to go to the factory ever again, but I can't quit, I've got four children to feed."

I looked at his thin face and wondered what I could do to help him.

"The threads are always getting stuck in the machine," he signed. "I try to watch. I look at them, but I don't see them. Then the boss comes over and yells at me. Everybody stares and they all shake their heads and say that Akbar's stupid. What do you think I should do?"

He'd asked me a clear question and I, Ishmael, needed to give him a clear answer. If I didn't help him, who would? My duty was not to think of Tina and my sisters, but of Akbar. I'd been born to serve him, so I had to save him. Suddenly I knew what to do.

"You have to die," I signed.

"What?"

"Die. Like the parrot. Fall down."

He didn't know what I meant.

"What do you mean? How? Fall down where?"

"Between the looms. Just keel over suddenly. Drop dead."

The next day five factory workers carried my father home. They laid him on his deathbed and left.

He immediately opened his eyes, grabbed his cane and his carpet-mending gear and escaped into the mountains.

I wonder where he went.

Golden Bell

Soon we'll run into Marianne.
We'll also get to know Golden Bell.
And we'll knock on the door of Dr Pur Bahlul.

 I'm going to save for a later chapter the subject of where my father went, what he did in the mountains and who he slept with during the months of his absence, because I don't want to let my imagination run wild. That's the reason I try to limit myself to actual events, to something that I myself have seen or heard or read in his notes. Consequently, I won't be chasing through the mountains after my father in this chapter. Instead, I'm going to let him wander off and do whatever he pleases, sleep with whoever he wants and build up his strength again, because difficult times lie ahead. In other words, I'm going to leave him to his own devices for a while and tell another story until he gets back.

. . .

The summer is over, but a few days ago the weather suddenly turned hot again. There's a lake about six miles from my house. I got out my bicycle and biked over to it, so I could swim and write in peace.

I went to the lake a lot this summer. I'd swim a lap, then roll out my mat and write.

The first time I went there was with Marianne, a woman I'd met two years ago in a literary café. She lived in Amsterdam, but was house-sitting for a friend. I'd noticed her before during the poetry nights at the café, without realising that she came to the polder especially for the poetry nights. She invariably read aloud the poems of famous dead poets. Thanks to her readings, I became acquainted with the masters of Dutch poetry, particularly J. C. Bloem. She's the one who introduced me to the following poem:

In Memoriam

The weather changes, autumn is returning.
Leaves gild the water as they have before,
And fall to earth, down to the shadowy yearning
Of living hearts. He'll see it nevermore.

How much he would have loved these dusky streets,
This atmosphere, befogged and sanctified,
Pavement, abandoned as the day retreats,
Turned damp and unfamiliar and wide.

But he was destined for the silent things
With which we live—not all of us so long—
The truths each heart expresses when it sings,
Until we sink, and with us sinks the song.

That season too was fall; the leaves return,
Though lives do not, once their brief day has fled.

We learned how cruelly human hearts can burn,
Standing in his still chamber, by the bed.

For me, this memory will not fade away:
So unlike sleep, death's utter lack of sound.
Life is a miracle renewed each day,
And each awakening a new life found.

And now I find myself back in this blessed
Season of fallen leaves on water, gleaming
Like the pale sun of dead days laid to rest.
But how much longer shall I go on dreaming?

This weary life of toil leaves us breathless.
And what remains? What's left worth longing for?
For him and me, an autumn that is deathless:
Sun, mist, and silence, and forever more.

I've included this poem in my book because of my father's un-expressed longings. Marianne explained to me that J. C. Bloem was the poet of longing and that he'd once described himself as "divinely unfulfilled".

Marianne also writes poems. I didn't know that until one evening when I happened to stop by the café on a non-poetry night. She was sitting at a table, having a drink. She was my age and this was the first time I'd ever spoken to her without other people around.

"Look who's here!" she said in a friendly voice. We began to talk and we've been friends ever since. I don't know if "friends" is the right word to describe our relationship. Anyway, one day she said she was going to the lake and asked if I wanted to come along, too.

I didn't know how to swim, but Marianne assured me I could learn.

"You *have* to learn!" she exclaimed. I went with her. The lake was in a quiet spot, and she and I were the only people there.

For one entire week we biked to the lake every day and Marianne taught me how to swim. On the last day she stood in the middle of the lake, spread her arms out wide and called, "Come!"

I swam and battled my way through the water until I reached her.

Then I clung to her and she clung to me.

Once more I laid my mat under the trees at the edge of the lake, in hope of getting some writing done. It was hot and muggy, so I thought, Why not go for a swim first? I waded into the water. It wasn't the first time I'd gone swimming by myself. Once I'd even swum five laps. I swam calmly away from the shore, but before I'd gone even a hundred yards, I had a sudden panic attack. I turned and headed back to the shore, yet no matter how hard I swam, I didn't seem to be going anywhere. I was seized with fear. I looked around, but there wasn't a soul in sight. All my swimming skills were instantly forgotten. I shouted for help, then shouted again, sure that I was going to drown. As I sank, I thrashed around in the water. All of a sudden my foot touched bottom. One hard stroke, then another, and I could stand up.

I knelt on the mat, lay my head on the ground, and wept. I had no idea why, or who the tears were for.

I gathered up my belongings, including the notebook, and biked home.

I'm usually strong and not easily frightened, but now, for the first time, fear has burrowed into the innermost recesses of my soul. Is it because I've been working on the notebook, writing a book in Dutch and going to classes, all at the same time? A heavy load. I've been working hard the last few months—not taking any breaks, spending day and night trying to whip this book into shape. That must be the reason. Fear has found my weak spot. I'll never go in the water again, or at any rate I'll keep my feet firmly on the ground until this book is finished.

The day I swam out to Marianne and clung to her in the middle of the lake, she gave me a book. Not then, but later, after we'd changed out of our wet bathing suits. It was a volume of poetry by the Dutch poet Jan Slauerhoff.

"Here," she said, "think of it as your swim certificate."

The title of one of the poems was "My Daughter Golden Bell":

At not quite forty, I had a daughter,
And quickly dubbed her Golden Bell.
In the year since she was born,
She's learned to sit, but not yet talk.

The poem goes on, though I've quoted only these four lines.

Maybe it's a coincidence, maybe not, but my youngest sister's nickname was Zanguli, which can be translated as Golden Bell.

Zanguli is not a pretty name for a Persian girl. Her real name is Mahbubi.

My father was afraid that his children would be deaf-mutes. So great was his fear that he wasn't even present at the birth of his first two daughters.

I remember when my youngest sister was born. I was standing at my father's side when the midwife laid the baby in his arms. He held her to his chest with one hand and pulled a tiny golden bell out of his pocket with the other. He rang it softly next to her ear. The baby opened her eyes and looked up at him.

"Did you see that?" he signed, glowing with happiness. "Did you see that? She's not deaf! She can hear!"

Then he handed me the bell and said, "You try it!" I rang

it softly and my sister opened her eyes for a second time and looked at me.

"Did you see that?" my father said again and he laughed out loud, so loud that she started to cry.

So that's how she came to be *our* baby, to belong to my father and me. And also how her name came to be Golden Bell in my father's sign language.

He had different names for all of us, and he changed them whenever there was a major change in our lives. For example, in the beginning I was called Mine.

When he put his right hand to the left side of his chest, everyone knew he was referring to Ishmael. Later he changed my name to The Boy Who Crawls Under the Blankets and Reads. When I went to the university, he called me The Man Who Wears Glasses. Two years later I became The Man Who Is Never Here. And after that I was no doubt known as The Man Who Went Away. But he never changed Golden Bell's name. She was always Golden Bell.

She was different from the start. Golden Bell immediately became my father's favourite daughter. She, too, had been born to ease my father's suffering. That's how nature—or the god of deaf-mutes—works.

As a baby, she used to crawl happily to the door the moment she heard his footsteps. She was a divine gift.

Later, when he came home exhausted from his work in the factory, she massaged his shoulders. When he was sick, she made him soup. Years later, when I was a student in Tehran, she brought him there for his very first visit and showed him around. (I'd promised to show him Tehran, but hadn't kept my promise.) She had a camera and she took pictures of him in various places. There was a good one of him standing by the statue of Reza Shah. She had put her arm around his waist and asked a passer-by to photograph them together. Then she'd taken him to the airport so he could see how planes fly. Every evening they'd gone to a movie theatre where a series of Charlie Chaplin movies was being shown.

Golden Bell was our great joy as well as our great sorrow.

A natural division had taken place in our family: Golden Bell and I were on my father's side, while my sisters Marzi and Enzi were usually on my mother's side. They seemed to get along better with Tina. Golden Bell didn't. Why not? I don't really know, but maybe we'll find out as the story unfolds. Still, one thing can't be denied: Golden Bell was my father's favourite daughter.

Now that we know who Golden Bell is, I'm going to go back in time so we can see what's happened to my father.

When he first came down from the mountains, I barely recognised him. He wasn't at all like the man I've written about in the previous chapters. He was older and smaller.

Late one evening there was a knock at the door. I switched on the hall light, opened the door and got a shock. He looked ill and he didn't seem to have a tooth left in his mouth. He stared at me—another cry for help. I took his arm and led him into the light.

"Open your mouth," I said.

He opened his mouth. His teeth were rotten: all black and broken. (How could I not have noticed that before?)

"It hurts," he signed. "It hurts all the time."

His eyes filled with tears. At last someone had noticed, at last someone had realised that he was in pain. It took me a few moments to remember who I was and what my function was in this household. I smoothed back his grey hair. "I'll take care of it," I signed. "Everything will be all right. I'll make the pain go away."

He bowed his head. Good God, he bowed his head to me in thanks.

. . .

We didn't have enough money to get his teeth fixed, but that was beside the point. What mattered was that *I* do something about the pain.

We had a few dentists in our city. We also had a clinic, but rich people, or anyone who could afford private care, avoided going there, because you had to wait so long to see a doctor or a dentist. Queues formed early in the morning. Some people even brought blankets and slept there overnight.

The queue for the dentist was the longest. Sometimes you had to sleep there three nights in a row just to reach the door. Once you got inside, the dentist simply pulled out your aching tooth and sent you home with a couple of painkillers. You had no right to any other treatment. I've seen old men reduced to tears by toothaches.

With such an inhumane system, how would I be able to help my father?

One morning, hours before school started, I went into town to find a dentist. There were three of them. As it turned out, they were all closed until ten o'clock. In the window of the first was a note stating that no new appointments could be made for the next two months. The second dentist had a fancy office with a big sign above the door: THE LATEST IN TECHNOLOGY FOR ALL YOUR DENTAL NEEDS.

You were supposed to call for an appointment, but there was only one public phone booth in the entire city. Besides, I'd never even touched a telephone.

After seeing their offices, I knew those two dentists would never let my father and his broken teeth through the door. So I set off for the last dentist. His office was in his home, just outside the city centre. It was an old, large house with a classical gateway. A simple sign said: PUR BAHLUL, D.D.S. MONDAY TO THURSDAY, 3:00–7:00 P.M.

I didn't have any money, but I was the son of a rather unusual patient, so I ignored the sign and the office hours. The dentist was probably still in bed, or reading his newspaper at the breakfast table. I banged the door knocker twice. No answer. I tried again. An old man, a gardener with a watering can in his hand, opened the door.

"What's wrong? Why did you knock so hard?"

"Good morning. I'd like to talk to Dr Pur Bahlul."

"Talk to him? What for? The office opens at three."

"I know, but I'd like to talk to him now."

"What about?"

"I'd prefer to discuss that with him."

He looked at me, thought it over, then said, "Stay here. I'll go and ask."

I stood at the gate for a long time, until the door was finally opened by a grey-haired man with a pipe clenched between his teeth.

"Good morning, young man. I assume you're looking for me."

"Good morning, doctor. I'd like to talk to you about my father."

"Your father. What's wrong with your father?"

"His teeth."

"If this is about teeth, you'll have to wait until three o'clock," he said and sucked on his pipe.

"No, it's not about teeth. It's about me."

"But also about your father's teeth."

"No, not just that, it's about his pain and . . . well, you see, I promised to make the pain go away."

"What else? Go on, tell me the rest."

"Well, I have to relieve the pain somehow and, uh . . . that's it, doctor."

He looked at me as he puffed on his pipe.

"Your name?"

"Ishmael."

"Last name?"

"Mahmud Ghaznavi Khorasani."

"Come on in. Follow me," he said.

I followed him past a rose garden, a bed of petunias and a row of apple trees filled with red apples. We went into a room with tall windows.

"Two cups of tea," he called.

His library was lined with shelves full of books. He pointed to a chair. "Have a seat."

A servant brought us tea.

"Tell me your story. You mentioned your father. What does he do for a living?"

"He's a carpet-mender."

"Where?"

"Everywhere. He doesn't have a shop, he just walks down the street calling, 'Farshi, farshi,' so everyone knows he's a carpet-mender."

"Why 'farshi, farshi'?"

"Well, he's a deaf-mute. He just calls out a word that sounds like farsh (carpet)."

"Ah, I see. And I gather he's having trouble with his teeth."

"Every tooth in his mouth is rotten. The pain has aged him terribly."

He struck a match, held it up to his pipe, inhaled deeply and sent the smoke spiralling into the air. Then he rummaged around in his drawer.

"I know you have to go to school. Here are some painkillers. Bring your father to my office tomorrow evening. We'll talk some more then."

"Thank you, doctor."

"There's no need to thank me."

I stood up.

"Do you read books?"

"Yes, doctor."

"OK, I'll see you tomorrow evening."

The gardener let me out. "Oops," I said, "I forgot to tell the doctor something." I retraced my steps.

"Doctor! May I come in?"

"Yes."

"I think you should know that I can't pay you. I mean, I'll pay you back some day, but not now. I should have told you that straight away. But I took one look at your library and forgot all about it."

"It's late. Go to school. We'll talk about it tomorrow."

Dr Pur Bahlul was arrested a year later. He was released from prison only after the revolution began. As it turns out, he was one of the most important theoreticians of the underground leftist guerrilla movement, but until his arrest, his role had been kept secret even from his own party members.

When nearly all the leaders of the underground movement had been arrested by the shah's secret police, Pur Bahlul, using his profession as a cover, was able to keep the party going for a couple more years. I was totally unaware of it at the time and only found out several years later when I myself became an active member of the party.

Over the next three months, Dr Pur Bahlul pulled out all of my father's teeth, one by one. My father, with his toothless gums and grey hair, was now truly an old man. We made an appointment to come back in two months. Dr Pur Bahlul checked to see if my father's gums had hardened, then measured his jaw and jotted down a few notes.

I'd seen dentures before, but it never occurred to me that my father would be fitted with a pair. I thought he'd have to drink soup for the rest of his life.

A few weeks later we came back for yet another appointment. My father sat down in the examining chair.

"Open your mouth," Dr Pur Bahlul gestured.

He did.

"Now close your eyes."

He did that, too.

The dentist took a set of dentures out of a plastic bag and, without looking at me or saying anything, inserted them in my father's mouth. Then he tapped him on the shoulder. "Look in the mirror!"

Oddly enough, I felt as though the person staring back from the mirror was not my father but me. It seemed to be my mouth reflecting that shiny row of teeth and me staring in astonishment at my mouth, which held something new and modern, something young that didn't fit with my old, worn face.

Now that my father was able to eat, he gradually put on weight. You could see that he felt like living again.

He was the first man in the mountains to have false teeth. In the summer, when we went to Saffron Mountain on our holidays, I kept having to tug at his sleeve to hurry him along, because every time he ran into an elderly villager, he'd take out his dentures and demonstrate how good and strong they were. He advised everybody to get a pair.

Sometimes I had to admonish him, "That's enough. Behave yourself. You're the father of three daughters. Put those teeth back in your mouth before everybody thinks you've gone crazy."

It didn't help. After that, he simply did it when I wasn't looking.

• • •

Dr Pur Bahlul sent me a bill for 3,000 toman. It was an enormous amount of money, which I'd never be able to pay. After all, my father earned only three toman a day.

"You have an obligation to pay the bill," the dentist said. "And you'll pay it down to the last penny."

"I know, doctor, but . . ."

Everything had already been arranged. He'd made an appointment for me with one of the editors at the city newspaper. If I agreed, I could work twice a week, for three hours a night, sorting letters from readers, editing them and getting them ready for print. I would be allowed to keep half of what I earned; the other half would go toward the dental bill.

It would have taken me years to pay off my debt, but fate intervened. A year later, I was heading towards his house with another book under my coat when I saw that his street was swarming with policemen. There were even three armed officers standing guard on his roof. The police held back the crowd and wouldn't let anyone into the street. I hung around to watch.

Half an hour later, Dr Pur Bahlul was escorted out of his house by three policemen. He was smoking his pipe. The policemen started to shove him into the waiting car, but he wasn't about to be shoved. He squared his shoulders, took a deep breath, stared into the crowd, then seated himself in the back.

The doors closed and he disappeared.

On Your Own Two Feet

We skip a few years,
*years in which Tina worked**
and Akbar was often gone.
But first Hannah's good name
has to be restored.

 I wondered where my father slept when he was in the mountains. I knew there was another woman in his life, and he knew that I knew, but it remained a secret between us. Now that I'm so wrapped up in his notebook, I'm reminded of her for the first time in years. I can't get her out of my mind. It's a pity I don't have a picture of her, that I have no idea what she looked like. I don't even know if she's still alive, though I suspect she is. You're less likely to die, in my opinion, if you have a secret

*Tina worked at home, mending textiles for the mill. Her job helped her to rid herself of the wolf.

to pass on. I think she'll go on living until she and I some-how manage to meet.

Here, in the silence of the polder, I'd like to utter her name, to shout it out loud, but I can't, because I don't know it. Someone in Saffron Village once told me that she was the daughter of a Russian immigrant and that she lived in a mountain village near the border of the former Soviet Union. Though I'd never met her or officially known of her exis-tence, she and I had a tacit agreement.

She did a lot to help the party. She frequently crossed the border with clandestine packages. And she sheltered a num-ber of important party members and smuggled them across the border at night.

I know she did it for my father. However, now that I'm able to look back at events more objectively, I've sensed, or rather realised, that to some extent she also did it for me—the son of the man she loved.

I think she also came to Golden Bell's rescue.

Is she the one who sent me my father's notebook? There was no return address on the package. No letter, either. Not a word.

What's her name?

Since she exists only in my memory, I suppose I can call her whatever I like. But what name should I give her? A Per-sian name? A Russian name? No, she already has a Persian or a Russian name. A Dutch name? I'll give her a temporary name. Hannah, for example. Aunt Hannah. Tonight, when it's dark, I'll go stand on the dyke, look out at the inky sea, and call her name: Hannah! Aunt H-a-a-n-nah!

I must call to her, otherwise this story will grind to a halt and the book will lose its momentum. That's all. I'm not going to say another word about Hannah.

And now my father and I are going to go to the bathhouse.

. . .

Whenever my father came back from the mountains after a long absence, Tina refused to let him in. She used to hand me a towel and a bar of soap and say, "Scrub him!"

Did Tina know about Hannah? I'm sure she did, though she never said a word about it to us.

My father knew he wouldn't be allowed in, so he always came back just before sunrise, when he and I could go to the bathhouse together. Since Tina wanted me to make sure he didn't bring back any diseases from the mountains, I used to get into the shower with him.

"Wash between your buttocks!" I signed.

He did.

"Turn around."

He turned around and I checked his body for lesions or rashes.

"Bend your head!"

He bent his head and I checked his grey hair for lice.

"OK, it's fine, you're clean."

Then I tied a towel around him and went into the prayer room.

Together with the other men, we faced Mecca and prayed. At the end, we turned around and, following a long tradition, greeted the person behind us. I always sat behind my father, so when he turned and put out his hand, I'd shake it and say, "May your prayers be answered."

But this time, when he turned to greet me, I wasn't there. I was standing beside the pillar in the bathhouse, watching the people pray.

"Why aren't you praying?" he signed.

It wasn't the first time I hadn't joined in the prayers. I'd stopped a long time ago. It had all started after I'd met Dr Pur Bahlul. He didn't pray, either.

I didn't answer my father's question.

He asked me again on the way home. "Why didn't you

pray?" I told him I'd explain later. I didn't feel like discussing God. I'd learned a lot from the books Dr Pur Bahlul had given me to read.

Late that night my father came to my room. He didn't say anything, but I saw the question burning in his eyes.

"Isn't it past your bedtime?" I signed.

"I can't sleep," he answered.

He looked at my new books, the ones I'd been reading while he was away. My bookcase contained several books that used to belong to Dr Pur Bahlul, but were now mine. He ran his fingers along the spines, as if he were checking out the titles.

"Sit down," I signed.

He sat back on his heels on the carpet. I sat down across from him.

"You asked me why I didn't say my prayers," I began. "But first tell me why *you* pray."

"What?"

"I said, Why do you pray? Why do you bow? Why do you touch your forehead to the ground?"

"Heaven," he pointed upward. "I do it because of Heaven."

"Heaven? What's in Heaven?"

"The Holy One," he signed.

"Which holy one? Tell me which one you mean."

He smiled, seemingly at a loss, and rested his hands on his knees. The discussion appeared to be at an end. Then he suddenly made his move, a counter-attack: "The Holy Book comes from Heaven. It was written by the great Holy One who lives up above. So there must be a Holy One in Heaven."

I shook my head. "The Koran doesn't come from Heaven. It's a book—a good book—but it has nothing to do with Heaven."

"Yes, it does. Kazem Khan told me so. And so did you,

Mine, The Boy Who Crawls Under the Blankets and Reads. You yourself kissed the cover of the book and washed your hands before you read it."

"You're right. I used to touch my forehead to the ground. Then I read these books and found out about other things, and they . . . wait a minute, let me start at the beginning."

I got up and hunted around for a book on outer space, one with lots of pictures of stars.

"Look at this picture. Can you tell me what it is or what it's about?"

No, of course he didn't know what it was. All he could see was a milky stripe, a trail, a path through the night.

"Come look!"

I opened the window. It was a dark blue night. Millions of stars were shining and the Milky Way was clearer than ever.

"It's a picture of this," I signed.

I wanted to tell him that in the beginning there was nothing and then suddenly there was a big bang, and after that everything was set in motion, everything started to move, just like the Milky Way, which consisted of lots and lots of stars and was still in motion. I did my best. I tried to tell him, in our simple sign language, all that I had learned. But he stared at me in perplexed silence, thinking, what on earth is he talking about?

In sheer desperation, I switched to something else, suddenly surprising him with a bit of everyday reality: "Did you know that the earth moves?"

"What?"

I gestured toward the stars, collected all those stars in my left hand, added the river that ran through our town, threw in the mountains for good measure, placed my father on top, squeezed them all together into a ball and then transferred that ball of matter to my right hand. I held it up in front of his eyes and suddenly let it explode: "B-o-o-o-m! Stars, stars, more stars, then the sun, then the earth, then the moon and then my father and then me . . . do you understand what I'm saying?"

No, he didn't understand. I didn't, either.

I took out a map of the world and tried to explain to him where we were on it. "Here, we're located here, on this little spot on the earth, and the earth is located here in the sky . . . Look, now I'm drawing the earth and the sun. We, you and I, are located here, but we can't see the sun. No light. Night."

I'd wandered far away, so far away that I could no longer connect these theories with my "not praying". I stopped.

"It's late, go to bed," I signed.

He left.

But later I noticed that he was still thinking about it. Sometimes, when he was in the right mood, he'd joke about it with Golden Bell. He'd pluck the stars from the sky, squeeze them into a ball, hold them up in front of her and shout "b-o-o-o-m!" Then he'd roar with laughter. Another time he saw me standing with a group of old men. He stamped his feet on the ground and signed, "The earth is round. And it revolves. You and me, us, we all revolve around the sun. And Ishmael has stopped praying."

My father went away again for a long time. When he came back, I was eighteen and ready to leave home.

In the last five years, our society had changed completely. The shah was firmly entrenched on his throne and in control of almost everything.

Oil prices had risen and the United States was helping him become the region's watchdog. The opposition had been crushed and the economy had started to grow—more jobs, higher salaries.

Everything was different. Even the seasons weren't what they used to be. The winters didn't seem as cold. Maybe that was because we'd bought a decent heater, or because we ate better—more meat, more fruit, more vegetables.

Tina no longer had to work. My father, who had gone back to mending carpets, now earned enough to support us.

Our remote city, which used to be controlled by the imams, was now divided among the Americans, who built a new refinery, the Germans, who revamped our railroad system, the Dutch, who dug our canals, and the Russians, who were building a tractor factory.

For the first time ever, we painted the doors of our house and replaced the front door, a worn-out wooden affair, with a sturdy iron one. We had the courtyard paved with yellow tiles. Tina was delighted with all these changes.

Imagine that your daughters had a deaf-mute for a father and a house with an ugly front door. Who would come to ask for your daughter's hand in marriage?

One chilly evening in autumn, I took hold of my father's arm and said, "Come with me. I have something to tell you."

The wind was blowing sand in our eyes and mouths. We needed to find a place where we could warm ourselves inside and out, so we went to a nearby teahouse.

"How are you, Ishmael?" the owner asked as he wiped the table. "What are father and son doing in my teahouse? Important business?"

"The autumn wind brought us here."

"Welcome. You're the finest boy in the area. If I had a daughter, you'd be the perfect son-in-law. You take good care of your father and your sisters. Boys these days have no respect for their parents. You're a good boy. This first round is on the house. And here's a bowl of fresh dates to go with it."

"Fresh dates in the cold autumn?"

"Oh, I just said the first thing that popped into my head. You see, you're different. You listen. Boys don't listen anymore. Here, scoot over towards the heater, where it's nice and warm. Praise be to Allah! You respect your parents."

It was the first time I'd taken my father to that teahouse. Maybe that's why he realised that I had something important to tell him.

"I've finished high school," I began. "I've stopped going to—"

"You've stopped going to school?"

"I've graduated. I don't have to go anymore. But I'm going to study somewhere else. What I mean to say is, I'm leaving home."

He sat bolt upright.

"Leaving home? Why? Where?"

"I have to read other kinds of books."

"Can't you get the books here?"

"It's not just the books. I have to go to another school, to a university, a big school in the capital, where the shah lives."

"OK, I understand that you're going to a big school in the city of the shah, but not what kind of books you're going to read."

"Books about light, for example."

"Light?"

"About darkness and light, about air, about aeroplanes, about—"

"Air? Aeroplanes?"

"Yes, air is very important. Aeroplanes can't fly without air."

My father thought it over. He had no concept of a university, didn't understand how a person could die without air, had no idea where Tehran was located and was puzzled by my field of study, but he did realise that something important was about to happen. He slumped back against the chair, exhausted.

"What's the matter? I'm not dying, I'll be back. The studying will be good for me, good for you and good for Tina."

"How long will you be gone?"

"Five or six years, I'm not sure, but I'll come home from time to time."

The owner plonked two fresh glasses of tea down in front of us.

"He's leaving," gestured my father.

"Leaving? Where're you going?" asked the owner.

"I've been accepted at the University of Tehran."

"The University of Tehran!" he exclaimed.

"Yes, but it's hard to leave my family behind."

"What's that you're saying? Hard? Leave them. Of course you should go!"

"He's going to learn about the sun," my father gestured. "He's going to read books about air, because air is important. If there's no air, you die, he says."

"What's your father saying?"

"Oh, nothing special, he . . . he's talking about what I'm going to study."

My father went on. "Did you know that at first there was nothing and then suddenly there was a big bang and then the stars began to glow? You didn't know that? I didn't, either, but Ishmael knows everything. He's very important, he's going to the city of the shah to study."

"What's he talking about?" the owner asked.

I laughed. "Oh, nothing special, he said that I'm going to study physics."

We drank our tea and sat for a while. I had another surprise in store for my father.

"I have to ask you to stop going away."

"What?"

"To stop going to the mountains, to stop leaving home."

"Why?"

"Because there has to be a man around the house when I'm gone."

"But I . . . I have to. I can't stop."

"I'm going to open a shop for you."

"A shop? For me?"

"Yes, a shop, a workshop, so you won't have to go from place to place. You can stay in your shop, and when people need something, they'll come to you."

This idea was more shocking to him than the fact that the earth revolves around the sun.

"What kind of a shop? I can't run it without you."

"Don't worry. Golden Bell will come and help you."

"Golden Bell?"

"Yes, I've already talked to her about it. She'll come to the shop every day after school."

The arrangements had already been made. The editor of the newspaper for which I was still working had helped me get a loan, and through friends of his, who worked for the municipal government, I was granted official permission to look for a shop in our neighbourhood.

My father had no choice. He couldn't believe the preparations were at such an advanced stage. On the one hand, he was delirious with joy. On the other hand, he had a secret. He insisted that he had to go away sometimes.

"OK, but only for a few days."

A month later my father, my mother, my sisters and I opened the shop. Golden Bell promptly sat down at "her" table. She had bought a mirror for my father with her own money. We all had on new clothes. I was wearing the suit that Tina and I had bought for me to wear to the university.

The shop was open. A dream had come true. Aga Akbar was standing in his own shop.

Giant Shadows

Soon after he moves to Tehran, Ishmael joins an underground movement. All contact with his father has to be broken. Akbar is forced to stand on his own two feet. Or perhaps Ishmael is the one who has to learn how to stand on his own.

 To my surprise, even here in the polder, people or events can have a direct, or sometimes indirect, bearing on my father's notebook.

Prince Willem-Alexander, for example, came to my aid.

The Dutch crown prince was interviewed on television. No fewer than 3.1 million viewers watched the interview, which was billed as the most important one of his life. The prince wanted everyone to realise that he'd become an adult, that he was now independent of his mother, the Queen. He wanted to show the Dutch public that he was ready to assume responsibility for weighty matters.

His lower lip trembled. Independence was apparently not at all easy. Still, it was a valiant attempt, in the presence of three million viewers, to step out from under the shadow of his dominant mother.

He emphasised the fact that he wasn't a mummy's boy, that he was a person in his own right.

"Is your mother your most important adviser?" the interviewer asked.

"Yes," he replied, "because I'm being groomed for her position."

"Which of your mother's characteristics would you like to adopt?"

"I'm Willem-Alexander, I'm me. I don't wish to adopt any of her characteristics. You can't adopt other people's characteristics."

The prince tried to keep the questions involving his mother to a minimum and to move on to the next subject, but the interviewer kept harking back to his mother.

What I liked about the interview was not so much the discussion as the underlying psychology. In the course of that long conversation, he said very little about his father. He never once managed to say his father's full name. It was as though the man didn't belong to the royal household, as if he were a ghost, a mere shadow.

I've seen the Queen on television several times and often listened to her on the radio. I even know some of her speeches by heart. For example, here's the end of one of her annual speeches to the Parliament:

As we reach the end of this century, it is time to take stock. Much that is good has been achieved in the Netherlands. Many people have contributed to that success. In an awareness of our strengths, while never losing sight of our weaknesses, this gives us confidence for the future. In the new century, too, we shall

all need to invest in the quality of our society and in international cooperation. The government will continue its unceasing efforts to achieve a strong economy and a vital society. In doing so, it will work with you, with other tiers of government, and with every member of society. I sincerely hope that you will discharge your responsible duties with dedication and commitment, in the confidence that many people join me in wishing you wisdom and praying that you will be blessed.

I can't remember even one speech given by her husband, Prince Claus. It's all a blank.

Of course I saw him on TV at the award ceremony when he took off his tie, but even though I was listening to his speech carefully, I didn't hear the words. Or, rather, I did, but his words didn't reach me, didn't get through to me. It was as if he used gestures rather than words.

I was accustomed to thinking of him as the father who didn't talk, as a watcher, an observer. Now that he was actually saying something, it didn't seem to fit my image of him.

I like the man. Whenever the royal family appears on TV—on the Queen's birthday, for example—I enjoy watching him, the father, walking circumspectly behind his sons with his hands clasped behind his back.

I like the Queen, too, when she takes her husband's arm and walks beside him with her head held high. If she ever angrily smacked him on the head and screamed, "You're a millstone around my neck. I wish you were dead, dead, dead," I'd despise her.

Tina did that once to my father. I heard her screaming, so I raced inside and saw her hitting my father over the head with her hands and shouting, "I wish you were dead, dead, dead!"

Suddenly she caught sight of me and her arms stopped in mid-air.

Later I heard from Golden Bell that it wasn't the first time Tina had hit him.

"I saw it with my own eyes," Golden Bell told me, weeping into the phone.

To this day, I can't forgive Tina for that. And yet she did a lot for my father, not the least of which was providing an element of stability in his life. She's suffered greatly and shown time and again that she can be strong in the face of adversity.

Although Prince Willem-Alexander didn't come out and say it in the interview, I could see that he had trouble with his mother's shadow. I have trouble with my father's shadow. If the prince thinks he's cast off that giant shadow, he's mistaken. You can never shake off the shadows of such influential people, not even when they're dead.

It only gets worse when they're dead. They come back into your life stronger than ever. They haunt you in your sleep.

Even from his grave, my father casts a shadow over my computer. When I went away to the University of Tehran, I decided to distance myself, both physically and mentally, from my father, but I couldn't. Somehow a new form of contact sprang up, more intense than ever.

When I left home, I thought my father would have to learn to stand on his own two feet. Suddenly I discovered that *I* didn't function well on my own. Not having to shoulder the burden of my father left me off-balance. I pretended to be strong when I actually wasn't.

My father was my strength as well as my weakness. Compared to other students, I was a man of experience, which is why I made rapid strides in the party. On the other hand, I was worried about my family, and that kept me from advancing any further.

At the end of my third year, my contact person ordered me to sever all ties with my family. Until then I'd been going home occasionally, but now I wasn't even allowed to phone. At his urging, I also dropped out of school. According to the party, a revolution was at hand and we needed to be prepared.

I was overcome with guilt at having deserted my family and was so concerned for them that I suffered a loss of self-confidence. I realised that I couldn't go on like this. It was time to discuss the matter with my contact person.

Before going on with the story, however, I'd like to say a few words about the resistance movement. Every Persian school-child dreamed of going to the University of Tehran. And yet we had a saying: "You can get in, but you may not get out again."

That's because the underground leftist guerrilla movement against the shah had its roots in the university. The movement's three main slogans were: "Down with the shah!", "Bread for the masses!" and "Long live freedom!"

The red banner on its underground newspaper read "Freedom or Death!" When I started at the university, there were dozens of shoot-outs on the streets of Tehran between the party's armed faction and the shah's secret police. Time after time, they uncovered the hiding place of the leaders, then moved in with helicopters and tanks. But the leaders never let themselves be taken alive. They fought until they had no more bullets left, then swallowed a suicide pill as the police burst in to arrest them. Every shoot-out was followed by an eruption of violence at the university.

It was in those turbulent times that I went through my personal crisis.

I made an appointment to meet my contact person at a tea-house in a remote area on the outskirts of Tehran. It was the first time I'd talked to him about my father. "I can't break the ties with my family. I have to stay in touch with my father. It's necessary for him as well as for me. Without that, I can't function properly within the party."

Permission was denied. It was too risky. If the agents of the secret police arrested me at my parents' home, I could endanger the party.

An idea flashed into my mind. "My father's shop, his disability, his contact with the villagers near the border could be . . . I mean, I could get him to . . . What I'm trying to say is that his shop and his knowledge of the mountains could be of use to the party."

The focus of the conversation had suddenly shifted. My contact person didn't comment further, but told me I'd be notified of the party's decision.

A week later I was unexpectedly summoned to a confidential meeting with Homayun, one of the legendary leaders of the resistance. We talked for a long time about my father, his contacts in the border area and his knowledge of the mountain trails. I was then given permission to meet my father in secret a few times a year. It was also my job to prepare him "in case the party needed him". What that meant, neither of us knew. In any event, the party leadership realised that it had a trustworthy deaf-mute in its service, who was prepared to do anything for his son.

At last I was allowed to secretly visit my father, whom I hadn't seen for a long time.

He was doing well, mostly because of his shop. Setting him up in a small business had been an excellent decision. Golden Bell had bought a good secondhand stove and had it moved to the shop. All year long, my father went around collecting twigs and branches for the winter like some doddery old bird. It made Tina furious. Whenever I called, she moaned, "Son, I'm ashamed of your father. He does one stupid thing after another. No matter where I go, I see him with a bundle of twigs on his back. He even climbs trees to snap off the dead branches. When I run into him in town, I have to hide my head in shame."

I laughed at the thought of him climbing a tree to snap off a branch.

"You can afford to laugh," Tina said angrily. "You're not here, you don't have to see him. I'm the one who's melting from shame like a candle. You're gone and it doesn't affect you in the slightest. I'm a mother, I've got three daughters at home and I have to—"

"There's no need to make such a fuss, Tina. You know how he is. We can't change him."

"Why not? You just don't want to. It's all your fault, you're the one who abandoned him. He listens to you, but you haven't said a word. Why don't you come and visit us, son? People need to see that my daughters have a learned brother and not just a stupid father. Listen to me! Come home! Your sisters' futures depend on it!"

Tina was right about one thing. My father did seem to be slipping. He was doing stupid things more often now. Well, not really stupid, but I don't know what else to call them. How could I get him to stop climbing trees? I couldn't be around to scold him all the time.

We had to face facts and accept him the way he was. Tina was unable to do that.

Despite his initial hesitation, my father was very proud of his shop. Wherever he went, he took the key out of his pocket and showed it to everyone, "Look, the key to my shop. Ishmael gave it to me. He's a student in the city of the shah. He's learning about airplanes. If someone pinches your nose and puts his hand over your mouth, you'll die, because air is very important."

The shop had been his salvation. He no longer had to roam the streets in search of customers. Nor did he have to hang around the house during the winter when he was out of work. He simply went and sat in his shop. That's why he gathered twigs and branches: they made him feel peaceful and secure.

He stayed in his shop till late at night. Who knows, a customer might drop by, or maybe Ishmael would turn up out of the blue one day.

On my way to the shop, I bought him a bag of firewood. The snow crunched beneath my feet. All was quiet in my old area—the lights in the windows had long been extinguished, the curtains drawn. Everything was in deep sleep, everything except my father's chimney. It was still smoking.

There was a soft yellow light in his window. I peeked inside. He was sitting on his carpet, next to the stove. His head was bent over a book, which was open on the low table in front of him.

My God! I thought. What's he reading?

He looked like a scholar. No, like an imam reading a book in a mosque. No, not that, either, more like a craftsman, a carpet-weaver, who was going to repair the book rather than read it. A couple of his customers' Persian rugs were rolled up on the table beside the book and on the wall was a large framed photograph of the shah in a military uniform.

I was startled. Why was the dictator's picture hanging in his shop? At first I was angry, but then it occurred to me that perhaps it was better this way.

I gently pushed open the door. It squeaked. I should oil those hinges, I thought. I slipped inside. My shadow fell over the book. He raised his head and looked at me, without a flicker of recognition. I took off my hat. A shy smile appeared on his face.

"I didn't recognise you with a moustache," he signed and stood up.

I thought he was going to hug me, but he didn't. He kept staring—at my hat, my glasses, my moustache. I held out my hand. "Why don't you shake my hand? Here, I've brought you some firewood."

He pointed, looking slightly embarrassed, at his pile of twigs and branches, then hesitantly shook my hand. He hung the bag of firewood respectfully on a hook and probably never touched it again.

"Why are you staring at me like that?" I signed. "Aren't you going to offer me a cup of tea?"

"Oh, yes, sit down," he pointed at the carpet, then corrected himself. "No, not there, wait a minute." He pulled out a chair and offered it to me. "Please be seated."

He thought I'd become a gentleman, a gentleman in a hat. I put the chair back and sat on the floor next to the stove. He poured me a cup of tea and stood hovering over me like a waiter. "Why don't you come sit by me?"

He did sit, but at a respectful distance and with his hands on his knees. It was what he wanted, so I stopped protesting.

"How're you doing?" I signed. "Are you pleased with your shop?"

"Yes, thank you, I'm pleased," he replied and bowed his head.

"And how's Tina?"

"She's fine, thank you."

I pointed at the photograph. "I see you have a picture of the shah in your shop," I said.

His eyes lit up. He started to say something, to offer an explanation, but changed his mind and kept sitting there politely on his knees. After a brief silence, he hesitantly signed, "How are you? Is everything all right?"

"Yes, I'm fine," I replied.

"Where have you been?" he continued. "Why don't you come home any more? Why don't you phone? Golden Bell is waiting for you to call. She's grown up. She asked me to tell you that she wants to see you. I know you don't have much time, that you have a lot of books to read, and I understand. But maybe you could give us a call every once in a while."

"OK, I will, but it's become a lot harder."

"What has? The books?"

"No, not the books. Well, yes, the books are hard, too. But take that picture on the wall, for example. Do you know who that man is?"

"He's the son of Reza Khan," he gestured proudly. "You know that. He's an important man with a gold crown on his head. He owns lots of horses and rifles and carries a pistol with him at all times. He's a very important man. All the carpet-weavers in the city have his portrait in their shops. Me, too, I bought a picture. No, wait, I didn't buy it, a city official brought it here and I had it framed. It's nice, isn't it?"

I didn't answer. He started to say something else about the picture, then suddenly sensed that I didn't share his enthusiasm. So, instead he said, "Do you think it's wrong?"

"Yes, no . . . I mean I'm talking about something else."

"But all the carpet-weavers like him," he hesitantly signed. "His picture is in all the shops. He's a good man."

"I don't agree," I signed.

"Why not?"

"I don't like him."

"No? Why not?"

"He's not a good man. He's no good."

He pointed at the portrait and was about to say something. Then he stopped himself. His hand dropped back into his lap.

"It's almost too complicated to explain," I said, "but I'll give you an example. Do you remember the policemen at my school who beat you over the head with their clubs?"

"Yes, I remember."

"Those policemen were working for the shah. In Tehran, at

my university, there are lots of policemen, too. They beat up the students, arrest them and throw them in jail. They even want to arrest me."

"Arrest you? Why? What have you done?"

"Nothing. Or, at any rate, nothing special. They don't want me to read certain books. Or to say certain things. They expect me to honour the shah, but I don't like him. They're keeping me under surveillance. They're hoping to catch me. That's why I can't come home."

"Oh," I read in his gesture.

"And you know what's worse? The policemen in Tehran don't wear uniforms. They wear ordinary clothes, just like you and me. You never know who to trust. I don't want them to recognise me, so that's why I'm wearing a hat. It's also the reason for the glasses and the moustache."

"How can you read books about light and air when there are so many policemen?"

I wanted to tell him that I wasn't reading any books about light and air at the moment, but I refrained. It would only hurt him.

"I'm going to tell you something else. Do you remember Dr Pur Bahlul? The dentist?"

"Of course I remember him."

"Do you know who had him arrested? The shah! He ordered his policemen to arrest the dentist! He's still in jail. All of his teeth have been broken. Do you understand what I'm saying? That's why I hate the shah. Important people—people like the dentist who read books—also hate the shah."

Was it all right to use simple examples to explain complex issues? Was it fair to saddle him with my personal opinions? Shouldn't I have left him in peace and simply accepted his opinions and his view of the world?

Now that I can look back on those years with more objectivity, I sometimes feel a twinge of regret. But only sometimes. There was no other way. He and I couldn't possibly hold different opinions. We had to be one, to share one ideology. I had to bring him close to me, close to the new reality in my life, so he wouldn't get lost in the unfamiliar world of his son. Suppose I was arrested? Suppose the secret police suddenly burst through the door in the middle of the night and searched his house because of his son's political activities and he had no idea what was going on?

I felt that it was my duty to explain the world to him. I had been appointed by family, friends, neighbours and even nature to be my father's guide, so I had to lead him as I saw fit.

Once and for all, let me make it clear—if only to myself—that if I'd had any other father, I might not have felt the need to join the movement, or at any rate I wouldn't have become so involved or gone so far. Being the son of such a father brought me, led me, propelled me in this direction. That's the long and the short of it. We had to adjust our steps to each other's stride. He had to stand by me and therefore by the leftist movement in which I was involved. It was time to let him know that we—my comrades and I—might need him some day.

"My friends and I are against the shah," I signed. "He has to go."

At first he didn't understand. He sat and stared at me, without moving. All of a sudden it dawned on him. His hands began to tremble.

"What do you mean, 'go'?"

"Just go! Down with the shah!"

"But he has a pistol strapped to his side!"

I thought it over. Should I or shouldn't I?

I hesitated for a few moments, then finally reached under my jacket and pulled out my gun.

The Dutch Dunes

We go to see Louis. Ishmael hardly
knows him, but that's not important.
There's a young woman in Louis's life,
whom Ishmael is destined to meet.

 I knew what sand was, and hills, too, but I had
no idea what Dutch dunes would look like or
how a person could go for a walk through hills
of fine sand.

I looked up the word in the dictionary:

dune \ 'd(y)ün \ *n—s often attrib* [F, fr, OF, fr, MD
dune—more at DOWN] **1:** a hill or ridge of sand piled up by
the wind commonly found along shores, along some river
valleys, and generally where there is dry surface sand during
some part of the year **2:** TWINE 5

• • •

I received a letter from a man named Louis, whom I'd met on the train.

It was late and I'd caught the last train home from the university. I stepped into a nearly empty car and saw a man sitting at the far end. Tired, I plonked myself down, closed my eyes and dozed off.

How long had I been dozing? I don't know. Suddenly I heard someone calling, "Sir!"

I opened my eyes and looked around. The man in the back was still the only person in the train. Had he said something or had I dreamed it?

"Would you care to join me?" the man asked. "I'm sitting here all by myself, too." I went over to him. He didn't look old enough to need a cane, but one was resting by his side.

"Where do you come from?" he asked.

"From Persia . . . Iran," I said.

"I thought so," he said, nodding happily. "That's why I called you over. I can sometimes spot an Iranian just by the way he carries himself. I spent years in Iran, working as a doctor."

"Oh, really? How nice!" I said.

I sat down.

"Let me introduce myself. I'm Louis."

The conversation quickly became more personal. He talked about his stay in the south of Iran, where the rich oil fields are. He'd been there at the beginning of the revolution, but the embassy had made him leave, much against his will, along with all the other Dutch citizens.

As with most chance encounters, we talked about how I'd ended up in Holland, what I was doing and what I thought of it.

After an hour-long conversation, he wrote down my address. I got out at my usual station and he travelled on to spend the night at a friend's.

A few weeks later a letter arrived. It was only after reading the first few lines that I realised who it was from. At the bottom of the letter he'd included a translation of a poem by Omar Khayyám:

We are no other than a moving row
Of Magic Shadow-shapes that come and go
Round with the Sun-illumined Lantern held
In Midnight by the Master of the Show.

I remembered how delighted he'd been to hear that I was studying Dutch literature.

He thought Persian literature was beautiful. When he was living in Iran, he'd known very little about our literature. Only after his return to Holland had he gone looking for Persian classics in translation.

In his letter he said that he very much hoped we could meet again and he invited me to go and visit him.

At first I didn't take his invitation seriously. I had several Dutch friends—Igor, a number of local artists and poets, a few teachers at the university—but this was the first time a Dutch person I hardly knew had asked me to his home. He lived in Agnet aan Zee. I looked at the map. It wasn't all that far away, but still I thought, no, I won't go, he probably wants to spend all night reminiscing about Iran and I'm not in the mood for that.

And yet my curiosity had been aroused by the final paragraph of his letter: "We have beautiful dunes here—the most beautiful in all of Holland. If you come, you can take a long walk through the dunes. I'm sure you'll enjoy it. I hope to see you."

Maybe it wouldn't be too bad. The name "Agnet aan Zee", in particular, sounded intriguing.

I could make a day of it, I thought, and go and visit the

sea. The first time I'd ever heard of the Dutch dunes was during one of my courses, when we were analysing an excerpt from Frederik van Eeden's classic *De kleine Johannes* (Little Johannes):

> *Oh, if only I could fly away from here! Far away, to the dunes, to the sea!*
>
> *Early every morning he asked [his dog] Pluizer if he could go back again to his house and to his father, if he could once again see the garden and the dunes.*

I called Louis and set off. On the way I bought a new translation of Sa'di's *Rose Garden*, since one of my professors had mentioned that a good Dutch translation had just been published.

I took the bus, really making a day of it. First to Lelystad, then to Enkhuizen, then to Alkmaar, then to Bergen and finally to Agnet aan Zee.

Who or what was Agnet? Or was it actually Agnes? I liked the combination of "Agnet" and "Zee". I imagined a woman sitting calmly on the beach, looking out at the sea.

Agnet aan Zee was not an ordinary Dutch village with a church and a square, but a harbour town. It looked a bit touristy, though it was fairly quiet. Maybe things picked up during the summer. Though it was cold, a number of German tourists had found their way there.

Finally, after walking around for fifteen minutes, I saw a sandy hill covered with tall grass—golden-yellow grass. The cold wind rippled the grass and made it even more beautiful. I'd never seen anything like these sandy hills of rippling grass. They had to be the dunes I'd read about in *De kleine Johannes*. I stood and stared at that amazing landscape. There were dunes, dunes and more dunes, as far as the eye could see! Just as in other places there were hills, hills and more hills. You couldn't tell where they ended or what was on the other side.

"Beautiful, isn't it?" I heard a voice behind me say.

I turned.

"Good afternoon," a man called from a window. I didn't realise it was Louis.

"Don't you recognise me?" he asked.

"Oh, now I do."

"Wait a minute, I'll open the door."

After a long while, the door swung open. Louis started to walk toward me, but after a few steps he lost his balance and nearly fell. I rushed over and took his arm.

"Thanks," he said cheerfully. "You thought I was going to fall, but luckily I never do."

I offered him my left shoulder and he placed the palm of his right hand on it. "You've got a strong shoulder! Go on inside. I'm glad you came."

How stupid of me not to have realised when we were on the train that he was disabled. I'd been so struck by his personality that I hadn't even noticed. Now I acted as though I'd known all along. As soon as we entered the house, he let go of my shoulder and took a few steps. I thought, Oh, oh, he's going to fall and bang his head against the wall. To my surprise, he didn't. He grabbed the chair, then the bookcase, and made his way through the room by going from one handhold to another.

"There's coffee in the kitchen, but I can't bring it here. I can walk, but not with a cup of coffee in my hand. So if you'll go and get the coffeepot, I'll pour. While you're at it, would you bring me my herbal tea?"

As I stood in his kitchen, I felt a strong liking for this unknown man.

I didn't feel like a stranger. Everything in his house—the

furniture, the chairs, the heater, the bookcase—all seemed familiar. I took my coffee and his tea into the living room and sat down. I was glad I'd come.

"What a beautiful view!" I said, pointing at the dunes.

"Yes, it is," he said. "But my wife's tired of it. She's been looking at those dunes for twenty-five years and now she'd like something else."

"What about you?"

"Me? I think it's as beautiful as ever. I've got a plan. In a few years I'll be totally bedridden. Before that happens, I'm going to have the house re-modelled. The upstairs balcony will be converted into a room with a big picture window. Then I'll put my bed by the window so I can look out over the dunes. Unfortunately, I won't have a view of the sea, but that doesn't matter. You can't have everything."

We chatted for a while about Iran and the kingdom of Persia, and about Persian culture and ancient Persian literature. Then I asked if he'd show me around upstairs.

"No, not me. You can take a look, though. I haven't been able to climb stairs for ages."

"I'll be glad to help you."

So we went upstairs. It wasn't easy, but we made it. Louis was pleased. "I can't believe it. How long has it been since I was up here? I can't even remember . . . it's been years, *years*, since I looked at the dunes from upstairs."

"Do you have any children?" I asked. "A son, perhaps?"

"Not a son. A daughter."

"Are you on good terms with her?"

"Yes, why do you ask?"

"How old was she when you got sick and couldn't . . . well, couldn't walk anymore?"

"It was a gradual process. She was a child when it started. Why do you want to know?"

I told him about my own father. I explained that, as a child, I had felt it my duty to stick as closely as possible to my father, so I could help him. In short, wherever he went, I went, too.

"My daughter's also been a big help. Thanks to me, she's got strong shoulders. Her left shoulder, in particular, is well-developed: muscular and strong. She's always been there for me. Always. She still drops by almost every evening."

Propping himself against the wall, he pointed at the dunes. "Look," he said. "There are twenty-one dunes between here and the sea. It's just behind the twenty-first dune. I haven't seen the sea in years. I used to go down to the beach every night after dark, but since I fell ill, I haven't had the strength or the courage to climb the dunes. It's now become a dream that will never come true."

"What has?"

"Walking to the sea one last time."

"You could pick a shorter route, use your cane, take your time and walk there step by step. Or you could ask your daughter for help."

"That's not what I mean. I want to walk across all twenty-one dunes. Go up and down the dunes in the dark, just like I used to. Anyway, it doesn't matter. Life isn't a bed of roses. Sometimes the simplest pleasures are suddenly impossible."

I couldn't stop thinking about his dream. It had a kind of beauty, a kind of challenge that appealed to me. The sea had become inaccessible to us both.

"You're awfully quiet," Louis said.

"I'm thinking of the sea. Of your sea, behind the dunes. It's a shame you won't be able to see it from your bed. It would be a real boon to an invalid."

"That's a nice way to put it."

I carried a chair over to the window and stood on it.

"I think I can see the sea," I said. "At any rate, I see a kind of blanket of blue stretching to the horizon. If you raise the bed a few feet, you'll have the sea right here in this room."

"That's funny. No one ever thought to bring the sea here by hopping up on a chair."

"Do you want to try it?"

"Don't be ridiculous!"

"What time of day did you used to walk through the dunes to the sea?"

"It's been so long I can't remember. Around dusk, I think."

"Shall we try it tonight?"

"Try what?"

"Going down to the sea together through the dunes, as soon as it starts to get dark."

"You're crazy," Louis laughed.

"No, I'm not. I know how to do it. I've had a lot of training."

"Training? What kind of training?"

"It's a long story. I used to be active in an underground movement and we spent a lot of time in the mountains. The Cuban revolution was our shining example. We hoped to swoop down from the mountains one day with thousands of sympathisers, like Castro, and conquer the cities and overthrow the shah. We trained hard for that great day. We learned how to carry dead or wounded comrades through the mountains, but we never got a chance to put our training to use. Trust me, I know how to support a man who can barely walk. I can get you up and down those dunes."

He didn't answer. He stared at me, then at the dunes.

"We'll go down to the sea on foot. Once we're there, we'll think of a way to get back."

As evening fell and the grass rippled in the wind, Louis put his left arm on my right shoulder and we began our journey to the sea. He quickly lost his daring. His atrophied muscles wouldn't cooperate. I changed position and offered him my other shoulder, but that didn't help, either.

"You see, it won't work," he sighed.

I showed him how to position his left arm so that I bore most of the weight. I thought he could hobble along like a comrade who'd lost his right leg, but still had enough strength to walk on his left.

"This ought to do the trick," I said.

It didn't. I remembered what our instructors had said. Our wounded comrades needed to believe they would reach their goal. Our job was to make them think about the city we were going to conquer, rather than their wounds. To think about the dictator we were about to overthrow, rather than the remaining miles.

"I've got a story for you, Louis," I said.

"OK, go ahead and tell me."

"I'm working on a book."

"A book?"

"Yes, I'm writing a book. A novel. In Dutch."

"In Dutch? That's interesting. What's it about?"

"It's about my father. Let me explain. My father kept a diary his entire life. He'd jot down a sentence, or a paragraph, or sometimes an entire page. But it's a strange book."

"What's so strange about it?"

"I can't read it."

"Why not?"

"Because he wrote it in an unknown language—a kind of cuneiform that he invented himself. I look at a passage, then try to read it and transcribe it. No, 'transcribe' isn't the right word. I try to translate it into Dutch."

"Translate it when you can't even read it yourself?"

"I'll let you read the book when I'm done."

And as we talked, we reached the third dune.

It was dark, but I saw a glimmer of hope in his eyes.

Between the third and seventh dunes I told him what I'd written so far.

"Let's sit down for a bit," said Louis.

It started to rain, a light drizzle.

"You said you sometimes blame yourself for using your father for your own ends," Louis said. "I don't know the details, but if I'd been in your position, I think I'd have done the same thing. Did he, in fact, do what you asked?"

"Yes, that's what hurts me so much now."

Gradually, I let Louis depend more on his own legs than on my shoulder. I wanted him to feel his old route beneath his feet. It was probably not very sensible, since he might seriously damage his leg muscles, but all I could think of was his dream. Suddenly I realised that I was doing the same thing to Louis that I had done to my father.

It was wrong of me to force him. It was wrong of me to do his thinking for him. So, I put my arm around his waist and let him lean on me again.

Now we were getting somewhere. I began to tell him the rest of the story.

"You used to work in Iran, Louis, so you know that our border with the former Soviet Union was more than 1,200 miles long. It was heavily guarded. We were afraid to go anywhere near the border—we'd have been arrested on the spot. My father, on the other hand, could come and go as he pleased. Everybody knew him. The gendarmes took no notice of him, so he could roam as freely as a mountain goat. He went wherever he liked. We knew that a revolution was at hand and we believed that the shah would be overthrown within a few years. We had a lot of contacts with the Soviet Union, but our communication had to be routed through Europe, mostly through East Germany, which was quite a long detour. We needed a quicker route. The party wanted to be able to send messages to the Soviet Union and get an immediate reply. We needed someone who could get up to the border and back. Someone like my father."

"Did he know that it was dangerous? That he could be sentenced to death if he were caught?"

"No, not really. I explained that it was dangerous and that he could be arrested. But he couldn't fully comprehend the danger."

"What exactly did he do for you—for the party?"

"I don't know. They didn't tell me. I was just supposed to give him a package and make sure he understood who he had to deliver it to. I would hide classified documents in his long black coat. He'd put it on and leave. Someone would be waiting for him at the border in another long black coat and they'd trade coats."

"That was cruel."

"I agree. Very cruel."

"Did you stop to think what would happen to him if he got caught?"

"Yes. You can see the danger, but you're so close to it that you're . . . well, blind. You've been mesmerised by the dream. You have a totally different mindset, so you see things in a different perspective. To be honest, I thought my father probably would be caught. I assumed they'd torture him to find out who his contacts were, but I knew he wouldn't cooperate. I explained that he couldn't tell anyone about his contacts. I told him that the only sign language he was allowed to use was: I don't know, I don't know, I don't know."

"That was very unfair," Louis said. "Hey, did you hear that?"

"Hear what?"

"The sea. We're halfway there. You can always hear the waves from here when there's a strong surf."

I held my breath so I could hear it, too. But the sound of the surf was drowned out by the rain.

The wind blew even harder, flattening the grass. A wet moon peeked out from behind a cloud, then disappeared again.

Louis resumed the conversation. "The border area was heavily patrolled, so why was your father never arrested?"

"Have you ever heard of Mahdi, the twelfth imam?"

"No."

"You must have heard about him when you lived in Iran. He's a messiah figure. People believe he's hiding in a water well near Saffron Village and that one day he'll come out and relieve the world of its suffering. The well doesn't ring any bells, either?"

"I'm afraid it doesn't."

"That's probably because you worked in the southern part of the country, where people aren't as religious. The sacred well is located in a remote spot on Saffron Mountain, not far from my father's village. My father thought of this well as the centre of the universe. As an earthly symbol of God. I'm not religious, or even vaguely superstitious, but I can't help thinking that my father's belief in Mahdi was what saved him."

Louis laughed.

"What's so funny?"

"Nothing. Forget it."

Now I, too, heard the sea. Louis's hand trembled on my shoulder.

"Two more dunes and we'll be able to see it," he said.

"Can you keep going?" I asked.

"*I* can, though I'm sure you're exhausted from having to drag me all this way."

"Yes, but I'm making up for lost time."

"What lost time?"

"All those months and years of training in the mountains with my comrades so we could conquer a city."

"Oh, everyone's lost that kind of time. It isn't really lost. Ultimately it all adds up to life's experience."

"The sea!" he suddenly exclaimed. "Can you see it?"

I couldn't make it out in the dark. It was still Louis's sea, not mine.

I held on to him and let him stare at the sea in silence. I noticed that he could no longer stand without assistance.

"Four more dunes to go!" Louis said. "We'll get there!"

The grass was wet and I was afraid he'd slip. I was so busy concentrating on where to put my feet that I didn't hear the sea. When we came to the last dune, he said, "My legs are numb."

"Maybe we should sit down and rest for a while," I said.

We sat for fifteen minutes. Then I helped him get up again.

"This time we're going to make it," said Louis.

We set off.

The sea was still new to me, unlike the desert.

Louis felt at home on wet sand; I felt at home on dry sand. The sea, the dunes, the grass, and the rain belonged to him, but the night belonged to me.

"When I've finished my book," I said to Louis, "I will no longer be living for my father, but for myself."

Just then I heard a woman's voice, shouting from the darkness behind the dunes: "Daddy, D-a-a-a-d-dy!"

"Over here," Louis called excitedly.

The silhouette of a young woman in a hat suddenly appeared on the moonlit top of the last dune.

"Daddy, how on earth did you get here?"

I looked at her. She grabbed her hat to keep the wind from blowing it away. The rain beat down on her.

She knelt by her father.

I heard her crying, then Louis pointed at me. She stood up.

There was another gust of wind. She grabbed her hat again and looked out toward the sea, to the place where I was standing.

Jamileh

The story brings us to Jamileh.
Jamileh needs a hiding place.

 One of the most important orders the party gave me was to provide a hiding place for Jamileh.

It was a huge responsibility. If I bungled the job, I'd never be able to redeem myself. If I couldn't guarantee Jamileh's safety, it would be a disaster, not only for the party but for my family as well.

Jamileh—the legendary resistance fighter whose heroic deeds were known to one and all—was more precious than gold. Her fate was in my hands. I would have to hide her so well that the shah's secret police would never find her.

No one ever thought the party could get her out of Ewin Prison, the shah's most notorious jail. To this day no one knows how she escaped from that hellhole. It's believed that she had help from an officer who had secret contacts with the party.

Before her arrest, Jamileh had been in a shoot-out. Seven leading members of the party had been killed, but Jamileh went on fighting. All of Tehran held its breath. She kept dozens of policemen at bay, until she ran out of ammunition. Then she swallowed a suicide pill. The secret police were determined to take her alive. They immediately pumped her stomach and flew her by helicopter to a military hospital.

At the same time, the shah was appearing on TV almost every night with a big smile on his face. He swore up and down in interviews that his secret police had wiped out the leftist movement once and for all. No party member or party sympathiser dared to make a move.

But now Jamileh had escaped. By liberating her from prison, the party had demonstrated that it was alive and well, and stronger than ever.

I was informed that I had an appointment with Homayun. (By the way, he was arrested after the revolution and executed on the personal orders of Khomeini.)

Homayun met me in the basement of a glass factory. He told me that Jamileh had been liberated from Ewin. Despite this earthshaking news, he spoke calmly, as if it were an everyday event, and that helped me rein in my excitement. "This is strictly confidential," he said. "No one else must know. The operation has been successful so far, but it's not over. We haven't issued an announcement yet and the police haven't said anything about the escape, either. We're planning to smuggle Jamileh across the border, but we need to hide her in a safe place for at least a week until we've made the arrangements. What about your father's shop?"

I could feel the tension in my neck and shoulders. This was a turning point in my life. The movement needed my help. I was being given a chance to determine the outcome of a singular episode in the history of the resistance. I knew the escape had been shrouded in mystery. I knew it was a fairy tale that would be handed down to later generations. I wanted that fairy tale to be told. But if anything went wrong, if the secret police dragged her out of my father's shop, it would be the end—for her, for me and for my father.

Fairy tales are not subject to the same laws as normal life. I had to think fast, give an immediate reply and instantly go into action.

"All right," I said. "I'll make the arrangements."

At nine o'clock that evening, I parked my car in a deserted garage outside of Tehran, on the road to Isfahan. I slipped behind the wheel of a red van that had been waiting for me and drove off.

My heart was pounding in my ears. For a moment, I couldn't concentrate. I'd never been so scared in my life. Then a truck honked and I snapped out of my daze, regained my self-control and realised that I was driving a van and that Jamileh was hiding in the back, lying beneath a couple of rolled-up carpets.

Jamileh was a pseudonym. Nobody knew what she looked like. During the revolution, Jamileh published her autobiography, in which she revealed that she'd been tortured and raped in prison. Her jailers had hoped to break her will, to make her betray her comrades. But time after time she'd shouted, "Down with the shah!"

Ten minutes ago she'd been a character in a fairy tale. Now I could see her in my rear-view mirror and talk to her.

"Hello, comrade," I called softly, looking in the mirror. There was no reply.

"Comrade! Are you all right?" I said a bit louder.

No answer. I thought she'd fallen asleep, so I drove on in silence.

My father and I had an agreement. He was supposed to

stay in his shop until midnight. When the clock struck twelve, he could turn out the light and go home.

The stores were usually open until nine, but my father liked to stay in his shop until late at night. Everyone thought it was perfectly normal. He had a storeroom, a kind of lean-to at the back of his shop, where Jamileh would be safe. It had a window that looked out over the river and the mountains. In an emergency, she could escape through the window.

"Comrade! Can you hear me?" I called again. In my mirror I saw something move beneath the carpets, but there was no sound.

I reached Senejan at a quarter to twelve. At five to twelve I saw that the light was still on in the window of my father's shop. I parked the car, switched off the lights and whispered, "We're here. Stay where you are, I'll be back in a few minutes."

I walked to the shop. My father had fallen asleep beside his stove. I gently touched his shoulder. He woke with a start and immediately sat up.

"Don't get up," I quickly signed. "I have something important, *very* important, to tell you. I have someone with me. A young woman. We have to give her a place to stay, for a week maybe, or even ten days. Listen carefully: no one must know she's here. If the police find out, she'll be arrested, and if she's arrested, she'll be killed. Do you understand?"

How could he understand such a condensed version of a long story told to him in the middle of the night?

"Who is she?" he signed.

"A friend. And I think she has a—"

I hesitated, wondering if I should tell him that she had a gun. I decided not to.

"What do you want me to do?" my father signed.

"Hide her here, in your shop."

"In my shop? How? Where?"

"In the lean-to."

"That's impossible, it's a mess and—"

"Give her an oil lamp and a book. Buy her a newspaper . . . or no, not a newspaper. Forget that. Nobody must know she's here."

"What if she has to go to the bathroom?"

"Give her a bucket."

"A bucket? I can't give a bucket to a woman."

I'd chosen the path of least resistance: my father's shop. Actually, there'd been no alternative. The party had been in such a rush to get her out of Tehran that I hadn't had a chance to think things through. Besides, I didn't know of a better place.

"She's no ordinary woman," I said to him. "She won't mind using a bucket. Stop looking at me like that. Give her a book to read and everything will be all right."

"Where is she?"

"In the car. Turn off the light. I'll go get her and bring her here. Meanwhile, stoke up the fire. No, wait, don't do that, we don't want anyone to see smoke coming out of the chimney."

I switched off the light and went out to the car to get Jamileh. It was an exciting—and also terrifying—moment.

I opened the rear door of the van. My hands were shaking. It was childish, I know, but I thought she'd leap out with her gun and say, "Lead the way, comrade!"

But she didn't.

"Could you please get out now?" I whispered.

She didn't move.

"Can you hear me?"

She moaned. In sudden panic I pushed aside the carpets. She couldn't sit up. I knelt beside her and felt her forehead. It was feverish.

"How long have you been sick, comrade?"

"I'll be all right," she said weakly.

I had always thought of Jamileh as a tall woman with a powerful build, but she was small and thin. I threw my jacket around her, hoisted her onto my shoulder and walked to the shop. My father was waiting by the window. He came running out and helped me carry her inside.

Together we stumbled through the darkness and laid her down on the carpet before the stove. My father rushed off to get her a glass of water.

In the light of the glowing embers, Jamileh opened her eyes and looked at my father as he handed her the glass.

"This is my father," I said. "He's a deaf-mute."

"I know," she said and closed her eyes again.

I shook her gently. "Are you all right, comrade?"

"I'm just tired," she whispered.

"Shall I get her some pills?" my father signed.

"Let's wait and see."

Now that she was sick, the whole picture changed. I couldn't leave her here with only my father to look after her.

"Go on home, Father, like you always do. I'll stay with her. Come back in the morning, with some milk."

My father had no choice but to do as I said. He went out, locked the door of the shop behind him and walked away. I stood at the window and watched him go. He had gotten old, small and thin.

I stayed with Jamileh, terrified that she'd take a turn for the worse, that I'd have to bring her to the hospital, that everything would go wrong.

I had to stop thinking these negative thoughts. Since this whole thing depended on me, I had to pull myself together, stay focused and wait it out.

I walked through the dark shop to the lean-to. There, by

the dim light of the moon, I shifted my father's things around and cleared a space for Jamileh.

Once that was done, I no longer felt so insecure. My father's shop was the perfect place to hide. But now I needed to rest. I sat down by Jamileh and held her hand.

Just before sunrise I heard the muezzin call:

Allahu Akbar. Allahu Akbar.
Ashhado an la ilaha illa Allah.
Hayye ala as-salah.

God is great. God is great.
Testify that there is no God but God.
Hurry to the prayers.

I could hear people walking to the mosque. I got up and cautiously peeked out the window. As usual, men and women were making their separate ways through the darkness to the mosque. I turned back to Jamileh and felt her forehead. The fever had gone down.

"Are you feeling better?"

She nodded. I heard my father's cough. He opened the door and slipped inside with a bulging sack on his back.

"Nobody saw me," he signed in the moonlight. "Is she better?"

"Yes."

"Here—a pillow, blankets, milk, pills," he signed. "I'm going to the mosque."

"I'll move her to the lean-to. She's better, but I'm planning to stay here until tomorrow evening. I'll lock the door from the inside. When you come back, go and sit in your usual place and start working. If she's completely recovered by tomorrow evening, I'll leave. Don't worry. She's strong."

• • •

Around noon, Jamileh opened her eyes and I was able to talk to her. I told her I could stay another day, but she didn't think it was necessary.

That evening I put her fate in my father's hands and left.

Meanwhile, back in Tehran, the party was spreading the news of Jamileh's escape. There were flyers everywhere. It was seen as a stunning victory over the shah.

During the night, sympathisers hung a banner from one of the buildings at the University of Tehran. It showed Jamileh as a strong goddess with a rifle slung over her shoulder.

The police organised a massive search. Everyone followed the news broadcasts in tense expectation.

I was working for a plumbing company at the time. I went to the shop as usual and worked like mad, hoping to make the time pass more quickly. I couldn't keep my eyes off a black telephone mounted on the wall of the workshop. Every time it rang, my heart began to pound.

On the third day, at around three o'clock, just as I was having my coffee break, the phone rang. I raced to pick it up.

"Hello?"

"Hello, could I please speak to—"

I immediately recognised Golden Bell's voice.

"Hi, it's me. How are you?"

"Fine. Father gave me this number. He wants to see you right away."

"OK, I'll be there."

I cut the conversation short in case the secret police had tapped the phone.

I'd written the number on a piece of paper and given it to my father. "If you need me urgently, give this number to Golden Bell—only Golden Bell—and tell her to call me from a public phone booth."

I drove off immediately. Something must have happened to Jamileh.

On the outskirts of Senejan, I waited for half an hour until it got dark, then headed for the shop. My father wasn't expecting me so soon. He jumped up and locked the door from the inside.

"What's wrong?" I signed.

"She was getting better. Then yesterday her forehead felt hot again and she stopped eating. She's still breathing, but she doesn't open her eyes any more."

I went into the lean-to and looked at Jamileh in the dim candlelight. She was lying under the blankets, sweating. I knelt beside her and checked her pulse. "Comrade! Can you hear me?"

She couldn't hear me.

"If we don't take her to the hospital," my father signed, "she'll die."

I didn't answer.

"She smiled yesterday," he went on. "I fixed her some soup on the stove. She held my hand. But when I brought a spoonful of soup to her lips, she suddenly fell asleep. You've got to take her to a hospital."

"I can't," I signed back.

He panicked. "She's going to die. I can tell. My mother felt hot, then all of a sudden she turned cold. She was dead. You've got to take Jamileh to a doctor."

It was the first time I'd ever seen him so upset.

"My first wife, too. She was also hot, very hot, then suddenly cold."

"Take it easy. Calm down," I gestured.

But he didn't. "You've got to drive her to the hospital, *now*!"

I stood there helplessly.

Suddenly my father had an idea. "Let's take her to our house," he signed.

"What?"

"I'll carry her home. Then I'll go and get a doctor."

"We can't."

"Why not?"

"I can't explain."

"Talk to Tina," he signed.

"Tina?"

"Yes, why not?"

I was going to have to share my secret with Tina. All the doors were closed, and Tina's was the only one I could knock on.

"OK," I signed. "Go get Tina."

I didn't know how Tina would react, but I was sure the news would make her gasp. She had done her best to shield my sisters from my political activities. She wanted her daughters to find good husbands, leave home without a hitch, have children, buy a house and live happily ever after. And here I was, knocking on her door with the legendary Jamileh.

Tina realised instantly that this was an emergency. I hadn't seen her in more than a year, so I thought she'd start by moaning, "Where have you been, son, why haven't you come to see us?" But she didn't. I thought she'd hug me and exclaim, "My, how you've changed!" But she didn't. She bustled into the dusky lean-to and shot me a quick glance. At first she didn't recognise me. Then she saw Jamileh, stretched out on the ground. I briefly explained what was going on. She grasped the situation immediately.

She was silent for a moment. Then another side of her came to the fore. Not the weak Tina, but the Tina described by Kazem Khan, the woman who cleared the snow from the roof and refused to let him in. To my great surprise, she knelt calmly beside Jamileh, took her hand and felt her stomach. Then she picked up a candle and peered more closely at her abdomen.

"I'm taking her back to the house. Then I'll go for a doctor."

"Tina," I said, "she escaped from prison."

"But she needs a doctor."

"You're right, but if the police . . . Oh, I see. Nobody knows who she is. You can simply—"

"I'm going to take her home and say that she's my niece, on a visit from Saffron Village."

Tina had found a simple solution to a difficult problem: Jamileh was sick, so Jamileh had to be examined by a doctor.

She wrapped her in a chador. "Carry her over your shoulder," she signed to my father.

I helped him lift her.

"Let's go!" gestured Tina.

She kissed my forehead. "Don't look so sad. It'll be all right!"

I stood and watched until they vanished into the darkness. There was nothing more I could do.

The Mahdi

The man who reads leaves the well.
Tina weeps.
We might even go with the faithful to
the holy city, where the mosques
have golden domes.

 Jamileh stayed in my parents' house for a month. For thirty-four days, to be exact. On the last night, Tina escorted her to the big mosque in the centre of town, where a taxi was waiting beneath an old tree to whisk her away.

Tina had taken good care of her. In her autobiography, Jamileh described the month she spent with my family as a wonderful and safe period in her life. To protect people, she didn't use real names in her book, except for Tina's. "Though there are many I would like to thank by name, the safety of those individuals depends on my discretion. Even so, one person deserves my undying thanks: the courageous Aunt Tina."

Jamileh had stolen Tina's heart and left behind a wealth of unforgettable memories. Tina couldn't stop talking about Jamileh, who was unlike any woman she'd ever known. Tina had taken good care of her and cooked delicious meals, so Jamileh had even put on a little weight.

"Jamileh sang and skipped around the garden," Tina told me later. "At first it seemed a bit out of character, but actually it wasn't. Sometimes she'd ask me questions . . ."

"What kind of questions?"

"About that country, that island. Quub or Qube, or something like that."

"You mean Cuba?"

"Yes, that's it. Jamileh asked me if I knew where Cuba was. I'd never heard of it. She told me about the lives of the people there. She said that they were healthy and that medicine was free, along with milk for children and old people's homes—all free. She told me that women had lots of rights. For example, if a woman didn't want her husband, she could kick him out of the house. She said that most of the bus drivers were women and that they even drove great big trucks. She was always talking about that man, what's his name? The one with a cigar in his mouth and a rifle over his shoulder."

"Castro?"

"Not him, the other one, the man with the beret."

"You mean Che Guevara?"

"That's the one. She told me about his adventures. How he fought and barely escaped with his life. And sometimes she told me jokes about the shah. You know, how even his soap was made of gold, and how he went to the bathroom with a clothespin over his nose rather than admit that he was making that awful smell. Oh, we had such good times when she was with us. She also got along well with your father.

"He showed her his old pictures, the ones of him and Reza Shah standing by the rock with his pick-axe on his shoulder. And he told her his stories of the cuneiform relief and the time the villagers cleared a path through the mountains for the train.

"Even though she didn't understand our sign language, she listened patiently to your father. Sometimes she tried to answer in sign language, but she never really got the hang of it and we roared with laughter."

Tina could go on and on about Jamileh. There was no end to her reminiscences.

After the clerics came to power, however, she saw Jamileh's stay in a different light. She believed that it had destroyed the lives of her daughters.

Regardless of Tina's opinion, one thing was sure: Golden Bell thought of Jamileh as her role model. For thirty-four nights, she had shared a room with Jamileh. Her visit was a turning point in Golden Bell's life.

Before the revolution, Tina had the usual expectations. She dreamed that two normal, decent men would come and ask for her daughters' hands in marriage. She didn't include Golden Bell in her daydream, since she had no control over her youngest daughter anyway.

Tina had always longed for the quiet life she'd never had. She dreamed of becoming a grandmother, of holding her grandchildren on her lap and telling them stories. Then Jamileh shattered her dreams.

The two men Tina had been waiting for appeared. When they asked for her daughters' hands in marriage, however, her daughters refused to marry such ordinary men. They longed for another kind of man. Tina wept.

"What do you *want*? Who on earth are you waiting for? A

Castro? A Che Guevara? A man with a cigar and a beret? God help me, I don't deserve this."

Only after the revolution did the men her daughters were waiting for finally appear. They were hardly Castro or Che Guevara, though they did have Che Guevara posters above their beds. And while they didn't smoke (cigars were too expensive anyway), they did stick an occasional cigarette in the corner of their mouths and talk about the revolution.

Tina's two oldest daughters didn't go to jail, but their husbands were arrested and imprisoned by the secret police of the new regime, the Islamic Republic of Iran. When they were finally released a few years later, they were broken, both physically and mentally. It was years before they could function normally again.

The revolution had begun. The masses had risen up against the shah. But it came from a totally unexpected direction.

One night, when I was in my father's shop, he said, "The man who reads is gone!"

"Who?"

"The holy man who sits in the sacred well and reads."

"Gone? What do you mean, 'gone'?"

Perhaps I should refresh your memory. The Shiites have been waiting nearly fourteen centuries for the Mahdi, the messiah figure who would relieve the world of its suffering and meanwhile waited in a well, reading books.

Reza Shah had covered up the well. He wanted to strike a blow for modernisation and, at the same time, curb the power of spiritual leaders.

But the mullahs refused to be suppressed. They stepped up their fiery resistance to the Pahlavi kingdom.

My father was more interested in the Mahdi's kingdom.

"Someone smashed the stone that used to cover the well," my father signed. "The sacred well is now open. The holy man is gone."

The well was located in a place of strategic importance: a military zone. Obviously, the fact that some religious fanatic had broken it open was not a coincidence. Something important was going on. The mullahs were declaring war on the shah.

"Do you know who smashed the stone?"

"Allah," he signed, pointing at the sky. "The Holy One himself. He wants to fix things. I've seen His footprints."

"What did you see?"

"I was in Saffron Village. I climbed up the mountain with the villagers and saw, with my own eyes, the imprint of his bare feet in the rocks."

"Footprints in stone?"

"Yes, you could see that he'd stepped out of the well and gone into the countryside. The villagers knelt and kissed his footprints. I kissed one of them, too. It smelled heavenly."

The holy man was free. One day the Mahdi, and not the leftist movement, would conquer the cities and overthrow the dictator. He had come to help the poor, lift up the weak, heal the sick and comfort the mothers who had lost their sons and daughters.

"People cried," my father continued, "and people laughed. They put the Holy Book on their heads, gathered at the foot of the mountain and turned to face Mecca. Then they split into groups and followed the footprints."

"Where did the footprints go?"

"To the city with the big, golden-domed mosque. To the city where the women all wear black chadors, the one where so many imams live."

He meant Qom.

So the Messiah had gone to Qom—the Vatican of the Shiites. I immediately drove back to Tehran.

Akbar No Longer Wants
to Be Deaf and Dumb

Once more pilgrims journey to the sacred well.
We go along with them.

 In the days when the holy city of Qom was in an uproar and believers flocked to it from every corner of the land, Tehran was undergoing a revolution of its own. Parties that had been suppressed for decades were springing back to life and letting their voices be heard. Everywhere you looked you saw flyers and posters, which had been distributed during the night and pasted on the walls.

The political prisoners, realising that the revolution had begun, went on a mass hunger strike.

In Qom, the situation had spun out of control. As soon as it got dark, the laws of the shah could no longer be enforced, only those of the mullahs. No policeman dared show himself at night. In other cities, as well, people began to speak out.

Saffron Village had its own story. From all over the country, the blind, the deaf and the lame were on their way to Saffron Mountain, so they could touch their foreheads to the Mahdi's footprints and beg to be healed.

Because the sacred well was inaccessible, the local imam had ordered that a makeshift shrine be built at the foot of Saffron Mountain. The sick, the deaf, the lame, the mute, the blind and the otherwise afflicted tied one end of a long rope to the bars of the shrine and the other end around themselves, and lay down twenty or thirty yards away. They fasted and swore not to break their fast until the Mahdi came and relieved them of their burdens.

It was unbelievably crowded. The deaf lay side by side and wept, the blind sat in another cluster and begged, the sick groaned incessantly and the retarded roamed in and out of the wailing masses.

The voice of the imam of Saffron Village blared over a loudspeaker, urging believers to pray to the Mahdi and beseech him, from the bottom of their hearts, to come quickly to their aid.

Golden Bell and I were hunting among the deaf-mutes for my father. We didn't know for sure whether he'd gone to Saffron Mountain. Golden Bell had phoned to tell me that he'd suddenly disappeared and our search had brought us to the crowd of pilgrims.

"I see him! He's over there!" Golden Bell exclaimed.

My father was lying on the ground with his eyes closed. Around his right ankle was a long rope, tied to the shrine like hundreds of others.

He had lost weight and let his beard grow, which made him look older. I sat down beside him and took hold of his wrist. He opened his eyes, surprised to see me.

"What are you doing here?" he gestured weakly.

"What are *you* doing here?"

For an entire week he had fasted and had drunk almost nothing. His lips were cracked and blistered. The imam came by, placed a wet, fragrant-smelling handkerchief on his forehead and murmured, "The Mahdi will soon come and bless you, my poor man!"

And then he moved on to the next one.

"Come on!" I said to my father. "We're going home!" I offered him my hand so he could pull himself up.

He refused to take it.

"Listen," I said, "you could die of thirst. Golden Bell, help me lift him up. I'm going to have to carry him."

He didn't want me to. He'd never resisted me like this.

"I've read him so many books," I said to Golden Bell. "About the universe, the earth, the moon, mankind. And now he's lying here like an illiterate peasant, like a deaf-and-dumb old man. He won't even look at me."

Golden Bell stroked his forehead, wet his lips with a damp cloth and shook him gently. "Come, Father. Let's go home. It pains me to see you so weak. Please open your eyes."

He opened his eyes.

"Tina's been crying," she signed. "Come home for a few days. You can always come back here again if you want to. Come, it'll be better this way."

He stopped resisting.

"Take his shoes," I said to her. Then I carefully lifted him up and carried him to the car, which was parked a mile or so away.

I laid him on the back seat and drove to Senejan. Ever since the revolution had begun, I'd been visiting my family from time to time, so now I drove him home myself.

Tina promptly made him some soup, moaning all the while, "Oh, the misery I've suffered because of that man. What did he think the Mahdi was going to do? Teach him how to talk? I hardly have any peace and quiet as it is. God help me if he starts to talk."

"That's enough, Mother," Golden Bell protested. "You shouldn't talk about Father like that."

"Why not? What am I supposed to say when my husband comes home half-dead?"

"Stop it, Mother, or I'll—"

"Or else you'll what? You aren't exactly an angel, either. I can be just as hard on you, if I have to. You're ruining my life. Now that your brother's here, I want to make a few things clear. Ishmael, I've lost control over your sister."

"Mother," Golden Bell replied, "why are you suddenly different now that Ishmael's here?"

"I'm no different than I usually am. But I need to say something to him before he rushes off again. Ever since that Jamileh came to stay with us, Golden Bell has been—"

"What's Jamileh got to do with it?" sputtered Golden Bell.

"—growing away from me. There, now I've said what I had to say."

I felt like an outsider. I wanted to take Tina in my arms and say, "You're right, but now you can stop being so scared. The years of hardship are over. I'll be coming home more often. Everything's going to be fine."

But I didn't. I couldn't. I realised that my heart had hardened.

"Tina," I said, "let me give Father his soup. We'll talk later."

I spooned some soup into my father's mouth, while Golden Bell wiped his chin with a handkerchief.

"Are you going crazy, Father?" I asked. "Why on earth did you tie yourself to that shrine?"

He said nothing, just smiled.

I slept at home that night for the first time in years. It felt strange. As if I were a stranger. My other two sisters were still at home; they weren't married yet. They had always thought of me as more of a father than a brother, which is why they didn't come sit by me as readily as Golden Bell did. If we'd had time, that would have changed, but we never got the time.

My father's grey beard made me realise that the revolution was taking him away from me.

The next day I talked to him and tried to explain that the Mahdi didn't actually exist. I should have saved my breath.

My father told me that, after his first wife died, he saw the holy man in the well with his own eyes. And the day before yesterday he'd seen a miraculous cure. "A blind man went to bed and when he woke up in the morning, he could see. The holy man had come and cured him in his sleep."

My father no longer wanted to be an illiterate deaf-mute. He wanted to learn how to read.

"OK, I'll teach you how to read," I said. "If you can wait a year, or half a year, I'll come back home and teach you myself. I promise."

But my words no longer had any effect. He was completely bewitched by the footprints in the rocks.

A few days later my father grabbed a cane and went out again to look for the holy Mahdi.

The Days Rush Past

*We fly over Saffron Mountain
with Khomeini.*

 We once hoped to transform our country into a paradise. But we didn't know, or perhaps didn't want to know, that neither the country, nor its people—nor we, for that matter—were ready for it. We were impatient, in a hurry, anxious to catch up with history, or even to outrun it, as if such a thing were possible. Actually, we deserved the regime of the mullahs. The events taking place in my country over the last century and a half had all pointed to the rise of a spiritual leader. History had pushed Khomeini to the fore. The shah was forced to go. The front page of the nation's leading newspaper announced in huge capitals: KHOMEINI HAS COME.

Such big headlines were unprecedented in Iranian journalism. So, when I laid the newspaper on my father's workbench, he immediately understood that something important was happening.

"The shah is gone," I said to him.

"Gone?"

I picked up a map. "He went to Egypt, then to the Bahamas and then to the United States."

Egypt? The Bahamas? The United States? He didn't understand.

The problem was that he couldn't see the connection between recent events and the shah's departure.

"And he's never coming back," I said.

"Why not?"

My father hadn't realised that, in following the footprints of the Mahdi, he'd helped to topple the shah.

"Khomeini is now sitting on the shah's throne."

He looked at me in surprise.

"Why are you surprised? You wanted Khomeini to come and the shah to go."

"Me? I didn't do anything."

"What do you mean, you didn't do anything? You took the shah's picture off the wall and hung up Khomeini's picture instead. You went out every day and demonstrated, together with thousands of people. Look in the mirror. You even have a long grey beard, like his."

"Like whose?"

"Khomeini."

He looked in the mirror, toyed with his beard and seemed to make a startling discovery.

"Where was Khomeini before now?" he signed.

It would be hard to explain in sign language. I knew I'd have to skip over the events of the last century.

"It's complicated," I said to him, "but fifteen years ago the shah forced Khomeini to leave the country. He went to live in another country, far away from here. Those two men were enemies. Now that Khomeini is back, he's made the shah leave the country."

That would have to do. I pointed to the newspaper. "It says here that three days from now, Khomeini will be flying to Saffron Mountain to visit the sacred well."

"Why the sacred well?"

"Because he wants to see the holy man."

"But the well is empty. The holy man is gone."

I couldn't explain that, either. "The well isn't empty," I said. "The holy man has come back. He's sitting in the well again, reading his book."

A helicopter circled above the crowd that had climbed up Saffron Mountain. Thousands chanted in unison: "*La ilaha illa Allah! La ilaha illa Allah!*"

The helicopter circled again, in response.

"*Salaam bar Khomeini!*" they roared in unison.

My father pushed through the crowd and climbed even higher. He wanted to be as close to the well as possible. I went where he went, and he helped me over the difficult mountain paths.

I was impressed by the mood of the crowd. In spite of myself, I had been swept up by the religious fervor. Although I didn't chant the slogans along with the rest, I mentally shouted "*La ilaha illa Allah*" like a true believer.

Khomeini was now flying directly overhead. I could see him sitting next to the pilot. He waved. Tears sprang to my eyes. I promptly hid my face so my father wouldn't notice and enthusiastically followed him up the mountain. I wanted to see Khomeini get out of the helicopter and kneel before the sacred well.

I knew this was an important moment in Iranian history. The helicopter hovered above the well and tried to land. Apparently, it wasn't easy. The pilot made three attempts to land on a slope. The fourth time, he turned the helicopter around and landed with the tail pointing down at the crowd. Thousands of people suddenly burst out: "*Gush amad! Gush amad! Yar-e imam gush amad!*"

Seven bearded mountain climbers clambered up to the helicopter with ropes and spikes to help the aging leader. Khomeini refused their assistance. Out of respect for the Mahdi, he wanted to walk to the well on his own.

But how was he going to get there?

The mountain climbers had to come up with another plan. They couldn't let Khomeini scrabble across the rocks in his brand-new imam slippers. That would be unthinkable!

So they opted for a long detour. All seven climbers surrounded Khomeini and guided him down, step by step, without being allowed to touch him. After almost twenty minutes, he finally set foot on the ground around the sacred well. He stumbled, and for a moment the crowd was afraid he was going to fall, but to everyone's surprise he caught himself and calmly straightened up again. The crowd roared, "*Salah 'ala Mohammad! Yar-e imam, gush amad!*"

He adjusted his black turban, smoothed down his aba, squared his shoulders—as if he were meeting God Himself—and walked calmly up to the sacred well. I expected him to look directly into it, but he didn't. Instead, he turned to the left and faced Mecca. He stood for a moment—no doubt reciting a prayer—then stiffly knelt and touched his forehead to the ground.

It was a political deed of the first order and at the same time a fairy tale that was taking shape before our eyes. Anyone who has read Sheherazade's tales of the thousand and one nights will understand what I mean.

Reza Shah had once come here to plug up the well. Now Khomeini was standing on the same spot. A kingdom had vanished and been replaced by the regime of the mullahs.

· · ·

Khomeini got to his feet. He reached into his pocket, apparently in search of something. Ah, his glasses, but this wasn't the right pair. He checked his other pocket, but didn't find them. He must have left them somewhere.

Khomeini put on the pair he did have and checked to see whether they would do. No, he couldn't see a thing. So he took them off and tucked them back in his pocket. Then he stepped up to the well, leaned over and stared down into its depths.

Apparently, he still couldn't see anything, because he quickly straightened up again. Then, once more, he leaned over and stared into the well. Clearly, he was looking for the Mahdi, but couldn't see him. Or could he?

He nodded three times by way of greeting, then began to speak into the sacred well. A hush fell over the crowd. Everyone knew that Khomeini was seeking the Mahdi's advice, that he was asking him how to govern the country.

How long did the conversation last? I don't know.

What did he say to the Mahdi? I don't know. However, he no doubt began with the following words: "*As-salaamo aleika ya Mahdi ibn Hassan ibn Hadi ibn Taqi ibn Reza ibn Kazem ibn Jafar ibn Baqir ibn Zayn ibn Hussein ibn Ali ibn Abi Taleb.*"

After a while he gestured for help. The seven bearded mountain climbers rushed over, lifted him up on their shoulders and carried him back to the helicopter. The crowd shouted, "*Khoda ya! Khoda ya! Khomeini-ra negah dar!*"

It was the dawning of a new era in Iranian history.

Time goes so fast! When I was little and went everywhere with my father, time seemed to stand still. The days crawled by, the nights were endless. Now I can see that it all went by in a flash.

. . .

I sit here in the polder and look out the window. I feel frozen in time, stuck at my computer forever. Luckily I know from experience that this, too, will pass.

In the meantime, Khomeini has disappeared, died, as if he never existed. One night he took off his aba, fell asleep and didn't wake up again.

The era of the sacred well is also over. The Mahdi has vanished. The well is empty. Wild pigeons build their nests on the ledges. Poisonous snakes coil up behind the rocks, wait patiently for the birds to leave, then slither into the well and eat the eggs. The pigeons come back, see their empty nests and weep.

This, too, will come to an end.

Autumn turns to winter and it snows on Saffron Mountain. For several months, the well is covered with a thick layer of snow. Then spring comes, the snow melts and the well fills with water. It's an anxious time for the mountain goats. They watch their young and push them away from the well, afraid they'll fall in.

The Soviet Union has also ceased to exist. If you were to stand at the top of Saffron Mountain and stare through your binoculars, you'd no longer see red flags and a checkpoint on the other side of the border, or gendarmes on this side. It's all gone. Everyone's gone. Including me.

I'm here, but where's the Mahdi? Perhaps he's also moved to the Dutch polder.

Sometimes I see in the distance the figure of a man, walking his dog on the dyke. I walk toward him, but no matter how fast I walk or run, I never catch up with him. So I let him go, along with his dog. We both need this polder.

It's peaceful here in the polder, unlike the rest of the world. The moment you turn on your TV, however, you realise that the quiet is deceptive.

Saddam Hussein occasionally flashes on the screen. Then the President of the United States says a few nasty things about him. By now everyone knows that under Khomeini's leadership we fought for eight years with neighbouring Iraq. Thousands died and thousands were wounded, on both sides. What was the war about? Nothing. Just the stupidity and stubbornness of two crazy leaders. Next, Saddam moved on to attack his other neighbour, Kuwait. America chased him out of there and he crawled back into his hole. But he keeps crawling out again.

I don't want to talk about Saddam. I just want to use him as a stepping stone to my father's notebook.

When Khomeini became the absolute ruler of Iran, the party wasn't sure how to react. We didn't trust him and were convinced he wouldn't tolerate a leftist movement any more than the shah had. We knew he'd outlaw the party at the first possible opportunity. Even so, we were anxious to make use of our temporary freedom. We therefore opted for a semi-legal existence. The party opened an office in Tehran, where a few leaders operated in the public eye. At the same time, however, the movement's most important activities were kept underground.

One of those closely guarded secrets was the location of the printing press and the place where the party's editorial board met. In those days, I was one of the editors.

I no longer remember the date, but my oldest sister was going to get married that day and I had agreed to drive home for the wedding. At about one o'clock, warplanes suddenly flew over Tehran, so low and so loud that everyone clapped their hands to their ears and ducked for cover.

Saddam bombed Tehran's airport. The war had begun. Instead of going to the wedding, I hurried back to the newspaper.

. . .

Iraqi planes bombed our houses one night, and we bombed theirs the next.

One evening, during the second or third year of the war, the phone rang. It was Golden Bell.

"Ishmael? Listen, Tina's not well."

"What's wrong?"

"She's been hit by a bomb."

"A bomb?"

"Well, she didn't exactly get hit, but . . ."

"When did it happen?"

"Last week, when the Iraqi planes started flying over Senejan. I think you'd better come up here."

How stupid of me. I should have phoned. I knew that Senejan had been bombed. I'd put the news in the paper myself. There had been a couple of deaths, but the planes had bombed an industrial area far from our house. How could Tina have been hit?

I reached Senejan in the middle of the night. The city was in darkness. Not a single light was on. A man racing away on a bicycle yelled, "Saddam's going to bomb the city tonight. He announced it on the radio this afternoon."

Everyone had fled into the mountains. How would I be able to find my family? I switched off my headlights and drove cautiously down the darkened streets to our house. I was hoping they'd left me a note. Just as I was about to park the car, a figure came out from under the trees.

My father. We couldn't communicate in the dark. He got in the car and gestured: "Drive! Get out of here!"

"Where's Tina?"

"I carried her up to the mountains on my back," I gathered from his gestures.

I drove off. Once we were in the mountains, I hid the car behind a boulder and turned on the inside light. "What's happened to Tina?" I signed.

"She was at the home of your sister Marzi, who, by the way, is pregnant," he signed back. "They were standing in the courtyard. Suddenly an airplane flew over the house and dropped a bomb."

"On her house?"

"No, on a nearby tractor factory. But one of the walls in Marzi's house collapsed. Tina thought the bomb was going to fall on the house. She pulled Marzi to the ground and lay on top of her to protect her. After the airplane left, Marzi got up. But Tina didn't."

"Was she wounded?"

"No. I mean, yes, her left arm was bleeding. But she didn't open her eyes. They took her to the hospital. I went with them, I saw her lying in bed. Her eyes were open, but she didn't know who I was. They had her strapped to the bed."

"Why?"

"The doctor said that otherwise she'd scream and beat herself over the head again. He gave her an injection. She was acting strangely. I think it had something to do with that airplane. The doctor gave her an injection every day to make her sleep.

"Five days ago I went to the hospital again. I was sitting on the chair beside the bed. Suddenly everybody started running out of the room. Tina opened her eyes and began to scream. I undid the straps, lifted her up, threw her over my shoulder and rushed out into the corridor.

"I found a doctor. Tina was still screaming, so he gave her another injection.

"'What should I do?' I gestured to the doctor. 'Take her home,' he said and gave me a bottle of pills.

"Outside, people were running away. I carried Tina all the way home."

"Is she all right now?"

"The wound has healed, but she still won't wake up and she's lost weight. I don't understand it. I think it must have something to do with that airplane, don't you?"

I started the car and drove to a farm, where my family had been given temporary shelter in the barn. Golden Bell came out just as I was parking the car.

"You found us!" she exclaimed. She held up an oil lamp. I kissed her and followed her inside.

I almost didn't recognise Tina in the dim light of the oil lamp. I checked the wound and it seemed fine. I couldn't work out why she was still so sick. Could the bomb have contained some kind of poison?

"Here, this is her medication," my father signed. He handed me a half-empty bottle of pills.

I looked at the label.

"It's Valium. How many have you been giving her?"

"Four or five a day," he replied.

Had the Valium been knocking her out?

"Here, keep the bottle in your pocket. We're going to stop her medication for a while."

"Isn't it any good?"

"I don't know. Come and help me carry her to the car."

"Are we taking her to the hospital?"

"No, to Saffron Village. She needs to be in a quiet place, far away from airplanes. I'll stay with you for a couple of days. If she doesn't get any better, I'll take her to Tehran."

The sun was just coming up as we drove into Saffron Village. We went to our summer house, the one my father had built in the time of Reza Shah. I hadn't been there for years, but Tina and my sisters often spent the summer there.

"Golden Bell, will you make Tina some soup? I'll make the tea. And Father, will you go get some fresh bread? I'm starving! Are you hungry, too, Golden Bell?"

My sister Golden Bell—the best, the prettiest, the sweetest sister in all the world—walked with such a cheerful bounce that I suddenly felt optimistic. Surely hope, health and happiness were on their way to our summer house! She picked up a basket and went off with my father to get some vegetables.

Tina lay like a corpse in bed. But all the signs—my burst of optimism, Golden Bell's cheerfulness, the light in my father's eyes, even the birds singing in the garden—pointed to Tina's recovery. Soon she would open her eyes and look around quietly, without screaming.

Suddenly I saw a white rabbit. We didn't have white rabbits in our part of the country, but there it was, sitting outside our door. It hopped around for a while, quite merry, then disappeared.

Now I was sure that things would soon be all right.

The next day, when a fire was blazing in the stove and the soup was bubbling away, my father gestured, "Look! Tina's trying to open her eyes."

I stayed for five days, days filled with the smell of soup, milk, fresh bread and burning logs.

We took care of Tina and walked around the hills, laughing at the antics of a little white rabbit.

Those days, too, came to an end.

Mount Damavand

*Let's climb to the roof of our country
and pray.*

 One night dozens of Iraqi airplanes appeared above Tehran and bombed the city for the umpteenth time. It was the heaviest bombardment to date.

Radio Baghdad regularly issued warnings that warplanes were going to bomb Tehran. The broadcasters also urged people to leave the city, so twelve million inhabitants took to their heels. Sometimes the planes came, sometimes they didn't. Saddam Hussein played the same game over and over again. People no longer knew whether to stay or go.

If you grabbed your children and fled, the planes didn't come, but if you stayed, the city was bombed. It was psychological warfare. When the planes did come, the nights were hell. They flew over the city with a terrifying roar. Your house shook, pictures fell from the walls, pots and pans bounced off the shelves, the cat crept under the covers, the baby cried and the bombs thudded to the ground, accompanied by the rattle of anti-aircraft guns. The all-clear finally sounded, only to be followed by the shriek of fire engines and ambulances. You'd rush outside to see which houses had been hit.

But that night, when dozens of planes bombed Tehran simultaneously, killing and injuring hundreds, Khomeini took advantage of the chaos. He ordered his secret police to arrest the leaders of the leftist opposition. For years they'd been pinpointing hiding places, so even before the Iraqi planes had finished, most of the important party leaders had been rounded up.

In the morning, on my way to an editorial meeting, I ran into one of my fellow editors. "We've got to get out of here fast. Almost all of the leaders have been arrested."

It meant the end of the party. I immediately went back to my flat to warn my wife, Safa, who took our daughter, Nilufar, to her grandmother's house in Kermanshah. Then I destroyed whatever documents were in my possession. After that, all I could do was wait.

So far I've said very little about Safa. That's because I don't want to stray from my father's cuneiform notebook. Otherwise I would also have written more about my sisters and about their husbands' tragic fate.

I met Safa at the university. She sympathised with the party, although she wasn't a member. She hadn't been the one to seek contact. If we hadn't met, she probably would have led a normal life, but because of me, she got involved in all kinds of underground activities.

Until the revolution broke out, we met in secret. We knew

that every rendezvous might be our last. The revolution made it easier for us to get together and we gradually dared to talk about the future.

The day after the fall of the shah, I had a date with Safa. I asked her to marry me.

Our wedding was a simple affair: just two of our friends who acted as witnesses and the civil servant who performed the ceremony. In such momentous times, when we were all so busy, a wedding banquet was out of the question. We celebrated our wedding in a café, talking with our comrades deep into the night.

Three weeks later I took Safa to meet my parents.

"This is my wife."

"Really?" cried Tina. "She's beautiful."

My sisters, surprised at this unexpected turn of events, embraced Safa. My father kept his distance. He knew I had a girlfriend, because I'd shown him a picture of Safa. In his eyes, however, the bride's health was of prime importance in a marriage. He scrutinised her from head to toe.

Not only did she appear to be healthy, she was also vivacious and sociable. I could see the approval in his eyes. Safa walked over to him and embraced him. And because she knew the story of his first wife's death, she took his hand and held it to her cheek. "See," she said, "I'm healthy."

What else? I can't imagine that my father would have written more about his first meeting with Safa.

She once spent a week with my family in Saffron Village. She reported that she'd had a wonderful time, that she'd quickly mastered our sign language and that she and my father had sat up late every night discussing the state of the world.

"The state of the world?" I asked.

"Yes. And we roared with laughter. I really laughed a lot."

"About what?"

"Oh, I don't know. I'd use the wrong signs and they'd burst out laughing."

She never got another chance to visit my parents.

When Safa was in the final stages of pregnancy, she invited Golden Bell to our apartment. After that, when we had to move again for reasons of security, Golden Bell no longer knew how to get in touch with us.

In the dark time that followed the arrest of the party leaders, Safa and my daughter went to Kermanshah. She was planning to stay for a few weeks.

As fate would have it, those few weeks turned into years. By the time Safa was finally able to leave Kermanshah, her whole life had changed.

She was forced to move to a new country, where everything—from the front-door key to the bathroom mirror—was different. The teapot, the floor, the ceiling, even the ground beneath her feet, all were different.

A KLM flight brought her to Amsterdam, where I welcomed her with a bouquet of red, yellow and orange tulips. We took a train from the airport and then a taxi from the station to 21 Nieuwgracht.

But let's go back to Tehran.

A week after the arrests we still didn't know how badly the party had been hit or what the movement was going to do next.

While we waited, the secret police did their utmost to break the will of the party leaders, subjecting them to various forms of torture, in the hope that they would eventually bow down before the mullahs. The prisoners were thrown in separate cells and not allowed to sleep or sit. For five days and nights, they remained on their feet. Every time they nodded off, they got a bucket of ice-cold water thrown in their faces. They were given nothing to eat but a bowl of soup. Banned from using the toilets, they were forced to go in their pants. To weaken their resistance even further, their captors put tape recorders in their cells and forced them to listen night and day to Khomeini's speeches. The torture went on until the prisoners agreed to kneel before the prison imam on TV, confess that they were Soviet spies and beg for forgiveness.

The regime wanted the opposition to see what it was up against.

Dr Pur Bahlul was arrested for the second time. Having spent years in prison under the shah, he was now flung in jail by the mullahs. He was forced to crawl to the prison imam on his knees and say, "*La ilaha illa Allah.* I repent. From now on I will follow you."

They wanted millions of viewers to see that he was worthless, a mere worm hoping to become a human being, if only the imam would grant him forgiveness.

At home alone, I turned on the TV to watch the evening news. An old man appeared on the screen. A sick man with a pallid complexion. I knew who he was, or thought I did. There were a few seconds of deliberate silence meant to put the fear of God into the viewers. This ominous pause was followed by an icy voice, announcing that, after the news, the Soviet spy, Dr Pur Bahlul, would confess his crime.

The news didn't last long, but it was the longest news broadcast I'd ever seen. The dentist finally appeared. I couldn't believe it. The old Dr Pur Bahlul was dead and gone. The devil stared out from his eyes. He claimed that he was a spy who had betrayed his country. He said that from now on he was a follower of Khomeini, and that Khomeini was God's earthly shadow. He repudiated his past, his party and his comrades, and knelt before the imam. Then he cried like a baby.

The party had been shattered, like an earthenware jar that falls to the ground. Hundreds of comrades were arrested, dozens were executed and hundreds more fled to the border areas and managed to escape.

During the shah's regime you could count on the support of the people. Even total strangers would take you in. During the regime of the mullahs, all that changed.

The shah had governed in his own name, but the mullahs governed in the name of God. Khomeini himself appeared on television and said that God's kingdom was in danger. He ordered his followers to keep a close watch on their neighbours.

Suddenly your country was no longer your own. You didn't dare take a step. You had the feeling that people were watching you from behind their curtains.

After the revolution I wanted to make use of my new-found freedom to travel around the country with my father. To board a train with him and journey to the oil fields in the south, where the gas flames shot up into the air and the earth was dark with oil. Do you see that? Do you smell that? Beneath our feet, beneath this soil, there was oil. Lots of oil.

I wanted to show him the giant tankers that transported the oil to other countries, but I never got the chance. Although he always looked in wonderment at our gas stove, he never found out where those blue flames came from.

I wanted to take him to our marvellous Persian desert, where the sand glistened in the sun like gold. I wanted to ride across the desert with him on a camel, stop in a remote place and eat a simple meal with the villagers: a bit of camel's milk and dry bread, a bowl of dates and a palmful of water that oozed gently from the heart of the earth.

I wanted to sleep beside him on the roof of a desert café, where you can reach up into the sky, with its unforgettable moon and millions of stars, and pull it over you like a velvety-blue blanket.

Unfortunately, I didn't get the chance to do that, either.

I longed for just enough freedom to go with him to Isfahan, to visit the mosques he knew so well and talked about so often. I wanted to take him to the centuries-old Sheikh Lotfallah Mosque, and even though I'd stopped praying long ago, I would have stood beside him and prayed with him and for him.

But my deepest wish was to climb Mount Damavand with my father.

Mount Damavand is the highest mountain in Iran and also the most difficult to climb. People refer to it as the roof of Persia. I no longer remember whether it's 18,934 or 18,349 feet high, but it has one very distinct feature: one side of the peak is always covered with a thick layer of ice and snow, and the other side is always warm. Once you're at the top, you can see that the summit is shaped like a bowl—a great, big, warm bowl. It's actually the mouth of a once-active volcano. If you put your ear to the ground, you can hear the volcano breathing.

It's dangerous to climb Mount Damavand in the winter. The best time is spring, when the storms have died down and the ice has not quite melted. Then lots of mountain climbers cautiously make the ascent. As soon as they leave the frozen mass of snow behind, they begin to sing love songs, such as this one:

To goft keh gol dar ayeh mu biyayom.
Gel-e alam dar amad kiy miayi?

You said you'd come to me the moment the flowers blossomed.
Now that every flower has blossomed, when can I expect you?

At the time of Dr Pur Bahlul's televised "confession", I didn't know what was going to happen to me. Would I be arrested, too? Would I end up in jail? Would I crawl to the mullahs on my hands and knees and beg them for forgiveness? I didn't know how much danger I was in, but I did know this: I didn't want to flee. My comrades and I might be required to lead the party through these difficult times.

First I had to leave my flat and go into hiding for a few days, to avoid falling into the hands of the secret police. Then I'd come back and see what was left of the party. I'd go looking for the rest of my comrades, so we could pick up the pieces. In the meantime, I had to get out fast. But where was I to go?

Suddenly, the answer came to me: Mount Damavand!

Even though it was winter, I might be able to make one of my dreams come true. I raced to the basement and gathered up my climbing gear, along with some hiking boots and warm clothes for my father.

I surprised my father in his shop.

"Do you want to come with me?" I asked.

"Where?"

"To the country's highest mountain."

"Now?"

"I have a couple of days off and Safa's at her grandmother's, so I thought the two of us might—"

"What'll I say to Tina?"

"Tell her you're going away with me for a few days."

Was my father too old to attempt such a difficult climb? He was an experienced climber, but he knew nothing about climbing techniques. Was I being irresponsible? Would my father have trouble breathing at that high altitude? We would see. I didn't want to stop and think about such things. It didn't matter whether we reached the top. I just wanted to be with him. Who knows, maybe this would be the last time we could be together. I might be arrested any day now, so I didn't want to miss the opportunity to make use of my unexpected freedom. If he couldn't climb that high, we'd simply turn back.

In that case, we could still take the train to the oil fields or ride a camel across the Kavir-e-Lut desert. We'll see, I thought, as we headed toward Mount Damavand.

If we drove all night, we'd be at Safar's before sunrise. Safar's Café is where the climbers meet, eat breakfast and form groups before starting up the mountain.

I'd already climbed Mount Damavand three times, but never in the winter. I was afraid that the café would be closed and there wouldn't be any climbers.

I saw a distant light and felt hopeful. At least Safar's was open. My father was quiet. He couldn't see the point of climbing a mountain for the fun of it.

There had to be a goal. You climbed a mountain to get to another place or to meet someone. Or you went up one side of the mountain and came down the other because a woman was waiting for you. He wanted to know why we were making the climb in all this snow.

I told him that we were going to try and reach the top. "But it's a difficult mountain. Have you ever climbed with ropes?"

"A couple of times," my father said. "You're the one who taught me how."

He was right. I'd forgotten. Once, when I was a student, I'd tried to scale a difficult wall on Saffron Mountain with him.

I heard the buzz of voices before I even opened the door to the café. To my surprise, Safar's was as crowded as it usually was in the spring. That was a relief. "Come on in," I gestured to my father. "Sit down." But there were no empty chairs.

Where had all these people come from? Why were they making the climb in the middle of winter? Surely they couldn't all be members of the party, hoping to escape reality for a few days?

It was so pleasant that you forgot the war and the imams. It was as if you'd closed your eyes for a moment and when you opened them again, you found yourself in another country, or on another planet.

The café smelled of fresh tea, fresh bread and dates.

People usually climbed the mountain in groups; nobody climbed alone. If you were by yourself, you went to Safar's and asked to join a group, which accepted you unhesitatingly.

I put down my backpack and introduced myself. I let it be known that I wanted to make the climb with my father and that we would prefer to join a group of experienced climbers, because he was a deaf-mute.

My father was surprised to find such a warm and friendly café in the middle of the snow. He felt happy and comfortable. Everyone went over to him, shook his hand and wished him luck with the climb. He thought all those young men and women were friends of mine.

One group promptly found two chairs for us. My father sat down and I went off to get our breakfast: omelette, dates, real butter, fresh bread, tea and sugar. Just what climbers need.

It was still dark when the groups left the café, one by one. The groups made sure to stay fairly close together, since they knew they'd need each other's help in the cold.

We climbed up to 3,000 feet, where, following an old tradition, we waited for the sun to rise. My father stood next to me. He didn't understand why everyone was staring at the sky.

Suddenly, the sun's first golden arrow pierced the darkness. Silence. Then there was a second arrow, and a third, and all at once a whole shaft of light. Finally, the sun burst into flames behind the top of Mount Damavand like a golden crown. My astonished father looked at me, then at the sun and finally at the mountain, looming over us like a solid mass of snow.

As soon as Mount Damavand had revealed itself to us in all its archaic beauty, we burst into a well-known song:

Damavand! Your Majesty! O ancient pride of Persia,
Lend us your strength. Make us as strong as you.
Help us to be steadfast in the face of hardship.
Teach us to trust ourselves just as you trust yourself.
You are our pride and glory, O Damavand!

You have to climb Mount Damavand to experience it for yourself. The eternal snow, the biting cold on your skin, the colour and smell of the ancient volcano, the thick layer of ice.

We climbed on in silence. With only a few short breaks, we could probably reach 15,000 feet by sunset. There we could pitch camp, spend the night and prepare for the difficult climb ahead.

But before we got to 15,000 feet, we'd have to scale a few tricky ice walls with spikes and ropes. Fortunately, my father and I were with a group of very experienced climbers. They took my father under their wing, so I didn't have to look after him by myself. They were patient with him. He climbed like an old mountain goat, which made the climbers chuckle. They got a kick out of his old-fashioned methods.

Once we pitched camp, he was no longer dependent on me. In fact, he didn't even have time to sit next to me. Everyone wanted him in their group, so they could talk to him around the campfire.

"We need an interpreter, Ishmael. Can you come sit over here?" someone called.

I didn't feel well. This time, the thin air was making me

dizzy. All I wanted to do was sleep, but I couldn't just crawl into my sleeping bag and abandon those millions of pearls in the sky.

Besides, now that the party had been dealt a crushing blow, I wanted to think quietly about my future: What would happen when I went back to Tehran? The party might have been decapitated, but it wasn't dead. We had lost, but we weren't vanquished.

First, however, I had to reach the top of Mount Damavand.

It was a cold, short night. We got up before the sun rose. I couldn't eat or drink. Even the thought of food made me sick.

We started the climb, in groups, while it was still dark. I was worried about my father. The higher we climbed, the thinner the air became. The moment I noticed that he couldn't go any further, I'd take him down to the first-aid tent.

As fate would have it, however, I was the one who needed help. After a while, I felt too weak either to climb properly or to look after my father.

"Will somebody please take care of my father?" I called in a faint voice.

"Your father's doing fine," I heard the leader of the group say. "Look after yourself."

After a while, my mind went blank.

My father, the party, the movement, the mullahs—everything was erased. My previous climbs had gone all right, but this time I felt incredibly weak. I kept my eyes glued to the brown hiking boots of the man in front of me and tried to follow his footsteps.

At some point, my legs almost gave out. An inner voice,

however, urged me not to fall, not to lose sight of those boots, but to keep going, keep going, keep going.

Mount Damavand had me in its clutches. It had suddenly turned into a giant and I was a sparrow—a weak sparrow in the palm of its hand. How long did I have to keep going? How many steps did I still have to take? That was all I could think of. The world was standing still, but I had to keep moving, to keep climbing. One more step, then another, and another.

All of a sudden there was silence. For a moment I heard nothing at all, then only faint sounds, sing-song words.

Summoning every ounce of my strength, I could hear that people were singing. I smelled the familiar odour of sulfur: the volcano. Then I went deaf again and it got dark—totally dark. I fell.

Apparently, I passed out the moment I set foot on the rim of the bowl-shaped volcano. The experienced mountain climbers knew I needed immediate medical attention. It was a while before I opened my eyes and realised where I was. Someone helped me to my feet and steadied me. My father.

I leaned against a rock. My fellow climbers were putting flags on the rock and taking pictures. In fact, I have one of those snapshots here on my bookshelf. You can't see that we're standing at the top, at 18,934 feet. It looks as if we're posed next to just any old rock. My eyes are closed and my father looks proud.

If you look at the snapshot without knowing the story behind it, you notice a strange thing: I look as sick as a dog, but my father is glowing with happiness. In fact, I was leaning against the rock and doing my best to keep from passing out again, so I could look at my father, who was mesmerised by the view.

He was looking in astonishment at a band of blue in the distance. I didn't have enough energy to explain that it was the Caspian Sea—the sea that lay between us and the Soviet Union. He admired a faint, dark-green stripe on the horizon, without knowing that it was the largest forest in Persia.

I wanted to tell him to look at the view behind us, where a chain of mountains stretched out to the end of the world, but I was too weak. I nodded off again and the world fell silent.

If they hadn't carried me quickly down to a lower elevation, I might never have woken up.

The next time I opened my eyes, I was lying on the ground. Somebody helped me to my feet. I'd been carried to the first-aid tent, but fortunately I didn't need any more medical attention. The natural oxygen was already doing its work and my body was starting to function normally.

At 13,000 feet, I was able to walk on my own again, though my father walked beside me, keeping an eye on me. "How was it up there?" I asked him.

He smiled. I could tell that he was worried about me. I put my arm around his waist, kissed the top of his head and said, "I'm fine. Soon I'll be walking like I always do."

"What a wonderful father!" everyone exclaimed. "We're enjoying his company so much!"

We had to keep moving so as not to catch cold. I hadn't eaten since breakfast the day before, which was why I'd run out of energy. Still, I did my best to keep up with the rest. After about five hours we arrived at a shepherd's hut, where tea was always available for the climbers, and where you could buy bread, milk and butter at reasonable prices.

Soon the group would reach the foot of the mountain, rest in Safar's Café for a while and then head home. I knew I didn't feel strong enough to drive.

Luckily, you could always rely on mountain climbers to help out. They arranged for my father and me to spend the night in the shepherd's hut, so I could regain my strength.

We hugged each other goodbye. Everyone shook my father's hand, took one last snapshot and left.

I'll never forget the night we spent in that hut. It was as if my father knew that I'd never again have a chance to get so much rest.

That evening, the elderly shepherd, using every gesture under the sun, had a conversation with my father. Then he turned to me and said, "I know how you can get your strength back. You need to take a bath. Your father, too."

"Here? A bath?"

"I have a magic bath. Actually, it's only supposed to be used by shepherds, but you're a decent boy, you respect your father. Come, I'll show you. Damavand gives back what it takes."

After a fifteen-minute walk through the crunching snow, the shepherd held up an oil lamp. "In here. This way."

We followed him through an opening in the rocks leading into a cave. Then, guided only by the faint light of the oil lamp, we walked about a hundred yards into the cave's inky depths. I could smell the sulfur from the volcano.

"Wait here," said the shepherd.

He put the oil lamp on a ledge.

"Now come look!"

I took a few steps forward, leaned over and saw a pool of steaming water.

"Feel it!" the shepherd said.

I stuck my hand in the water.

"Oh, nice and hot."

"I'll leave you to your bath," the shepherd said, "and come back for you in an hour." He left.

In the yellowish glow of the oil lamp, the cave seemed magical. My father helped me into the bath, then carefully got in himself.

I wanted to stay there for ever.

The End of the Road

Ishmael has no idea where the road leads.

 The Dutch poet Rutger Kopland knows what he's talking about when it comes to mountains. I now live in the polder, but I know that I left myself, or rather *us*, back in the mountains, just as accidentally as all the rest.

In this attitude, as they lie
here, it seems perhaps
an attitude, it looks perhaps
like staying, but

whereas they rise up and
descend all around us, like
earthen bodies, asleep,

with the snow dripping off
their flanks and new falls
covering them again,

it is only as though we
could abandon ourselves,
invisible in this herd.

Mount Damavand had become a memory. One of my dreams had come true and I felt good.

The trip had helped me to think things through. I resigned myself to my fate and opted for my fatherland. I drove back to Tehran with my father. Then I brought him to the bus station and bought him a ticket. "This bus is going directly to Senejan. You don't have to change buses. The driver knows where you're supposed to get out. It'll be a long time before we see each other again. Have a good trip and give my love to everyone."

"Can you phone us?" he signed.

"Not for a while."

"Will you be coming to see me in the shop?"

"No."

Only then did he understand why I'd been so anxious to go to Mount Damavand with him. He looked as though he thought we'd never see each other again. I took back my words. "I don't know, I'll try to come for a visit."

I hugged him and the bus left.

Two days later I had an appointment to meet my contact person. Had he been arrested? Had he gone into hiding? Had he fled the country? All I could do was hope he'd show up.

We had a secret code. I was supposed to drive past a certain school once a week and check the fence on which the students chalked their graffiti. If the word *salaam* was scrawled on the fence, it meant that all was well and I was to meet him at the appointed place. If the word wasn't there, I was to try and find it on the wall of another school. If it wasn't on that wall, either, I knew that I was in danger. In that case I was supposed to go into hiding immediately and report to another place two days later to meet a new contact person.

Fortunately, the word *salaam* was on the fence. *Salaam*— greetings, hope and best wishes, all rolled into one.

We embraced. "*Salaam,* comrade! *Salaam!*" It was as if there'd been an earthquake and your friend had been pulled out of the rubble without a scratch.

In a café, he told me his story. The party had been wiped out. Nothing was left of the leadership. We no longer had a national committee. A small central committee had been formed, but we'd have to work in total secrecy. Nevertheless, we needed to show the imams that the movement was still alive.

The next day I was informed of my new duties. The party no longer had a printing press. My job would be to publish the party newspaper, though on a smaller scale. It was up to me to make the arrangements.

What arrangements? There was almost nothing to arrange. All we had was an old stencil machine, stashed away in a salvage yard somewhere outside Tehran.

I was to fetch the machine, repair it and get to work.

Where was I to keep the thing?

At home, in my own flat. Safa and my little girl would serve as a front.

Involving my family in the printing operation was not the wisest thing to do, but it was pointless to refuse or protest. Who would I protest to? Myself?

I was to run off 3,000 copies of a news sheet once a week and deliver them to another contact person. Under normal circumstances, this would have been impossible, but these weren't normal circumstances. We were ready to fight the clerics with our bare hands.

Still, the hardest part was yet to come. Freedom fighters place great demands on themselves when the need arises. In my case, the hardest part would be having to work out of my own flat.

I considered the drawbacks. How would I get that heavy machine up to the fifth floor without being seen? What if someone came out of one of the apartments and asked, "What's that?" Even if I got it safely upstairs, an antiquated machine like that was bound to make a lot of noise.

What I dreaded most, however, was having to tell my wife about it when she came back from Kermanshah.

I briefly fought an inner battle. I had to choose or, rather, I had no choice. I chose the movement, which meant leaving my family in the lurch. Setting aside my doubts, I phoned my wife and told her that we wouldn't be able to see each other for a long time.

Women have always surprised me. I thought my wife might object, might say it was out of the question, that she wanted to come home and that I couldn't involve everything and everybody in my wild dreams. I thought she'd say, "Forget it, I'm coming home."

But she didn't. I sensed that she was crying. For whom? Herself? Our daughter? She had the right to a normal life. And yet I knew my wife was also crying for me, since she was the only witness to my dreams.

My wife was a normal woman who embraced life and wanted a peaceful existence. I couldn't give her that. Not then, at any rate. Later on I did, when she moved to Holland, but by that time she'd paid a high price: she would never be able to go home again.

. . .

I drove out of town to pick up the stencil machine. After about an hour I arrived at the salvage yard, where various people were poking through wrecked cars in search of parts. Since I had no reason to go into the office, I walked directly to the shed at the far end and pushed open the door. It was dark inside. I lit a match and turned on the light.

The stencil machine was in the corner, covered with a thick layer of dust and grime. I wrapped it in an old blanket. It was too heavy to lift, so I dragged it across the ground to my car.

What were we doing? What was *I* doing? This wasn't an act of resistance—it was a suicide mission. At any moment, a couple of men from the secret police might stop me and yell, "Hands up!"

I was reminded of Don Quixote. He tilted at windmills; I wrestled with my stencil machine.

When I reached the car, I looked around for help. A young man happened to be passing by.

Together we lifted the machine and put it in the trunk. Then I locked the car and walked to a teahouse at the edge of the village. After all, I couldn't carry the thing up to my flat in broad daylight.

Late that night, when everyone was in bed, I hoisted the heavy machine onto my back and staggered up to our apartment, one step at a time. It was risky. I was terrified that one of our neighbours would open a door and see me on the stairs, but no one did.

In the bedroom, I eased the machine off my back and set it down on the bed. I tried to straighten up again, but couldn't. Movement of any kind was out of the question, so I spent the next quarter of an hour bent over, on my knees, until the pain subsided.

To this day I'm still plagued by backache. Sometimes, when I've been sitting at my computer for too long, I feel a jab of pain when I try to stand up. I have to hunch my shoulders, then slowly straighten my back.

I put the stencil machine in the wardrobe and tried to insulate it so the noise couldn't be heard outside. It didn't help. The entire wardrobe jiggled and bounced, and the din echoed around the room.

The whole thing was a disaster. The machine hadn't been designed to run off so many copies. It might do for a country schoolhouse that needed only twenty or thirty copies a week, but not for me.

The paper got stuck, the ink leaked and the roller squirted ink all over the place. The stencil tore easily, and whenever that happened, I had to type up a new one.

I could put up with all of this, but not with the racket. It was the kind of noise that would make people ask, "What's that man doing in there?"

How long could I turn on the radio or the vacuum cleaner to mask the noise? I'd print a couple of hundred pages, then run out to see if the neighbours had noticed anything. Day after day I hid behind the curtains, watching until our next-door neighbour had left for work and his wife and their two children had gone off for their daily visit to her mother. As soon as they were gone, I'd race to the wardrobe and begin stencilling like mad in an attempt to catch up on the backlog.

Safa and I had deliberately kept our contact with the neighbours to a minimum. Still, they might wonder where she was: "Hey, we haven't seen the wife for ages," or "What's our neighbour up to, he's at home alone a lot of the time."

During the day, I closed the curtains and pretended I wasn't at home. Sometimes I didn't leave the flat for days.

If I knew the neighbours were away, I ran the machine on electricity, but in the evenings I had to work it manually. I switched on the nightlight and churned out copies until morning. Then I delivered the news sheets to my contact person and received the next assignment.

Buying paper and ink was also a dangerous undertaking. Paper had become scarce during the war and the mullahs had seized control of printing supplies. You could only buy them in a special store in the mosque, which also sold vital foodstuffs, such as rice, sugar, cooking oil and tea. Not only did your request have to be approved by your local imam, but your purchase was supervised by a couple of bearded fundamentalists.

So, I bought paper and ink on the black market, where you often paid ten times the going rate.

The first two months, the printing went well and I finished the news sheets on time. Fear, however, gradually took hold of me. I slept badly. I had terrible nightmares and woke up every morning with a headache.

We were banging our heads against the walls of the mullahs, presumably to let them know that we were still alive and not afraid of them. And yet I was afraid. Not of being killed, but of having them break my spirit so much that I'd be prepared to kneel before them.

In reality, our resistance was having little effect. I no longer believed in what I was doing, and that scared me, too.

I kept going, but reality was stronger than I was. Every time I went out the door, I was hoping, deep in my heart, that I'd never have to return. I didn't even care if I had a car accident and ended up in the hospital.

I did my best, though. I cranked out the news sheets and delivered them on schedule every time. Then one night I ground to a halt, just like the stencil machine. I just couldn't take it any more.

· · ·

I explained the situation to my contact person. He didn't understand. I had the feeling that he was looking at me with contempt. He must have thought I was trying to save my own skin, now that things had got dangerous.

I told him that our resistance was ineffective, that we should accept the fact that the mullahs had won and save our strength for later. As much as I believed in the party and was prepared to sacrifice myself, I had to conclude that our current methods weren't working.

He said he would pass my advice on to the central committee.

A week later I heard what I expected to hear: the committee didn't agree. If I wanted to quit, my name would be put on the non-active list and I would have to sever all ties with the party.

Sever all ties? That wasn't what I wanted. I couldn't opt for a safe life while my comrades continued to battle the mullahs. How could I just sit there, comfortably watching TV with my wife and child, while an imam announced that "The police have arrested the last of God's enemies. A stencil machine was found in their hiding place."

It was too late for me to lead an ordinary, bourgeois life. My comrades were right: we had to say no to the mullahs who had brought the Iranian people to their knees. We had to say no, to shout no! Even if no one heard us now, because sooner or later we would be heard.

Now that I had made my opinion known to the party, I felt better. I went back to work.

Six weeks later, I drove to the usual place to deliver the news sheets to my contact person, but he didn't turn up. He was supposed to be waiting for me by the phone box in the loading zone behind the Tehran bazaar.

Normally, when I saw him, I parked my car in the lorry-loading area, got out and opened the boot, as if I were an ordinary businessman. My contact person then wheeled a cart over to the car and took the boxes from me.

This time, however, he wasn't there. I drove around the car park for a second time, just to make sure. There was still no sign of him.

Yesterday afternoon, everything had been OK. The word *salaam* had been written on the fence. If something had happened, it must have happened after that.

There was no reason to panic. My instructions were to come back in an hour and try again. If he failed to turn up this time, something was definitely wrong.

I parked the car and went into a teahouse. Time seemed to stand still, so I tried walking around a nearby park. After fifteen minutes, I'd had enough, so I joined the crowds in the bazaar and did my best to work up an enthusiasm for the jewellery. This didn't make the minute hand on my watch move any faster, so I sat down in another teahouse, drank a few more glasses of tea and skimmed through the old newspapers on the table.

At last an hour was up. I left the teahouse, got in my car, drove past the phone box and looked to see if he was there. No, still no one. I drove a couple of hundred yards farther, turned around and checked again. No, not a soul.

My instructions were to leave the vicinity immediately and go to an emergency meeting place. If my contact person hadn't been arrested, I'd find him there.

I drove to a café outside of town. If all was well, he'd be sitting by the window, and when he saw me, he'd come out and get in the car.

I drove slowly past the café. There was no one at the window. I turned around and drove past again.

Was I scared? Not then. I had a strange, mixed-up feeling. Like a person who'd shouldered a heavy burden for a long time and suddenly had the weight lifted. Even though it was gone, he still couldn't stand up straight.

I felt anxious, but fear hadn't gained the upper hand. Something had definitely gone wrong: either the police were on his tail or he'd been arrested.

What was the next step?

I drove away quickly, because when the police arrested someone, they tortured him until he divulged the names of his contacts.

There was one last ray of hope. I had to wait until the next morning, then make my way to one final meeting with a woman I didn't know, who would re-establish my contacts with the party.

For security reasons, I couldn't go home that night. I left the car in a car park and spent the night in a hotel. If this last contact person failed to show, I would have reached the end of the road.

The designated place was a nursery school in the middle of Tehran. At eleven-thirty in the morning, a woman was supposed to be sitting in a car out front reading a newspaper. If I saw her car, I was to park a few streets away, walk back to the school and wait along with the parents until the doors opened and they went in to collect their children. When everyone had left, I was supposed to ask, "Are you waiting for someone, too?"

If she answered, "Yes, I'm waiting for someone, too," I was supposed to get in the car and she would drive off.

I drove past the school. A few cars were parked outside. There was even a woman at the wheel of a car, though she wasn't reading a newspaper. I parked and walked back to the group of parents waiting on the sidewalk. I checked out the woman in the car. She looked more like a mother than a political activist. It's not her, I decided. Or was it? Maybe she wouldn't take out her newspaper until everyone had left. The school doors opened and the parents streamed in. To my dismay, she got out of the car and went in, too. Five minutes later, all the cars had driven away.

Five minutes after that, the janitor locked the heavy iron gates.

I didn't want to believe it, but I knew we were finished. The clerics had caught up with us.

I had reached the end of the road.

From then on I wasn't sure what I was supposed to do.

Had I walked into a trap? Were the secret police watching me this very moment? Were they following me so they could nab the others?

In any case, I had to move fast. The most important thing was to get rid of the boxes in the boot as quickly as possible. Then I'd think about the next move.

I jumped in my car and drove off. Oddly enough, though the police could have been on my tail, I was suddenly less scared. My first priority would be to dump the boxes. After that, I'd have to get rid of the stencil machine in my flat.

I looked in the rear-view mirror to see if I was being followed, then drove down a couple of streets and doubled back so I could check the cars behind me. No one seemed to be following me. I got on the motorway, drove as fast as I could, got off a few exits later and waited by the side of the road. Not a car in sight. It would be safe to get rid of the news sheets. The only question was how. Should I toss them in a rubbish bin? I couldn't bring myself to do it. A rubbish bin was no place for something I'd risked my life to produce.

I saw a bridge. A river would be a good place for my news sheets. I drove under the bridge and waited until there weren't any cars. Then I opened the boot, took out the boxes and threw them into the river.

I stared at them as the current carried them downstream. Where did the river go? It flowed into a large salt lake near the holy city of Qom.

There was no time to waste. I drove straight home. If the police had arrested my contact person yesterday, I had precious little time. Only the greatest of heroes could hold out for more than a couple of days in the torture chambers of the mullahs. A few of my comrades had chosen to die rather than name names.

My instructions were simple: clean up and get out.

First the stencil machine, then the car.

There was no sign of any suspicious activity near my flat. No strange cars were parked nearby.

I parked, lingered deliberately by the door, then went up the stairs. It was hard for me to accept that my printing operation had come to an end. I gathered up the documents and the ink, stuffed them in a bag and put them in the car, leaving the boot open. Then I hurried back upstairs.

I dragged the machine out of the wardrobe, wrapped it in a blanket and tipped it onto the bed.

I was afraid that if I bent down and lifted it on my back from the bed, I'd never be able to straighten up again. What if my back muscles seized up like they had the last time and the pain was so intense that I couldn't move? There had to be a better way.

I shoved the table next to the bed, then stood on the bed and manoeuvred the machine onto the table. That was better.

I remembered reading about a mother in France who, when she saw her child trapped beneath the wheels of a lorry, lifted up the lorry and pulled her child to safety.

I bent down and lifted the stencil machine onto my back, then staggered to the door and the stairway. It didn't matter if anyone saw me now. Holding the machine tightly with one hand and gripping the banister with the other, I started carefully down the stairs.

A flat door opened. I heard a man's footsteps. Don't panic, I said to myself.

"What are you doing, neighbour?"

"Just carrying something to the car," I calmly replied.

"What on earth is it?"

"Would you mind giving me a hand? I don't want to ruin my back."

I sat down on one of the steps and lowered the machine.

"Why didn't you ask me for help?" he said.

"I didn't want to disturb you. Besides, I didn't know if you were home."

The two of us carried the machine down the stairs.

"Whew, it's heavy," he moaned. "What the hell is it?"

"Just . . . uh, er . . . a piece of junk," I said as casually as possible. "A kind of hobby of mine. You know . . . uh, er . . . repairing old machines. Life's expensive and the extra cash comes in handy. But there's not much room in my flat, so I'm . . . uh, er . . . getting rid of the junk. Here we are, the boot's open. Thanks, I appreciate your help!"

We lowered the machine into the trunk. My neighbour went back upstairs. I slammed the boot shut and drove off.

A Christmas Tree
in Akbar's Notebook

*Take my coat. It's cold on the other side of the
mountain.*

 After I'd written about stowing the stencil machine in the boot of my car, I put down my pen
and went to my local shopping centre. It dawned
on me that it was December. The last December
of the century.

There was a man selling Christmas trees in the square. I
watched as he unloaded his trees, and a couple of children,
with a nod from their mother, picked one out. The shop windows were all decorated. I hadn't really noticed them before.
Somehow Christmas seemed different this year, as if this
were the first Christmas I'd ever spent in Holland. Why had I
paid so little attention in the past?

I bought a tree—a light green fir. My wife usually took

care of such things. Why did I suddenly become aware of the holiday preparations and why did I buy a tree?

When I took it home, my wife exclaimed, "Look, Ishmael bought a Christmas tree!"

Was it just a coincidence?

Maybe I was relieved to be nearing the end of my father's notes. Now that the Dutch version of Aga Akbar's notebook was almost finished, I wanted the book to have a Christmas tree—one decorated with coloured lights, angels, hearts . . . and golden bells.

These last few weeks had been so tiring that I needed to get away. In past years we'd packed our bags and gone off to visit friends in Germany, Belgium, England or Sweden. This year I wanted to stay in Holland. We went from one travel agency to the next, hoping to book a cabin for the Christmas holidays, but the travel agents stared at us in disbelief. At this late date?

I'd read all kinds of maths books when I was studying physics, so I knew that, according to the laws of statistical probability, there had to be at least one cancellation among the thousands of bookings.

Sure enough, there was. Somebody had just called. The cabin was expensive and too big for the three of us, but luckily my wife was good at resolving problems like this. She immediately phoned a friend of hers, who said that she and her daughter would be delighted to spend the holidays away from home. We were all set.

We left and I brought my father's notebook along, hoping to finish the story.

The cabin was located on a campground in Friesland, somewhere between Drachten and Leeuwarden. When we got there, the fog was so thick we couldn't see the surrounding countryside. For the rest of the afternoon and evening, we looked out on grey fields.

I liked the idea of celebrating Christmas and the New Year with my wife's friend and daughter, because it would add to the festive spirit. We started to decorate the house. As it turned out, we could have left our Christmas tree at home, because the cabin already had one.

We agreed that if I did the grocery shopping, the women would do the rest, which meant I could work for a few hours every day. I wanted to have the book done before the new century began.

"Where are you?" my wife called.

"Here, upstairs."

"Come on down. I'm making coffee."

I came down.

"I was looking out the upstairs window," I said. "The cabin seems to be floating on clouds. There's grey fog everywhere. I don't think it's ever going to lift. What are you lot planning to do?"

"We haven't decided yet," my wife said. "After we've unpacked, we might go into town with the children. Do you want to come along?"

"No, I'd rather stay here. According to the camping guide, there's a village with a café about three or four miles away. I think I'll walk there."

They decided to take the bus to Leeuwarden.

I put on my hiking boots, grabbed a writing pad and set off to find the café.

Although I followed the route given in the guidebook, it came to a dead end at a river, or maybe it was a lake. Anyway, a ferryboat suddenly loomed up out of the mist. A bearded old man slowly steered the boat toward the shore.

"Get in," he said in some kind of dialect.

"Get in? Where are you going?"

"To the other side."

"But I want to go to the café."

"Get in!" he said.

I got in.

"I thought you could walk all the way," I said.

"You can," he said, "though in that case you should've taken a different route."

After a few minutes the ferry reached the other side. The ferryman pointed: over there. Through the fog I saw a faint gleam of light.

It was a quiet village, consisting of two rows of old and not very large houses. In the village square, I saw a café with a Heineken sign. I peeked inside to see if anyone was there. An old man, presumably the owner, was standing behind the bar. Otherwise the room was empty.

"Are you open?" I called from the doorway.

"Sure. Come on in!" the owner said.

I went and sat by a window, so I could look outside.

"How about a cup of coffee?" I said.

The café was quiet—a good place to write.

"Do you need cream and sugar?" the owner asked.

"Black is fine. No, wait, with cream, please."

I took out my pen and notebook and began to write.

Now that the stencil machine had been safely stowed in the boot of my car, I drove off. How would I be able to get rid of the thing in a busy city like Tehran?

Actually, considering the danger I was in, I shouldn't have been driving my own car.

I wanted to do everything right. Not like a frightened rabbit, but like a freedom fighter who's reached the end of the road. If I left the stencil machine on the pavement and tiptoed away, I'd not only feel like a coward, but the machine would no doubt wind up in the hands of the secret police. I wanted to avoid that for two reasons. One, they would dust it for fingerprints, and two, they would conclude that we'd abandoned it because we were scared—so scared that we were dumping everything and running away in panic.

I was of two minds. Deep down, I rejoiced at the prospect of being liberated from the stencil machine, but at the same time I didn't want to let it go. It seemed as if my life were inextricably bound up with the machine. As long as it was in the boot of my car, I had an anchor. The moment it was gone, however, I would be adrift—a nobody, superfluous.

No, I refused to throw it away. Someone might need it later on if the party ever decided to start printing again. Why not take it to the salvage yard where I found it?

I'd have to hurry. It was five-thirty, and I didn't know what time it closed.

On the way there, I thought about what I would say. Maybe I wouldn't say anything, just drag the machine back to the shed where I'd found it. I decided to play it by ear.

It took me an hour to reach the salvage yard. A light was still on in the office. I parked the car and got out to see if the gate was locked. It was.

"Is anyone there?" I shouted. No answer.

I looked to see if there was a back entrance by the shed, but there wasn't. My only alternative would be to leave the stencil machine at the gate and drive off.

Just then the office light went out. I waited. A figure emerged from behind the wrecked cars, but I couldn't tell if it was a guard or an office worker. As he came closer, I could see that it was an old man in a cap—clearly the guard.

"Good evening," I called.

"Good evening," he said with an Afghan accent. No doubt one of the thousands of Afghan refugees who had fled to our country.

"Are you looking for someone?"

"No. A couple of months ago I took a stencil machine out of the shed. I don't suppose you know anything about that?"

"No."

"It doesn't matter. I don't need it any more, so I brought it back, but the gate was locked. I've got it out in the car. I live far away, so I'd rather not make another trip. I'd appreciate it if you'd let me put it in the shed."

He thought it over.

"Who let you have the machine?"

"A friend of mine arranged it. He said I could just take it out of the shed. It's an old machine that should actually be scrapped. That's why I've brought it back."

"OK, go and get it. But you can't take it to the shed—it's too dark back there. Just put it down here. I'll bring it to the shed myself tomorrow morning."

"Thank you."

I hurriedly opened the trunk, hauled out the stencil machine and lowered it to the ground. Then I dragged it in its blanket over to the gate and left it just inside.

"More coffee?" the café owner asked.

"Yes, thanks. It's good coffee."

"Are you keeping a journal?"

"No. Yes. I mean, I suppose it's a kind of journal."

"You write fast. Have you lived in Holland for long?"

"I may write fast, but I make lots of mistakes. When I go back home, I'll have to go through it all again and correct it."

"Your Dutch is good. Where do you come from?"

"Iran. Persia."

"No kidding! Look, I've got Persian carpets on my tables. Not real ones, of course, but nice all the same. They brighten up the place, make it look smarter. Well, I won't disturb you any more. I expect you're staying at the campground."

"Yes, I'm here with my family."

The fog had lifted. The villagers were walking down the main street in festive clothes. A group of older men, about my father's age, came into the café. They greeted the owner, then started talking loudly to each other in dialect. It made the café a lot more cheerful.

The owner brought me a fresh cup of coffee and said, "I suppose you won't be able to write any more with all the—"

"No problem. I'll manage."

Now that I'd disposed of the stencil machine, my instructions were to park the car somewhere and abandon it.

You agree to follow instructions like these without realising you might actually have to carry them out one day.

I had to do as I was told. Otherwise I could endanger the lives of others. I knew a lot about the party and I knew where a number of my comrades lived. If I were arrested, the police would drag the information out of me, bit by bit. This was no time for hesitation. A deal was a deal. I had to dump the car.

Without a car, though, how was I going to get around? And what were my next instructions?

As I drove through the darkness, I had a brilliant idea: I could park the car at my father's house. No, that was no good. It might sit there for months. What about behind the shop? There was a tiny plot of land where nobody ever went. It would be perfectly normal for a car to be parked there for a long time. Spare parts were so hard to find during the war that people often left their broken-down cars outside their homes.

I turned the car around and took the road to Senejan. I'd arrive in the middle of the night, which was good, because my father would be at home and the streets would be deserted.

. . .

It was almost quarter to one when I reached the city. I drove to my old neighbourhood. I saw a dog sniffing at a dustbin, but when he heard the car, he crept back into the darkness. I drove past my parents' house. The curtains were drawn as usual, but the lights were on. Were they still awake? Tina's silhouette suddenly moved across the curtains. She's up, I thought. What's going on? I felt a sudden urge to stop, but the house was off-limits. Whatever was going on behind the curtains was no longer my concern. And yet, I thought, it ought to be possible to drop in for a moment, say hello and leave.

I parked the car and was just about to get out when I saw my father's silhouette on the curtains. He threw up his hands and disappeared.

I had no right to know what was happening in their lives. I'd better go—I had come here for another reason. I started the car and drove to my father's shop.

I was used to seeing a light on in the window. This time it was dark. I drove slowly past the shop, then turned right at the corner so I could park behind it. Because I didn't want to wake the neighbours, I stopped, switched off the engine, got out and tried to push the car the rest of the way. It wasn't easy, but I finally managed to push it under an old tree. Suddenly there was a flicker of light in the window of the lean-to where we'd once hid Jamileh.

I thought I must be mistaken, that my imagination was playing tricks on me.

I took out the vehicle registration papers and locked the car doors. What should I do with the papers and the key? I probably wouldn't need them for a long time. Maybe never. I went over to the lean-to so I could slide the key and the papers through a crack in the window frame.

Tomorrow, when my father saw the car behind the shop, he'd realise what had happened. Eventually he'd also find the key and the vehicle registration papers in his lean-to.

The papers slipped easily through the crack, but the key wouldn't fit. Since the window frame was rotten, I gouged out a hole with the key, then pushed it through. As the key fell to the ground, I caught a glimpse of a shadowy figure inside. "Don't worry," I whispered quickly, to calm whoever it was. "It's OK. Everything's all right."

Who could it be? Golden Bell? A friend of hers? Did my father know? I had no idea and it was none of my business. I was the stranger here. I needed to disappear, to get away from my father's shop.

I'd left my flat, got rid of the stencil machine, and abandoned the car. Next I had to dispose of myself. I'd never expected to be in a situation like this. Since I realised that the police might pick me up if I headed into town, I started walking in the opposite direction.

An hour's walk put the city behind me. I saw the mountains, then the snowy peak of Saffron Mountain. I felt like an apple that had fallen from the bough. It could never be put back. My only option was to follow the path to the other side of Saffron Mountain. Flee my country? I'd never given it a moment's thought.

How could I leave my father, my mother and my sisters? I hadn't even said goodbye to my wife and daughter. No, the least I could do was to call Safa and let her know I'd be gone for a few months—maybe more, maybe less.

I retraced my steps to my old neighbourhood, where there was a phone box. I dialled the number of Safa's grandmother. My wife would know immediately that it was me. Who else would call in the middle of the night? She picked up the phone after only a few rings.

"Hi, it's me," I said hurriedly. "How are you? How's Nilufar? Listen, I've only got a couple of coins. I just wanted to let you know that I'm going away for a while."

"Going away?" she said sleepily. "For how long? Where?"

"I don't know. But I have to go. I'll let you know as soon as I'm safe. Say hello to Grandma for me. I love you."

"Me, too. Good luck."

Reality was cruel. We had to keep the conversation short—she knew that. You had to put your emotions on hold. Political activists weren't allowed to make long phone calls. You were supposed to deliver your message in a few short words, then hang up.

I always thought that at such a moment my wife would say, "Wait, you can't just leave us like this! OK, I suppose I have only myself to blame, since you made your choice years ago. I should have known you'd sacrifice me so you could follow your dream!"

But she didn't say anything of the kind. To my surprise, she was relieved that I was going. She must have instinctively felt that the path to Saffron Mountain was the only path to *her* liberation as well.

As I was leaving the phone box, I saw people walking down the street and realised that it was Friday.

My father, like all good Muslims, always went to the bathhouse before sunrise and then to Friday prayers in the mosque. It was a ritual he'd followed his entire life. When I was little, I used to go with him. He woke me every Friday morning and handed me his towel and various toiletries in a toilet bag. Then he set off at a brisk pace, with me following sleepily behind.

I looked at my watch. The sun would rise in half an hour. If I hurried, I could catch him somewhere between the bathhouse and the mosque. I headed for the mosque. It was no longer dangerous to walk or even run through the dark city, since everyone would think you were hurrying to prayers.

. . .

I went into the mosque along with the other men and peeked through the window of the prayer room to see if my father had arrived. He hadn't. So I turned and walked back in the direction of the bathhouse.

What if today, of all days, he wasn't coming to the mosque? What if whatever was going on in our house had kept him away?

As I came out of the side street, I suddenly saw his silhouette and recognised his footsteps. He walked with a kind of shuffle, especially now that he was old.

I ducked out of sight. He passed me by, lost in thought. I trailed after him, then gently tapped him on the shoulder. He turned. "*Salaam*," I signed.

He looked at me in surprise.

"What are you doing here?" he signed back. "Have you been to the shop?"

"I need to talk to you," I signed. "I've come to say goodbye."

"What?"

"I'm going away."

"Where?"

"To Saffron Mountain. And then to the other side."

"The other side?"

He was silent. He knew what that meant. When he was a child, he used to see people sneaking through the almond grove in the dark and asking for food on their way to the other side. He'd also seen the gendarmes arrest numerous men and women, and watched as they were handcuffed, pushed into jeeps and driven away.

"When are you leaving?" he signed.

"Soon, before the sun comes up."

"But you don't have any food. Wait, I'll go get you some bread." He hurried off toward the bakery, which was always open early on Fridays.

Did my father realise what it meant to flee one's country? I hadn't expected him to react so calmly. Perhaps he was going to the bakery to give himself time to think.

He came back with a long flat bread, which he folded in half like a newspaper and wrapped in a handkerchief before handing it to me. "Here, you'll need this."

We walked out of the city and headed toward the mountains.

In the glow of a streetlamp I told him briefly what had happened: that my comrades had been arrested and that the secret police would catch me if I didn't leave. I explained that I'd left my car under the tree behind his shop and shoved the key and the vehicle registration papers through the window of his lean-to. I watched his face to see if he knew that someone was in the lean-to. There was no reaction.

I wanted to ask him about it, but decided not to. If he knew, he could have told me, and otherwise it was probably Golden Bell's secret, in which case he didn't need to know. So I let the matter drop.

The sun would soon be up and for the first time ever my father would miss his Friday prayers.

"Aren't you going to the mosque?" I asked.

"No," he replied.

I realised then that he understood what my going away meant.

We came to the cemetery, the one the mothers went to early in the morning. They arrived with carpets under their arms to visit the graves of their executed sons and daughters.

In those days, many of the young men and women who opposed the mullahs were being executed. At first the families weren't allowed to bury their children in a cemetery. Later on, this rule was changed, but the families were forbidden to visit the graves, which is why the mothers stole through the darkness to the cemetery on Friday mornings.

I walked hesitantly beside my father to the grave of my

recently executed cousin and friend Jawad. I knelt by his grave and tapped his headstone with a pebble to wake him up. "Good morning, Jawad," I said. "I'm going away."

The sun rose above Saffron Mountain. My father took off his coat.

"Here, take it. It's cold on the other side of the mountain," he signed.

"No, you keep it, or else you'll catch cold," I signed back.

He refused.

To this day I still have his coat—his worn black coat—in my wardrobe.

He pointed toward the mountains. "You know the way. You won't have any trouble getting to the top of Saffron Mountain. When you get to the other side, keep moving, because the sun never shines on that side in the afternoon and the wind blows hard at night.

"Don't stop and rest when you get tired, but keep moving. You mustn't forget that. And stay away from the railroad, otherwise the gendarmes will be able to follow your tracks.

"When you get to the top, take the other path, the one the mountain goats use. Then no one will be able to see you, not even with binoculars."

I wanted to say that I was only going away for a little while and that I'd be back soon, but the words stuck in my throat. I wanted to look into his eyes, but he never gave me the chance. Instead, he looked down at my feet and said, "You aren't wearing the right shoes, but you'll manage."

I wanted to hug him, but he didn't give me the chance to do that, either. He pointed to the top of Saffron Mountain and said, "Go!"

I started climbing and at every turn I looked back at my father, still standing at the cemetery gate.

The Cave

A New Road

"Loss is an experience that eventually leads to a new road, to a new opportunity to think of things in a different way. Losing is not the end of everything, but merely the end of a particular way of thinking. If you fall in one place, get up again in another. That's a cardinal rule of life."

Those were the words of the Persian poet Mohammad Mokhtari, a comrade of Ishmael's, who refused to flee. His body was found behind a salvage yard outside Tehran. According to Western news reports, he was strangled by the secret police.

 Ishmael left. He took the path to Saffron Mountain and Aga Akbar remained standing at the cemetery gate until he could no longer tell the difference between Ishmael and the rocks.

Akbar knew from experience that once people vanished to the other side of the mountain, they never returned. But where did they all go?

If Ishmael thought there was no alternative, he had to leave. But what was Akbar going to tell Tina?

The sun had risen and the mothers had slipped away from the cemetery. An old woman with a cane hobbled over to Akbar. "Good morning, Aga!" she said. "What on earth have you been staring at for so long?"

"*Salaam*," Akbar gestured. "I've been watching the sun rise over Saffron Mountain. You can see dark clouds on the other side. It's snowing over there."

He had to hurry home. He'd never come back from the mosque so late. Tina would be worried.

She was waiting for him at the door. "Where have you been?" she cried. "Where's your coat? Why didn't you buy any bread? Where's your toilet bag?"

Oh, the toilet bag! Where had he left it?

"I'll tell you inside," he gestured. "Come in, shut the door and lock it! Where's Golden Bell? Call her! I have something important to tell you. He climbed the mountain. He left. He's gone."

"What are you talking about? Who climbed the mountain? Who's gone?"

"He disappeared into the mountains. To the place with the red flags. Where's Golden Bell? Call her! I told him to stay away from the railroad tracks, otherwise the gendarmes would be able to see him through their binoculars."

"Golden Bell!" Tina called. "Come here, I don't understand what your father's saying. He came home without his coat or toilet bag, he didn't bring us any bread and he's rambling on about someone who's gone. God help me, that man comes home every day with a different story! Akbar, what did you do with your coat?"

Tina immediately knew what he was talking about, she just didn't want to believe it. She needed to have it confirmed by someone else. Golden Bell came in.

"He's gone," Akbar signed.

"Really? When?"

"He's on his way to Saffron Mountain."

"Ishmael's gone, Mother," Golden Bell said.

Tina sat down and burst into sobs.

"You should be glad he's gone. Imagine what would happen if the mullahs got hold of him. I mean it, Mother, don't cry. If he takes the right route, the gendarmes won't catch him and he'll be free. He can do it. He knows the way, he knows how to stay out of sight. Don't cry, Mother. You should be praying for his escape with all your heart. Sit down, Father. Here's a glass of tea. Drink it, it'll warm you. Tell me what happened."

He took the tea, sat down and signed: "I was on my way to the mosque this morning when someone tapped me on the shoulder. I turned around and saw Ishmael. He said he was going to the mountains, but he didn't have any warm clothes, or any bread, either. Oh, I think I left my toilet bag in the bakery . . . Anyway, he's not wearing the right shoes."

Golden Bell sat down beside him. "It'll be all right. He'll manage."

They were sitting so close together that Tina couldn't follow their sign language. "What are you two talking about?" she said angrily. "Are you trying to keep something from me? Is this another of your father–daughter secrets?"

"Sorry, Mother, I didn't mean to—"

"Oh, yes, you did," Tina snapped. "I'm fed up with all the secrets in this house. I've had enough of father–son secrets. And of your secrets, too, Golden Bell. Where will all that secrecy lead to? Nowhere. Just look at what's happened to your brother. He's probably in the hands of the gendarmes right now! Oh, my God! Ishmael!"

"Mother, please don't shout. Before you know it, the neighbours will be at the door."

"Let this be a lesson to you, Golden Bell. Wake up, open

your eyes! Your brother, your great example, is gone. You'll be next. I wish—" She burst into loud wails.

"There's no need for hysterics, Mother," Golden Bell said. "Ishmael hasn't reached the border yet. He's still got a long walk ahead of him. Here's your chador. Go and pray for him. That's all you can do for him now. Father, go to your shop as usual. I'll be along in a little while."

Akbar got to his feet. "He'll phone us when he reaches the other side," he signed. "The people over there are different, you know, and they . . . where's the map?"

"This is no time for maps!" Tina shrieked. She took her chador and stomped out of the room.

Ishmael didn't phone. Nor did they get a letter from him. He wasn't allowed to write or make phone calls. People who fled to the Soviet Union knew better than to get in touch with their families. A letter from the Soviet Union? A hammer-and-sickle postmark? A Lenin stamp? It was unthinkable!

Every time the phone rang and Tina rushed over to pick it up, Akbar looked at her.

"No?"

"No."

Every time the postman went by the shop, Akbar gestured: "No letter?"

"No, no letter."

However, they were almost certain that he hadn't been arrested. Safa's friends had told her to expect neither letters nor phone calls.

Three days after Ishmael's departure, Akbar went to Saffron Village. He took a mule and rode from village to village, asking the elders if the gendarmes had made any arrests in the last few days. No, they hadn't, and the elders would surely have heard about it if they had.

Months later, in the middle of the night, when they were

least expecting it, the phone rang. Tina clambered out of bed and picked up the phone. "*Salaam,*" she said.

"*Salaam,*" a man replied. "Are you Ishmael's mother?"

"Yes," she said, terrified. She thought it was the police.

"I'm a friend of Ishmael's. I'm calling you from Berlin. I wanted to let you know that he's all right. He's in Tadzhikistan. He might be coming to Berlin, but not for a while. When he does, he'll contact you himself. Would you please pass the news on to his wife? Goodbye."

Before Tina could say a word, he hung up.

"Who was that?" Akbar enquired.

"Ishmael! Oh, my God! No, it wasn't Ishmael himself. Yes, he's all right. We've got to call Safa right away."

In those days the Soviet Union was struggling with problems of its own. Gorbachev was trying to salvage whatever he could with his policy of glasnost. Russia could no longer welcome comrades from its neighbour to the south and international solidarity was a thing of the past. Comrades like Ishmael who had escaped to the Soviet Union used to be the responsibility of either the government or local party officials. They were offered a wealth of opportunities. They could attend a university, for example, or they could visit collective farms and factories and broaden their horizons. Now there was no question of opportunities. The entire social system had been turned upside-down. All across the country people were busy trying to save their own skins. Ishmael ended up in a small flat with seven other Iranian refugees, all stuck in the Soviet Union with no future. So much for his dreams. It took him months to realise where he was and what had happened to him.

Russia was going downhill fast. He had to get out.

A fellow refugee told him how to exploit the chaos to travel to East Germany. Thanks to an old comrade who'd lived in the GDR for years, he managed to obtain a temporary travel permit.

The moment he set foot in East Berlin, he went to a post office and called his wife. Her grandmother picked up the phone.

"Hello, it's Ishmael."

"Who?"

"Ishmael. Safa's husband."

"Oh, Ishmael! How are you? Safa's not home right now. She's at work. Nilufar's here, but she's asleep. I'm taking care of her. Yes, she's fine. What about you? Is everything all right?"

"I'm in Berlin now. I'll call again tonight."

Next, he dialled his parents' number. Tina answered the phone.

"*Salaam,* Tina. It's me, Ishmael."

Poor Tina, she nearly fainted.

"Can you hear me, Tina? How are you? Sorry I didn't call before, but I couldn't. Anyway, I'm in Berlin now. I have to keep this short. Where's Father? Where's Golden Bell?"

Tina wept.

"Why haven't you said anything? I can't talk long. Is Father there?"

"No, he's at the shop."

"What about Golden Bell?"

"She isn't home, either."

"Just my luck. Well, it doesn't matter. I'll call again soon. I've got to hang up now. So, everything's OK? Good. I promise I'll call back."

Tina didn't tell him that the reason Golden Bell wasn't at home was because she was in prison. Or that Aga Akbar was sick and everything was far from "OK". His call came so unexpectedly and went so fast that Tina didn't have a chance to tell him anything. But she wouldn't have told him the truth even if she'd had more time. He couldn't do anything about it and it would only have upset him. Bad news could wait, Tina reasoned. In the meantime, there was no need for Ishmael to know.

She hung up, flung on her chador and hurried to the shop to tell Akbar the good news.

"He called!" she signed to him through the window.

"He did?"

"Yes!" she said and went in.

"What did he say? Is he all right?"

"Yes, he's fine. He asked about you. And about Golden Bell."

"Did you tell him that Golden Bell—"

"No."

"Why not? He's her brother. He should be told."

"I just couldn't do it. I cried and forgot what I was supposed to say. My hands were shaking. I couldn't bring myself to tell him."

"Is he going to call again?"

"Yes. He can phone us now. Golden Bell will be so happy to hear that he's called. I'll tell her on Friday. No, wait, why don't you tell her in sign language? That way, the guards won't be able to understand. Just say that he phoned. Keep it simple. I'm going to Marzi's and Enzi's now to tell them that he called. There's no need for you to stay in the shop. You look pale, Akbar. Do you feel sick? Come on, let's go home. I'll go to Marzi's later."

Golden Bell had been arrested six weeks after Ishmael's escape. No one knew exactly how it happened.

One evening she simply didn't come home. Tina immediately feared the worst. She'd always known there was a chance that Golden Bell would be rounded up one day, like all the others. But she'd expected the police to come in a jeep and drag her daughter out of the house.

Now that Golden Bell hadn't come home and no jeeps had pulled up to the door, Tina was even more frightened. What should she do? Should she alert the rest of the family or should she sit back and wait? Don't panic, she thought, it's early yet.

Tina and Akbar stayed up until long after dark. Golden Bell didn't come home, nor did she phone.

Tina had heard from people whose children had been arrested that the secret police immediately sent a couple of agents to search the house. It suddenly occurred to her that she should get rid of any incriminating evidence. She jumped to her feet.

"Go get a cardboard box," she signed to Akbar. "We have to get rid of Golden Bell's books. The police will be here soon. Hurry, we need that box!"

Tina had learned how to read, but the books in Golden Bell's room were far too difficult for her. Which books were all right and which were dangerous?

"Put them all in the box!" she gestured.

"All of them?"

"Yes, all of them!"

She got down on her hands and knees, felt around under Golden Bell's bed and pulled out a bag. It was filled with papers. She glanced through them to see what they were about, but they were too complicated, so she stuck them in the box, too. Then she searched the wardrobe.

"Don't just stand there, Akbar! Look in the pockets of her clothes! Take everything out."

While Akbar inspected Golden Bell's clothes, Tina rolled up the carpet and checked to see if anything was hidden underneath. No, nothing.

"Come on, let's go! We have to take the box somewhere."

"Where?"

"I don't know. We can't keep it here, though. Pick up the other end, I can't carry it by myself. No, wait. We can't throw away the books. What if Golden Bell comes home? She'll never forgive me for throwing them out. I know, we can put them in the shed in the almond grove. If she does come home, we can always go and get them again, and if she doesn't . . . Lift up your end of the box, Akbar, and be careful."

They carried the heavy box to the front door. Tina opened it cautiously and peeked outside.

"I don't see anyone," she said. "Let's go."

They walked to the end of the street, where they had their garden, and made their way through the darkness to an old, dilapidated shed. The door was open. Tina hid the box beneath the gardening equipment and shut the door. "Let's go home!" she gestured.

"Thank goodness that's done," Tina said when they were safely back home.

"What should we do next?" Akbar signed.

"Nothing. All we can do is wait and see what tomorrow brings."

"I was wondering—" Akbar began.

"What is it now?"

"Nothing."

They sat quietly for a long time. Neither of them wanted to go to bed. Golden Bell might come through the door at any moment.

Tina heard footsteps. Maybe it was the police! She leapt up and peeked through the curtains, but it turned out to be their neighbours going to the mosque for their morning prayers.

"God help us, it'll be daylight soon and Golden Bell still hasn't come home! Where should I start looking?"

She'd always known that Golden Bell would never lead a normal life. Golden Bell would never have a home, a husband, a child, a cat, a kitchen, a—

"I was wondering—" Akbar began.

"What is it this time?"

"Golden Bell left a few . . . I mean, if the police come, do you think they'll look in my shop? Golden Bell left some things in the lean-to."

Tina slapped her forehead. "What did she hide in your shop?"

"Papers," Akbar signed.

"What kind of papers?"

"Those printed things."

"We have to go to the shop, but we can't go now, everybody's awake."

She peeked through the curtains again. "I guess it doesn't matter. We can walk along with everyone else. Come on, now is as good a time as any."

She put on her chador.

Tina and Akbar walked calmly out of the house and headed toward the mosque with the others.

"Turn left at the corner and go to your shop," she signed. "Don't switch on the light. I'll tag along with the other women until we reach the mosque, then I'll double back to the shop."

Akbar did as he was told. When he reached the shop, he took out his key, stuck it in the lock, opened the door and slipped inside. He waited in the dark for Tina.

It didn't take long. She struck a match and signed, "Go get the oil lamp . . . No, wait, a candle is better."

Akbar trotted off and came back with a candle stub. Tina lit it and went into the lean-to.

"Where are they?"

"I'm not sure. I didn't take much notice."

Holding the candle in one hand, Tina groped around with the other until she came upon a stack of papers in a cardboard box. She held one of them up to the candle and read a few lines. It didn't make any sense to her, but she could see that it was a flyer. She thrust it into Akbar's hand. "How could you be so stupid?" she angrily signed. "Stupid, stupid, stupid!"

She got down on her knees and searched some more. She pulled a typewriter out from under a table. "How will I ever be able to get rid of this? Oh, Akbar, Akbar, you're ruining my life!"

Tina crawled through the darkness on her hands and knees. Behind a wooden box she found a few cans of spray paint. It was the first time she'd ever seen graffiti spray. She carefully picked up a can and examined it in the dim candlelight. "What on earth is this? Oh, my God, stay back, Akbar! Don't touch the thing, it might explode! Get me a plastic bag. OK, now put it in the bag. No, wait, I'd better do it myself."

She picked up the cans one by one and put them in the bag. "Golden Bell," she moaned, "you've not only ruined *your* life, but also mine."

Then she turned to Akbar. "Hurry up! Where's my chador? I'll take the papers, you take the typewriter. Hide it under your coat. Or wrap it in a rag. No, a carpet. Hurry! I'll carry those dangerous-looking cans. Now go! Follow me down to the river!"

It was light outside, though the sun hadn't come up yet.

By the bakery they ran into some men hurrying home with fresh bread.

"*Salaam aleikum!*"

"*Salaam aleikum!*"

Tina turned down a side street, towards a grape arbor, and Akbar trailed along behind her. Fifteen minutes later they came to the river.

Tina hunted around and found a heavy rock, which she put in the box of flyers. She took off her headscarf, tied it around the box and lowered it into the water. Then she gingerly picked up the bag of spray cans. She filled the bag with water, tied it shut and pushed it gently away from the shore. It floated briefly along with the current, then sank.

"Don't just stand there!" she snapped at Akbar. "Throw the typewriter in, too!"

But Akbar couldn't bring himself to do it. He hesitated.

So Tina picked up the typewriter, walked down to the river's edge and threw it as far as she could. It splashed noisily into the water, but Tina fell to her knees. "Ow, my back!" she cried. "Come here, Akbar! Hold my hand! I can't breathe. No, don't touch me, don't come near me. Golden Bell, look what you've done to me!"

She began to cry. After several minutes, she was finally able to stand up again, with Akbar's help. She held his arm and they slowly made their way home.

At eleven o'clock that same morning, two agents of the secret police walked into Akbar's shop. Akbar hadn't felt up to going that morning, but Tina had insisted: "Go to the shop as usual and do your work. We mustn't do anything out of the ordinary, or people will realise that Golden Bell didn't come home last night."

Akbar was sitting at his workbench when the shadows of the two men fell across the carpet he was mending. Startled, he raised his head and began to stand.

"Don't get up," one of them gestured.

Akbar sensed that these were the men Tina had been talking about. The other agent went around the shop, inspecting things. He moved aside the carpets on the workbench and peered into a box on the shelf.

"Your daughter, the girl who helps you in the shop, where

is she?" the agent asked, in rudimentary sign language.

Despite the man's clumsy signs, Akbar knew what he meant.

"What did she do in your shop?" the agent continued.

"I don't know what you're talking about," Akbar signed.

"Your daughter," the agent gestured more emphatically. "Daughter, earrings. Green earrings. Long hair. Breasts. You understand? What did she do here? Who else came to your shop?"

Akbar knew he wasn't supposed to say anything, but he was upset by the man's crude gestures. It was Golden Bell's long hair and green earrings he was describing. He must have seen her without her chador. Surely that was impossible?

Though Akbar was inwardly seething, he managed to sit calmly in his chair.

"He doesn't understand what you're talking about," the other agent said.

"He understands all right. Show him the photographs."

The other agent went into the lean-to.

The first agent took a couple of pictures out of his coat pocket. He thrust the picture of a man in front of Akbar's face. "Do you know this man?"

"I don't understand. Let me get my wife."

"Sit down. Look at this picture. Have you ever seen this man in your shop? Did he have any contact with your daughter? Did he—"

"I don't understand. You have to send for my wife," Akbar gestured for the second time.

"I bet you'll understand now. Here's another picture. I'm sure you'll recognise *her*," he said with a smirk. And he showed him a picture of Golden Bell with her hair in a tangle and her face covered with cuts and bruises.

That did it. The man had violated the inviolable. Akbar snatched the picture out of his hand, leapt to his feet and pushed the man aside.

The agent backed up a few steps, pulled out a gun and yelled, "Sit down!" But that only made things worse. Akbar grabbed a stick and started hitting him, shrieking all the while, "GEEEEE OUOUOU!"

The other agent rushed out of the lean-to and was about to grab Akbar from behind, when Akbar wheeled around and whacked him on the shoulder with his stick. The agent doubled over in pain.

Akbar hurried outside and began shouting: "MYYYY GOOLGOOL EAEAEAR RRRGGG!"

Shopkeepers raced outside and passers-by rushed to his aid. "What's wrong?"

"In there. Those men. A picture. Golden Bell. Her hair. Her earrings," he gestured.

No one knew what he was talking about.

The situation had got completely out of hand. The hated agents of the secret police slinked off to their car and disappeared.

The shopkeepers brought Akbar back to his shop.

"What did they want?"

"That man had a picture in his pocket. Golden Bell's long hair. Her green earrings. And her . . . How could he have seen her green earrings? Do you understand?"

"No," said the grocer.

"Golden Bell didn't come home, I mean, she got home late last night, but my wife can tell you more. And that man pulled out a gun. He had the picture in his pocket. Suddenly I got mad, I picked up a stick and hit him. The other agent was about to grab me from behind. I hit him hard on his . . . the picture, where's the picture?"

"I think we'd better get his wife," the baker said. "He's upset about something."

· · ·

Ishmael phoned a few more times, but Tina couldn't bring herself to tell him that Golden Bell was in prison. Instead, every time he called, she told him that Golden Bell just happened to be away at that moment.

"Tina, it's hard for me to phone. I can't do it often. I'll try again tomorrow evening at around seven," he finally said. "Tell Golden Bell, because I want to talk to her. And can you ask Father to come home earlier tomorrow night? I want to hear his voice. He's all right, isn't he?"

"We're old. Some days are better than others. But he's doing fine. He's working the same long hours he always has."

That was a lie, because at that very moment Akbar was lying ill in bed. Tina had deliberately stood with her back to Akbar so he wouldn't notice that she was talking to Ishmael, but he sensed that she was hiding something. He struggled to his feet, walked over to Tina and signed, "Who're you talking to?"

"Our next-door neighbour," she replied.

Akbar could tell that she was lying.

"Is it Ishmael?" he signed, and he began to say out loud, "Ismaa Ismaa Ismaa Agggaaa Aga Akkekebaaraa."

"Tina!" Ishmael yelled into the receiver. "Is that Father?"

Akbar grabbed the phone and started telling him Golden Bell's story in a trembling voice: "I I I crrrr sh sh sh is gogogo I I I Akka am iiin bedbedddd ohohoh shop shop is clo sh sh sh is gogogo oh nonono." Then he handed the phone back to Tina, wiped away his tears and went back to bed.

Sobbing, Tina told Ishmael the truth. She told him that Golden Bell was in prison, that after six months they'd finally been given permission to visit her once a month, that Akbar had collapsed by the cedar trees and the neighbours had carried him home on their shoulders.

. . .

Akbar went back to his shop, but he had trouble working.

"My head doesn't feel right," he told Tina. "I keep weaving the wrong flowers into the carpets I'm mending."

"You just need to concentrate. If you make mistakes, we won't earn any money. Go to the shop and work calmly and quietly. It'll all come back to you."

A month later, when he didn't come home from work one day, Tina went looking for him. She found him lying on the carpet with his cuneiform notebook beside him. He had fainted. Tina ran to the bakery. The baker immediately called an ambulance and Akbar was taken to the hospital. "Your husband needs to rest," the doctor told Tina. "Work will kill him."

After a week, Akbar was released from the hospital. He now walked with a cane.

He hated sitting around the house, so one morning he shuffled to the shop with his cane, unlocked the door, moved his chair over to the window, sat down and tried to do a bit of work. In the afternoon he walked to the cemetery and sat by the grave of his nephew Jawad. From there he looked up at Saffron Mountain. When evening came, he went back home. "Where have you been?" Tina burst out. "What will I do if you fall?"

He went in the house, picked up a pen and crossed off another day on the calendar. Then he counted the number of days left before they could visit Golden Bell.

On visiting days he got up at the crack of dawn, grabbed his cane and walked the six miles to the prison on his own.

Tina used to beg, "Don't do it. It isn't good for you. Why don't you take the bus, like I do?"

But Akbar never listened. "It makes me feel better. You don't have to worry about me. I don't walk fast. I stop and rest along the way."

When he got to the prison, he usually sat in the teahouse on the square until the bus arrived with its load of visitors. The moment he saw Tina, he stood up and went over to meet her.

Akbar always took along a few skeins of yarn that he'd dyed himself, because Golden Bell was knitting socks, mittens and a warm robe. Since she was ruining her eyes in her dark cell, Tina brought her fresh vegetables and lentils. On a previous visit, Golden Bell had asked them to bring her walnuts and dried figs.

"What do you need those for?" Tina said. "You don't get much exercise, so don't eat too many figs."

"Don't worry, Mother, I won't."

And so, the months and the years went by. The Berlin Wall fell and Ishmael ended up in the Netherlands, in a house in the polder. He had a place to sit and a window through which he could look out over his past.

These were difficult years, but he wasn't sorry he'd escaped or made the political choices he had. He'd learned a lot, he'd had all kinds of experiences and he'd even enjoyed life. Golden Bell's imprisonment, however, was a constant source of pain and worry. He also felt terribly guilty.

It was winter. Early one morning Akbar grabbed his cane and set off for the prison.

In the spring or summer he always ran into farmers walking out to their fields to work the land. "*Salaam*, Aga Akbar, how are you?"

"Better."

"And your daughter?"

"Fine. She knitted me a cap and some mittens for the winter. She's even weaving a carpet. She says that when it's done, she's going to sit on her magic carpet and fly away from the prison," Akbar signed. "Fly away," he repeated with a laugh, and he waved his cane in the air.

In the spring he usually sat down, drank a cup of tea with the farmers, rested for a while and then walked on.

But in the winter it was difficult. He couldn't stop to rest, because it was too cold. He didn't mind, though. He spent the whole time talking to Golden Bell in his head and that kept him from feeling the cold in his feet.

On his last visit he'd noticed that Golden Bell was getting old. Her face was lined and her shoulders were slightly stooped.

Maybe he was mistaken and they weren't really stooped, but he signed to Tina anyway, "I've noticed that Golden Bell has a stoop. Have you noticed it, too?"

"No, but it must be from all that sitting. With four or five girls crammed into one tiny cell, there's not much room for her to move around. She'll have to do a lot of walking when she gets out. That'll straighten her back."

"When is she going to get out?"

"I don't know, Akbar. They don't tell us things like that. Maybe soon, maybe not for a long time."

"How long is 'a long time'?"

"Oh, honestly, Akbar, how would I know? Maybe so long that *I* won't be able to walk any more."

He felt saddened by her answer.

As he walked toward the prison, Akbar pondered her words. Long, Tina had said, maybe so long that she wouldn't be able to walk any more. By that time, Akbar thought, I'll probably be dead.

Golden Bell's hair was turning prematurely grey. But she was clever and strong, so Akbar hoped she'd survive for years. When she was finally released, she'd still have a long life, she'd still be able to work and maybe even have children. Akbar felt sure Golden Bell would manage all right, since she'd read so many books.

Tina didn't want Akbar to feel so sad. She told him that everything would be OK. "If you suffer from too much sadness," she said, "you'll fall down again and die. And if you die, you won't be able to visit Golden Bell any more and then Golden Bell will cry in her cell for ever."

Tina also said that if he died he'd never see Ishmael again, either. "Maybe we'll all go and visit Ishmael when Golden Bell gets out of prison," Tina said. "We'll take a plane!"

Who knows? Maybe one day they would.

"Where does Ishmael live?" Akbar asked.

"He lives in a country that doesn't have any mountains," Tina said. "It's always cloudy there, the wind is always blowing and he lives at the bottom of a sea."

"At the bottom of a sea? A *sea*?"

"Yes," Tina said. "They pumped out all the water. Now there are trees growing on what used to be the bottom of the sea and cows grazing on the grass."

It didn't make sense to Akbar, but that's where Ishmael lived.

As he plodded on, Akbar thought about the fact that Golden Bell was more patient than Ishmael. She explained things to him with endless patience.

Ishmael always talked to him about big things—the sky, the stars, the earth, the moon—but Golden Bell always talked to him about little things.

Once she picked up a stone. "There are tiny things moving around inside," she said.

"Inside a stone?" Akbar couldn't believe it.

"Yes. Little tiny things that revolve around each other," Golden Bell explained, "the way the earth revolves around the sun."

He still couldn't believe it. "That's impossible," he signed. "A stone is just a stone. If you smashed it with a hammer, you wouldn't see a thing. No earth, no sun."

Golden Bell handed him a hammer. He smashed the stone. "You see, no sun."

"Make it even smaller," she said.

He did it. Smaller and smaller and smaller. He banged away at that stone until it was just a heap of sand and it couldn't get any smaller.

"The sun is inside the tiniest grain of sand," Golden Bell said.

Akbar laughed out loud.

She's smart, he thought as he neared the prison. She gets all of that from books. He remembered another of Golden Bell's explanations. One time she laid her head on his chest and said, "Boom, boom, boom."

"What do you mean, 'boom, boom, boom'?" he signed.

"Here, just under your ribs, you've got a motor," she replied.

"A motor?"

He laughed, but she opened a book and showed him a picture of the motor under his ribs that went boom, boom, boom.

The prison was on a hill. By the time Akbar reached the square in front of the prison, the sun had come up. He was early, so he went to the teahouse to wait for Tina. The owner brought him a cup of tea and asked him if he wanted to eat anything.

"Bread and cheese," he gestured.

He looked out the window at the snow-covered mountains and at the tiny windows of the prison cells. Golden Bell is in one of those cells, he thought. She knows I'm waiting here in the teahouse. Soon I'll be able to see her and she'll ask, "How are you, Father? Did you walk here? You shouldn't do that, your knee will start acting up again. Why don't you take the bus?"

"I don't like the bus. I can't think because of those smelly exhaust fumes. Walking gives me a chance to think."

He hates it when a guard stands next to Golden Bell and keeps his eye on her during the whole visit. Tina says he ought to ignore the man, simply pretend he's not there. But he can't.

One time he motioned to the guard to move aside.

Tina immediately tugged at his sleeve. "Don't do that! They might not let us see her again."

Visiting hours are short, the time flies by. "Don't complain," Tina says, "it's better than nothing."

Akbar saw the bus go past the teahouse and stop at the bus stop. He watched the visitors get out.

He saw Tina, carrying the vegetables she'd bought for Golden Bell. She's having trouble walking, Akbar thought. He hadn't noticed it before. She's getting old, he realised.

Political prisoners were not allowed to have any visitors except their parents. When the gates opened, the parents poured into the visiting room and stood behind a wall of bars. The prisoners were lined up behind another set of bars, about five feet away. Since everyone talked at the same time, you had to shout to make yourself heard. You also had to be quick, because there wasn't much time. Any unspoken words had to be left unsaid for another month.

Sometimes a mother's scream cut through the tumult. There was an immediate hush, because they all knew that when prisoners didn't appear, it was because they'd been executed. Visiting hours were a torture to the parents. They died a thousand deaths before their sons and daughters appeared behind the bars. Will he be there today? Will she be there today?

Akbar wasn't aware of this possibility. Tina had spared him the anxiety. But she was always on tenterhooks until she saw Golden Bell.

The inner door opened. The guard led the prisoners to the bars, but Golden Bell didn't appear—her place remained empty. Tina wanted to scream, but she didn't dare. Akbar saw the vegetables trembling in her hand. Tina fainted and Akbar panicked.

Two guards grabbed Tina under the arms, dragged her across the floor and took her outside. Akbar hurried after them, then turned and went back in.

"Where's my daughter?" he signed to a guard standing on the other side of the bars. The guard didn't answer.

"Golden Bell, my daughter," he quickly gestured, while glancing anxiously at Tina, who was lying by the gate.

The guard pretended not to see him.

At the end of visiting hours, the guards sent the parents away.

"You, too! Get out!" the guard gestured.

"I haven't seen my daughter."

"Get out!" the policeman yelled, pointing at the door.

Akbar didn't want to go. The policeman grabbed him by the arm, "I told you to get out!"

Akbar clamped onto the bars and shouted, "M-y-y-y G-o-o-o-l!"

Three guards yanked him loose and pushed him out the door. He lifted his cane and was about to bring it down on the head of a guard, when he suddenly remembered what Tina had said, "Don't get angry. Don't talk to the guards. And don't hit anyone in uniform. If you do, they'll kill Golden Bell!"

Akbar lowered his cane, smiled and gestured, "OK, I'm leaving."

The other parents were waiting for him outside. They crowded around him.

"Well? Did you see her?"

"No! They shoved me out," he gestured.

"Such rudeness. They're not people, they're animals," one mother muttered.

"Where's my wife?"

"A couple of women are taking her home," a man gestured.

"Is she all right?"

"Don't worry. They'll take care of her."

Akbar didn't know what else to do. Everyone was whispering that Golden Bell had probably been executed.

"But in that case, the family should have been informed," one mother murmured.

"They're worse than you think," another one said. "They want you down on your knees. Only then will they tell you they've murdered your child."

"In the bus on the way here," another mother whispered, "I heard that the guards had been combing the mountains all night with police dogs and searchlights, looking for some prisoners who had escaped."

"Really?"

"Apparently three prisoners have escaped."

"From the mullahs' prison? Are you crazy?"

"I heard it, too," another man said warily. "People were talking about it in the teahouse."

The mothers covered their faces with their chadors and continued to stand in little groups, talking.

Akbar was standing off to the side by himself.

Two jeeps with armed guards and dogs drove down the hill and stopped in the square.

"Get out of here!" shouted one of the guards. "Go home!"

The mothers hurried off to the bus stop, where the fathers were already waiting for them.

The bus had gone and the square was empty. An icy mountain wind swept through the square. Akbar stood at the bus stop. He was hoping the prison imam would come out.

In that case he'd walk up to the imam, kiss his hand and throw himself on his mercy: "Golden Bell didn't come. And my wife fainted. Do you perhaps know what—"

The prison gate swung open. A female guard came out, wrapped in her chador. She walked over to the bus stop.

Akbar recognised her. She was the daughter of one of his

customers. He nodded to her in greeting and she nodded back.

"My daughter," he hesitantly gestured. "She didn't come."

The woman glanced up at the prison and moved a few steps away from him.

"My wife fainted," Akbar went on. "I asked the guard where Golden Bell was, but—"

The woman looked anxiously at the gate, then at the tea-house.

"Your daughter is gone!" she signed, concealing the gesture beneath her chador.

"Gone?" Akbar gestured in surprise.

"To the mountains," the woman signed and she hurried over to the approaching bus.

Footprints

*It's hard to tell whether they're
animal tracks or footprints.*

Darkness had fallen and Akbar's house was
abuzz with activity. Neighbours kept dropping
in. They were all sure that Golden Bell was one
of the escaped prisoners, though they had no official confirmation.

They told each other that Golden Bell had been preparing
her escape for months, knitting warm clothes out of Akbar's
yarn and hoarding a supply of nuts. Still, it was hard to believe.

Tina, surrounded by family and neighbours, was beside
herself with worry. Marzi and Enzi tried to reassure her.

"There's no need to act as if Golden Bell is dead, Mother,"
Enzi said to her. "I have the feeling she's still alive. She might
even have reached the top of Saffron Mountain by now."

"The top of Saffron Mountain?" Tina wailed. "She can't have

escaped. I know my daughter. Would somebody please go and ask what's happened to her? Would somebody please find out?"

"She might have escaped," Marzi said. "Everyone knows that the guards have been out all day searching the mountains. Try to pull yourself together, Mother. Even if they've been cap—"

"Stop!" cried Tina, putting her hands over her ears.

There was an abrupt silence. Suddenly Tina noticed that Akbar wasn't there.

"Hasn't Akbar come home?"

"Maybe he's gone to the shop."

The neighbours whispered among themselves. "Do you understand what it means if they really have escaped?" said one.

"Let's hope the guards don't catch them," said another.

"I wonder if they can survive in the mountains. It's freezing cold and Golden Bell isn't an experienced climber."

"Oh, but she's tough! My guess is that they had outside help. They'd have to be crazy to head for the mountains. Maybe there was a car waiting for them outside the prison."

"They say that Golden Bell put on a black chador, then simply walked out the gate and disappeared."

"That's impossible."

"Why not? Didn't she say she was weaving a magic carpet so she could fly away?"

"Just thinking about it makes me tremble."

"Marzi! Enzi! Where are Bolfazl and Atri?" Tina asked. "Would somebody please go see if Father's come back from the prison?"

The next-door neighbour was making soup and the woman from across the street was making tea. She poured glasses for everyone and brought them around on a tray. Marzi put on her chador and went to see if Akbar was in his shop.

Bolfazl and Atri, the husbands of Marzi and Enzi, arrived a

little while later. They'd gone to the imam in the hope of find-ing out what was going on.

"Well?" Tina cried, as she leapt to her feet.

"Nothing," said Bolfazl. "Every door in the world seems to be shut. We haven't been able to reach anyone."

"Here, have a cup of tea," said Enzi. "We'll just have to wait. There's nothing else we can do."

The door opened. Marzi came in and said that Akbar wasn't back yet.

"Not back yet? Oh, my God," cried Tina.

She grabbed her chador. "I'm going to go look for him. I'm afraid he's fallen again. Bolfazl, Atri, will you come with me?"

"Sit down, Tina," said Enzi. "Don't get excited. The men will find out where he is."

"You see?" Tina cried. "I've told him a thousand times to take the bus, but he never listens."

"Maybe he stopped off at a friend's," Enzi said. "Let's phone a few people first. If he isn't there, the men can go and look for him. Sit down, everything will be all right."

Three men—Tina's sons-in-law and one of the neighbours— put on warm coats, grabbed a couple of lanterns and went out into the darkness to look for Akbar.

They walked toward the prison, scanning the snow to see if he'd fallen. They asked every person they ran into if they'd seen him.

"Excuse me, have you seen Aga Akbar?"

"Aga Akbar?"

"Yes, the carpet-mender. You know, the deaf-mute."

"The Akbar who walks to the prison?"

"Yes."

"I often see him, but not today."

They went on, until they ran into an old farmer, pushing a cartload of wood through the snow.

"*Salaam aleikum,*" they said.

"Good evening, what are you gentlemen doing out in this cold?"

"We're looking for Aga Akbar, the carpet-mender."

"Oh, the man with the cane who walks to—"

"Yes. Did you happen to see him today?"

"No. I've been inside."

In the distance they saw the bus coming down the mountain. They held up their lanterns. The bus came to a cautious stop at the side of the icy road.

"Aren't you going to get in?" the driver called out the window.

"No. We're looking for Aga Akbar."

"Which Aga Akbar?"

"The carpet-mender."

"You mean the deaf-mute whose daughter is in prison?"

"Yes, have you seen him?"

"I think so."

"Where? When?"

"I'm not sure. This morning? This afternoon? Maybe around eleven, or was it twelve? Anyway, I think I was heading up the mountain when I saw him, but I don't remember where."

He turned to his passengers. "Has anyone seen the deaf-mute carpet-mender today? No?"

The bus drove off. The men went on looking.

"Something must've happened to him," said the neighbour. "Maybe we ought to contact the police."

"The police! Do you think they would help us?"

"Let's go on for a couple of miles," said Atri. "There's a garage just outside the next village. We can ask there. Somebody must have seen him!"

A cold wind blew down from the mountains and brought the snow along with it.

"I don't understand how a sick man like Akbar can walk all this way," said the neighbour.

"He's strong."

"Yes, but he's sick."

"He walks very slowly and doesn't push himself," said Bolfazl. "He rarely takes a bus or a taxi. He may be sick, but he's stronger than I am."

"It looks like the garage is closed," said Atri. "Nobody's out on these icy roads tonight."

Still, they went on walking until they reached the garage.

"Oh, good, there's a phone box," Bolfazl said. "I'll call home. Who knows? Maybe he's returned by now."

Marzi answered the phone.

"It's me, Bolfazl. Has he come home yet? No? We've looked almost everywhere. OK, we'll keep on looking. I'll call if we find him."

"The garage owner lives in the village," said Atri. "He must have seen him. Let's go to his house."

They walked to the village. At the grocer's, they asked where the garage owner lived. "A few streets away," said the grocer, "in a house with a big iron door."

The doorbell was broken. Atri picked up a rock and banged it against the door. A dog barked.

"Who's there?" a woman called.

"Sorry. Is the—"

The door opened and the garage owner himself appeared.

"Excuse me for disturbing you so late at night," said Atri, "but we're looking for the carpet-mender who walks to the prison. Do you know who I mean?"

"Sure. Aga Akbar. I know him well. He mended one of our carpets. He always waves when he walks past on his way to the prison. Why? Has something happened to him?"

"He walked to the prison this morning, but he hasn't come

home yet. He's got heart problems, so we're worried about him. We've been searching all along the road. Have you seen him today?"

"I saw him walking toward the prison this morning when I was working in the garage, but I don't remember seeing him come back. You should ask the people in the teahouse on the square by the prison. Have you got a car? No? It's a long walk. Just let me grab my coat and I'll drive you there."

The garage owner fetched his jeep and the men got in.

"Akbar's a good man," he said as he drove. "People say he brings luck. He mended my carpet so well that you can't even tell it's been mended. His life hasn't been easy, but we're living in a crazy world now. It's wrong to put women and girls in jail. Allah is sure to punish us for that. Even the shah didn't dare lock up women, but the imams do whatever they want."

The teahouse was dark, but the garage owner knew where the teahouse owner lived. He drove toward the mountains. After a few miles they saw the lights of a village. He parked in front of a house on the village square.

"Mashhadi! Hey, Mashhadi, are you home?" he shouted up at a lighted window on the second floor.

The teahouse owner looked out of the window. He recognised the jeep and came downstairs.

"Welcome, come in. What can I do for you?"

"Can you help these people?" the garage owner asked. "They're looking for Aga Akbar, the carpet-mender. You know, the deaf-mute who walks with a cane and goes to visit his daughter in prison."

"I know who you mean."

"He hasn't come home. He's got health problems, and they're afraid he's fallen down somewhere. They've searched the whole road. I thought you might have seen him."

"You're right, I have. He always waits for his wife in my teahouse. This morning he had breakfast and when she came, the two of them went to the prison. But after that? I haven't the faintest idea. Let me think . . . Yes, I saw him again after visiting hours. He was standing at the bus stop, talking to a woman."

"Then what happened?" Bolfazl asked.

"The bus came, but Akbar didn't get on. He stood there for a while, staring up at the mountains. That's all I remember."

"Where on earth could he have gone after that?" Bolfazl wondered.

"Maybe he went to visit someone?" Atri suggested.

"No, he knew Tina had fainted."

"So he must have headed home," Atri concluded.

"No, I don't think so."

"Then where did he go?" the neighbour asked.

"Well, I think he went uphill instead of downhill."

"Uphill?"

"Yes, into the mountains," Bolfazl said.

"Into the mountains?" the neighbour asked, in surprise.

"Perhaps he did," Atri said. "It's entirely possible."

"May I ask you a question?" Bolfazl said to the teahouse owner. "According to rumours, a few prisoners have escaped. Do you happen to know anything about that?"

The teahouse owner looked first at the garage owner, then at Bolfazl. "I'm sorry, but I prefer to mind my own business. I have five children, so the answer is no, I don't know anything about an escape. I saw the carpet-mender standing at the bus stop and that's all I can tell you. I'm sorry."

"That's enough," the garage owner said. "They have an answer to their question. I don't want to get mixed up in this, either, but the carpet-mender is a decent man. That's why I brought them here. Don't worry, we're leaving."

The teahouse owner went back into his house and locked the door.

The garage owner started his jeep. "I don't know what

you're planning to do," he said, "but I'm going home. Please forgive me for not helping you more."

"You've already done a lot," Bolfazl said. "Thank you. We'd appreciate it if you could give us a ride back to the square."

He drove them to the square and they got out.

While the three men waited at the bus stop, they talked about what they should do next.

"We can't give up yet," Bolfazl said. "Let's search the mountain path."

"That's like looking for a needle in a haystack," the neighbour said.

"I know Akbar," Bolfazl replied. "If he thought Golden Bell was in the mountains, he'd go looking for her."

"Surely he wouldn't go into the mountains with all this snow?" the neighbour said.

"That's what I'd do if I were in his place," Bolfazl said.

"This is no time for talk," Atri said. "Let's start up the mountain. He can't have gone far with his cane."

They took the mountain path, shining their lanterns on the footprints in the snow.

"This one was made by a soldier's boot," Bolfazl said. "And that one and all of those, too."

"What about these?" Atri asked.

"They were made by ordinary shoes. We should follow them."

"The prison guards must have followed them, too," Atri said.

"I don't think so," said the neighbour. "This isn't the route you'd take if you were escaping from prison."

"Why not?" Bolfazl asked.

"Because your footprints would show up clearly in the snow," the neighbour explained.

"If you were in danger and had no other options, you'd want to get up the mountain as quickly as possible."

"I don't agree," the neighbour said. "My guess is that they took the paved road to the village, then went on to the next village and so on. If they're smart, they'll hide for a few days, then go into the mountains."

At that point, the soldiers' footprints stopped and only one set of footprints went on, gradually merging with those of the mountain goats.

The men climbed higher and higher until they came to a path that could be traversed only by nimble-footed mountain goats and mountain climbers with ropes and spikes. It also happened to be the path that led to the cave with the cuneiform relief.

"He must have taken this path," said Bolfazl.

"With a cane?" said Atri.

Bolfazl knelt in the snow and inspected the tracks by the light of his lantern.

"The mountain goats come here in search of food," he said. "Most of them don't dare go any further. It's impossible to make out a human footprint among all these tracks. I think we'd better turn back."

They arrived home with their darkened lanterns in the middle of the night. The women received them in silence. No one dared cry, no one dared speak. The night had swallowed up Akbar and Golden Bell.

Daylight broke through the window. The sun rose slowly, but brought no news. The days came and went, and so did the nights, and still there was no news.

Then, on one of the first days of spring, when a shepherd was out looking for grass for his flock, his dog began to bark. The shepherd hurried over to investigate. There, between the rocks, he found the body of an old man, his grey hair glinting like polished silver in the freshly fallen snow.

The Cuneiform Notebook

 This is the end of Aga Akbar's story, though not the end of his cuneiform notebook. Unfortunately, the last few pages are indecipherable.

It's hard to know where he wrote those last few pages.

At home?

No, probably not.

They're completely illegible. Perhaps he wrote them in the mountains, by a craggy cliff, which he'd helped Golden Bell to climb.

Which he'd helped Golden Bell to climb?

No, that's impossible.

Anyway, you can see that he wrote the last few pages in difficult conditions.

He no doubt wrote them in the snow, in the freezing cold.

Nothing more was ever heard of the escaped prisoners. To

this day their fate is unknown. Perhaps Akbar did find them in the mountains. Perhaps he told them not to follow the railroad tracks and showed them the path that would lead them to Saffron Mountain.

Perhaps he said to Golden Bell, "Once you reach the cave, go into it as far as you can. Go all the way to the back until you can no longer stand. On your right you'll see a ledge and on that ledge there will be bags of raisins and dates and dried fruits. Take those, along with the warm clothes and flashlights for mountain climbers in need, and go even farther into the cave. Go all the way back until you can crawl no longer. There you'll be safe. Stay there for several days until the guards have stopped searching the mountains."

In all likelihood these were the last few sentences in Akbar's notebook.

He must have kissed Golden Bell goodbye. "Now go. You don't have to worry about me. I'll dig a hole in the snow and wait here until tomorrow. Then I'll make my way back. It's a good thing I'm here, because if the guards come, I'll shout as loud as I can and you'll know what's going on. Have a safe journey, my child."

Did Golden Bell and the other escaped prisoners ever reach the cave?

It's entirely possible. Just as it's possible that they slept in the cave's recesses and never woke up again.

A hundred years from now, or maybe three hundred years from now, they will awaken, like the men of Kahaf, whose story is told in the Holy Book:

And so it went until the men of Kahaf finally sought refuge in the cave. "Grant us Thy mercy," they said.

In that cave We covered their ears and their eyes for years.

And when the sun came up, the men saw it rise to the right of the cave. And when the sun went down, the men saw it set to the left, while they were in the space in between.

They thought they were awake, but they were asleep.

And We turned them to the right and to the left.

Some said, "There were three of them, and a fourth watched over them."

Others, hazarding a guess, said, "There were five of them, and a sixth watched over them."

And there were those who said, "There were seven of them." No one knew.

We woke them, so that they might question one another.

One of them spoke: "We have been here for a day or part of a day." Another said: "Allah alone knows how long we have been here. It would be best to send one of us to the city with this silver coin. We must be careful. If they find out who we are, they will stone us."

Jemiliga then left the cave with the silver coin in the palm of his hand.

When he reached the city, he saw that everything had changed and that he did not understand the language.

They had slept in the cave for three hundred years and did not even know it. And some say there were nine more.

One day Golden Bell will wake up.

She will leave the cave with a silver coin in the palm of her hand.

And when she reaches the city, she will notice that everything has changed.

Glossary

Allahu akbar. La ilaha illa Allah: God is great. There is no God but Allah.

ankahtu wa zawagtu: the words recited during the wedding ceremony that officially declare the couple to be man and wife.

Baba Taher: a mystic poet of the first half of the eleventh century. Every Persian can recite a few of his quatrains about love and death.

Eqra be-asme rabbeka alazi khalaqa . . . el-qalam: "Read! In the name of thy Lord and Cherisher, Who created, created man out of a mere clot of congealed blood. . . . He who taught the use of the pen." This is the first sura of the Koran to be revealed to Muhammad. Gabriel brought it down to him from Heaven, and even though Muhammad was illiterate, Gabriel asked him to read the text. Once he had read it, Muhammad's mission had officially begun.

Hafez: medieval Persian poet (1326–90), whose poetry is cited as a sacred text and learned by heart. No Persian household is complete without a volume of his poetry.

hekaya: ancient Persian stories.

ibn: son of.

jawid shah: long live the shah.

Jomah Mosque: The so-called Friday Mosque, one of the oldest mosques in Iran.

Kahaf: a well-known story in the Koran. A number of men who are being persecuted for their beliefs seek shelter in the *kahf*, or cave. Exhausted, they fall asleep. When they awake, they see that their hair and beards have aged. It seems they've slept for three hundred years.

Kazem Khan: *Kazem* is the name of one of Muhammad's successors; a *khan* is a nobleman.

Khata: The Persian name for Northern China, the region from which Iran's Mongol conquerors came. "Moon-faced," or Mongolian, beauty became an archetype in Persian poetry. But the women of *khata'* (with an almost identical pronunciation) are women of sin.

Khatun: Mrs.

Khayyam: Omar Khayyam (1048–1122) is known in the West mainly as the author of the *Rubaiyat* and numerous quatrains.

Lalehzar Mountain: named after the wild red tulips that grow on the mountain slopes.

Mahdi: the promised one.

Naqsh-e-Jahan Square: the oldest square in Iran.

Sa'di: medieval writer and poet (1213–93) whose *hekayas* represent the apogee of Persian language and literature. His book *The Rose Garden* can be found, like that of Hafez, in every Persian household.

Saffron Mountain: named after the red and yellow flowers that cover the mountainside in the autumn.

Sayyid: Sire, Mr (a term of address accorded to descendants of Muhammad).

Sheikh Lotfallah Mosque: one of the most beautiful mosques in Isfahan.

sigeh: under Shiite law, a man may have a maximum of four wives. In addition, he's allowed an unlimited number of temporary wives, who make a marriage contract for a period ranging anywhere from one hour to 99 years. These *sigeh* have no inheritance rights.

Acknowledgments

 The poems by J. C. Bloem and P. N. van Eyck have been translated for this edition by David McKay. The poet Jan Slauerhoff based his poem on the classic Chinese poem "Golden Bells" by Po Chu I. The Multatuli passage has been taken from Multatuli, *Max Havelaar*, translated by Roy Edwards, London: Penguin Books, 1987. The poem by Rutger Kopland, part of a series entitled "Suppose", has been taken from Rutger Kopland, *A World Beyond Myself*, translated by James Brockway, London: Enitharmon Press: 1991.

TRANSLATOR'S NOTE: The passages from the Koran and Shiite prayer books are not reproductions of the actual Arabic texts but have been adapted by the author. They should, therefore, be regarded as retellings, or as snatches of texts remembered by the characters, rather than as direct quotations.

I wish to thank Diane Webb for her editorial advice and R. M. McGlinn for his assistance with the translation and transliteration of Farsi into English.

The HOUSE of the MOSQUE

KADER ABDOLAH

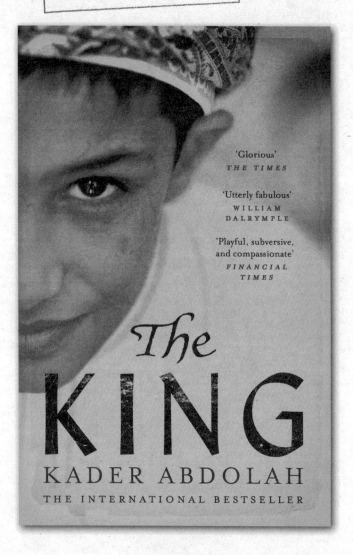

'Glorious'
THE TIMES

'Utterly fabulous'
WILLIAM
DALRYMPLE

'Playful, subversive,
and compassionate'
*FINANCIAL
TIMES*

The
KING

KADER ABDOLAH

THE INTERNATIONAL BESTSELLER

'A modern epic'
Independent

CANON‖GATE